THE BOOK OF
GAHERIS

THE BOOK OF GAHERIS

An Arthurian Tale

Kari Sperring

NEWCON
PRESS

NewCon Press
England

First published in the UK by NewCon Press
41 Wheatsheaf Road, Alconbury Weston, Cambs, PE28 4LF
April 2023

NCP 303 (limited edition hardback)
NCP 304 (softback)

10 9 8 7 6 5 4 3 2 1

ISBN:

978-1-914953-48-4 (hardback)
978-1-914953-49-1 (softback)

Cover art and internal illustration by Fangorn
Cover layout by Ian Whates

Minor editorial meddling and typesetting by Ian Whates

The opening section of this book "Serpent Rose" is dedicated to

Moira J Shearman, always.

朋友的眼睛是最好的镜子

The best mirror is a friend's eyes.

The Book of Gaheris in *toto* is for

Karen Kelly, who has always been my ideal reader.

Ultreia, peregrina!

Incipit

One

The boy hung on the railings, toes gripping the lower bar through thin cloth soles, upper bar pressed into his stomach, elbows making a pivot to rock him back and forth, back and forth. He no more noticed the shiver in the rail than the warm hand of the sun, toasting the back of his neck: his senses were full to the brim. He gazed at the tourney field, inhaling excitement with every breath. The last joust... He clasped his hands. The last one... His knight, the rose knight, *must* win. He could not speak for the hope of that: he must, he must, *he must*. His eyes bored into the back of the squire handing up water to the knight. If only he were older, that could be him. *Oh, come on, you must win this.* His hair flopped forward, tickling his cheeks: irritated, he shook his head. His mother leant forward, voice anxious, trying to draw him back down onto his seat. But he could not be still.

The squire took away the cup and offered instead the final lance. The rose knight took it, steadied it against his armoured thigh as he lowered his visor. *Oh, please.* The boy pitched further forward, grinding his elbows into the wood. *Please, God. I'll learn a new psalm.* His middle brother would sneer at that. But he didn't care. God understood him. God had made knights.

On the field, the horses gathered pace, kicking up sawdust. A confusion of sound and speed and metal, and then... A thud, a moment of stillness, and one knight tumbled to the ground in a plume of dust. Who was it? Who? The boy could not breathe for the waiting, clinging on to his rails. The dust cleared, and the crowd began to cheer. The winner had drawn up at one end of the course, the stub of his shattered lance still in his hand. A tall young man, a shade too thin for his shoulders, dressed in blond mail and a white surcoat. A knot of roses was emblazoned on his breast. As the boy

7

hung there, the knight pushed up his visor, looked back down the field. The boy quivered with delight. For a moment, their eyes met, and his knight grinned at him, laughing, still breathless and a little startled. The boy gazed back, too happy to smile, and rendered up his heart as the prize.

TWO

It was too hot in the stand, too hot and too dusty. Lady Elen of Nordgwalia tugged at her sleeves, one eye on the queen, the other on her youngest son, Lamorak, perched on the railings. Too hot and too awkward and not at all where she wished to be. Not fitting. She thought longingly of her still-room back at Rhuddlan, its coolness, its silence. She should not have to be here. It was not fitting. Three boys, and a petty kingdom without its lord, and no husband. God was not kind to widows. She straightened her veil, and hoped no one had noticed her fidgeting. She had no interests in tournaments, however well-staged, nor in the banquets that followed them, nor any of the court frivolities, but they must all be endured for the sake of her three sons. At her side, the eldest patted her hand kindly. Her rock, Aglovale, calm and unknowable at twenty two. The middle one, Percivale, had somehow evaded duty to browse the king's library. On the railings, the youngest pitched further forward, rocking alarmingly. She frowned. A dangerous life altogether, this business of knighthood, and one that would take all three away from her. It had already taken her husband, dead in war, and now Aglovale and Percivale were drifting away. She glanced sidelong at her eldest and he smiled, naming for her the combatants on the field. Kay, the king's seneschal, and Gaheris, brother of the famous Sir Gawain.

Brother of Gawain. Elen sighed. Her Lamorak was watching this Gaheris with adoring eyes,. Gawain's brother. One of those endless Orkneys who might – or might not – have killed her husband. Well, perhaps the king would be pleased. He wanted peace and affection between his lords, and an end to feuding. He wanted the war widows and orphans to attend his courts and share its jollities. It was so very hot. So dusty.

On his railing, Lamorak teetered and she reached out a hand to catch him back. He twitched free of her, ignored the caution in her voice. The battling knights kicked up more dust, and she raised her veil. At least it would soon be over, this knocking of one man into the dirt by another. She gazed at Lamorak. His jerkin was marked, and the sun had caught the back of his neck. He stared at the field, oblivious. The war had taken her husband, and it was not enough. The peace would take away her sons. Out on the field, someone had won, and Lamorak was rigid with excitement. She reached out to him, hesitated and withdrew her hand.

Three

I rinsed my mouth and spat surreptitiously into the sawdust. The stuff had got everywhere, into my eyes, under my nails, down the back of my mail. It itched abominably. I wanted a bath and a long cold drink. Instead… Up in the shady stand, my foster-brother caught my eye and pulled a face. A lot of comfort he was. Still, things were going well, just as he wanted. Even the dowager lady of Nordgwalia was here, sitting in the row of honour just below the queen. She looked as hot and bothered as I felt, and not a lot prettier. Arthur was going to have his work cut out there. In front of her, her youngest son was trying to break his neck, teetering on the railing. He had his eyes fixed firmly on my opponent, our newest knight, Gaheris of Orkney. Arthur would like that, no doubt, if the youngest of the Pellinors was to form a crush on one of the Orkney clan. Lady Elen certainly would not. I pulled down my visor, as my squire handed up my lance. Enough time to worry over politics later, after I'd dealt with young Heris. The dust had got into my helm, too, making me cough.

We faced one another, one on each side of the cane and cloth barrier. Heris fiddled with his reins. He wouldn't have expected to find himself here, not at this stage of the tourney. I straightened my shoulders as the flag came down, and set my heels to the flanks of my horse. Heris sat awkwardly. His mail was probably too tight: he'd done even more growing lately. I levelled my lance at his shield, aiming for the centre of his new rose knot device. Here it came… I felt the impact, as the dust rose up about us, blindingly.

Something slammed into my back. I gasped, and found myself down. So much for debutante nerves. I pulled myself to a sitting position and eyed Gaheris thoughtfully. Up in the stand, I could hear Arthur laughing.

I nodded to Gaheris, and his face cleared. Another one like Arthur, a born worrier. He looked away, and I followed his gaze as he locked eyes with a child hanging on the rail, and, quite suddenly, smiled.

Four

On the wide green swathe below the castle, the tourney stands stood tall in the sunlight. Multi-coloured pennants told over the names of host and guests, knights and wanderers. In his high seat, the king gazed out over the field and tried to conceal his anxiety. It was so uncertain, his five-summer crown: sometimes, he felt he was more juggler than king. Everyone wanted something from him, and no one wanted to see any other make a gain. His client kings tested their bounds and his justice; the loyalties of his young knights were yet to be fully tested. If he might only teach them all to trust, to respect, to understand each other, in place of their comfortable feuds. If he could only divert their aggression into the pursuit of mercy or law or skill. In the seats below him, he saw the dowager lady of Nordgwalia, four years widowed by one of those feuds. Her shoulders were stiff with tension: her hands fidgeted in her veil, or twitched towards her youngest son where he perched on the railings to watch the knights fighting.

It was easier with the young ones. They had fewer prejudices to overcome. But even so…

Out on the field, the king's newest knight looked nervous, wriggling in his saddle. His mail-shirt was just a little too tight. He just had to stop growing, it was getting embarrassing. He hoped he wouldn't make a fool of himself in this final bout. Not in front of the king. Not, more worryingly, in front of his eldest brother Gawain. He gulped down the cold water offered up to him by a squire, and tried to concentrate. This was only a game, the king had said so, but Gawain would care if he did something stupid. Such a thing might reflect poorly on the king. He bit his lip. Competence was called for, and a cool head, and above all that grace which held amity over rivalry and peace above resentment. He steadied his horse, tried to steady his hands.

A child on the railing was watching him with taut intensity. He neither knew nor cared that Gaheris' beloved brother might have bereft him of his father. All he saw was the joy and the skill and the glory. His mother tugged on the back of his jerkin, afraid for his bones, sensing the battle that had begun for his heart.

The knights charged in a flurry of dust. The king held his breath. He hoped he could count on Gaheris, but one never quite knew with the Orkneys. And Heris… Sometimes he had the oddest habit of saying exactly what he thought. There was a thump, and a crack of broken wood, and one knight fell. Arthur smiled. Poor Kay. He hated tourneys at the best of times. He would need his pride soothing tonight. Arthur glanced sidelong at the Lady Elen, at the Lord of Lys, at all the other rivals of the Orkney kindred. Set faces, one and all… His eye fell on the child Lamorak, still clinging to his rail, and he exhaled. The boy and Gaheris were gazing at each other, united in astonished delight. Perhaps, after all, there was hope.

PART ONE:
SERPENT ROSE

One

"Again!" Lamorak rolls to his feet, brushing straw from his shoulders, and looking hopeful. He's sixteen years old and fairly new to court. For all that, he's quick to learn how to get his way. I've seen the same look on greedy spaniels.

"No."

"Oh, come on."

"No, Lamorak. I've got other things to do. Go and ask Kay: he's master-at-arms."

"I don't want to ask Kay. Kay doesn't *like* me."

"Ask one of your brothers, then. One of *my* brothers? One of Sagremore's brothers?"

"You're making fun of me! Gaheris, you're my only friend."

"No, I'm not. You have plenty of friends."

"The only person who has time for me, then. Gaheris, *please.*"

"No. Go and ask Aglovale."

"I don't want Aglovale. I want you. You're far more..."

"... Stupid?"

"Sympathetic."

"Oh, that's a new one. I like that. Gaheris is sympathetic. Spelt g-u-l-l-i-b-l-e." I pick up my jerkin from the newel post and start to put it on. "No, Lamorak."

He has snake's eyes, long and cunning and yellow. They watch me reproachfully for a moment, then he turns his back. "It doesn't matter, anyway." He goes to the door, rests his head on the frame. "Forget it."

He sounds as though he's thinking of crying. That's another move I've learnt to recognise. I hesitate, with one boot on. "Lamorak, listen. I have duties to attend to, and you should be in the tilting yard practising knightly ways, not up here learning to wrestle."

He doesn't look round. He's not to be assuaged so easily. "Kay's in charge of training, and Kay doesn't like me."

"So? It's hardly personal. Kay doesn't like anybody. He told me yesterday that I was the most uncoordinated fighter he'd met this side of a duck. And I've been knighted ten years. It's just his way."

"But he makes me feel so worthless."

"Well, ignore it. You're already far better than I was at your age. He's just trying to make sure you keep working."

He turns, tears gone. "D'you really think so?"

"Yes. Kay…"

"No, about me. Am I really any good?"

His moods are ridiculous. Like talking to a woman. Smiling, I finish putting my boots on, and say "Yes, I think you're very good."

"For my age?"

"Don't fish." Lamorak looks plaintive. "Saint Anne! No, not just for your age. In comparison with all of us. Oh, you're not up to Lancelot, or my brother Gareth, but… You're certainly as good as I am – better, probably, though that's hardly difficult – you'd give Bors a run for his money, or Dinadan…" I tail off. "You're fine."

I'm very slow, sometimes. Lamorak's eyes light up, and he blocks my exit, grinning. "Then I hardly need Kay's training, do I? So we…"

Like all that family, he's built slight and wiry. It's easy enough to turn him, with a hand on his shoulder. "Who's that, with the blue cockade?'

"Sir Gareth. But…"

"But nothing. Gareth's out there, working with Kay. And if he needs it, you do. Yes?"

"Yes… But surely you… "He looks up over his shoulder at me.

'I have to go." I can stare him down, sometimes… After a minute, he shrugs, and swings out onto the ladder. He's only made me an hour late. I wait for him to reach the bottom before stepping out myself. With my weight, there's no point in taking risks. Halfway to the stable gate, he pauses, and looks round at me.

"Gaheris?"

"Umm?"

"Am I really better than you?"

"What a great achievement! Yes, I expect so." He's frowning, as though that troubles him. "What of it?"

"You always do that..." I want to start walking again, but he puts out a hand to stop me. "Will you fight with me, then? Swords?"

"Not now."

"No, but..."

"You won't learn anything. Better to ask Aglovale."

"Gaheris?" He sounds, I don't know, somehow anxious. His hand is on my arm, shaking it like a child. "Please?"

I sigh. What can one do? "All right. Swords." He takes the hand away, bouncing. "But, Lamorak..."

"Yes?"

"*Tomorrow.*"

There are four of us in all: four tall northern sons of Lot, tolerated in this southern land for our mother's kinship with Arthur. Most people think there are three, mind you; or think only three worth mentioning. I recall my aunt, speaking to the king of Dyfed, "Yes, my husband's nephews are a credit to us all. Gawain's a tiger in battle, and Gareth's beautiful – and pious, too – and Agravaine's *so* clever. Oh, yes, and there's Gaheris. He's... dependable."

Spelt gullible. There are worse things. My brothers make enemies, and other people watch out for it. That evening, in the refectory, Gawain glowers and the servants keep clear. It's me he's angry at, for all that. Halfway down his third cup of ale, he sets his knife down, all of a sudden, and stares. "It must stop. D'you hear me?"

Inevitably, I've a mouth full of bread. I say "What?" – it comes out more like "Umphg?"

"Spending so much time on the youngest de Galis. It attracts the wrong kind of attention. And he's a wastrel." He gestures to where Lamorak is barely visible underneath one of the waiting maids.

I look. His hair's a mess, and the girl has her hand inside his shirt. "He's young, Gavin."

"He's got no sense. Now, our Gari..." I catch his eye and look quizzical. "All right, Gari's exceptional. But I..."

"Lady Mahaut."

"I didn't say I was perfect, but..."

"Lady Avise. That girl from..."

"*Stop* it, Heris. All right, he's young. But his family..."

"He can't help who his family is."

"He's taking advantage. You know it." I have never been able to stare Gawain down. "I want you to stop letting him."

"He's not. And anyway, it's harmless."

"His father murdered ours."

Despite myself, I look around before answering. Our father's death has never been a safe subject here. I drop my voice as low as I may, and say, "It was war, Gavin. No one knows for sure. You know that. It could have been Balin. Urien admitted he didn't actually *see* Pellinor..."

"Might have murdered ours, then. Little difference. You're asking for trouble."

I look across at Lamorak, fondling the girl, and sigh. If we carry suspicion and envy from generation to generation, we'll never truly have peace. Ten years ago, the rash youngsters were Gavin and me. One young fool is very like another. Perhaps Lamorak feels my gaze: he looks up, and smiles. I smile back, and, beside me, Gawain thumps the table. A goblet jolts and falls, spilling wine into my lap. Gawain sighs heavily, and hands me his napkin. "Honestly, Heris."

"I'm sorry."

"Hmm." He pauses, chewing on a bite of meat. "Then there's your wife."

"Oh?" My wife's in love with my brother Gareth. She's never forgiven him for preferring her sister. "I know Luned isn't happy."

"D'you wonder at it, the amount of time you spend with her?"

It's on the tip of my tongue to suggest I take a solo trip to one of my manors, but Gawain's expression suggests that this may not be quite the time for flippancy.

"You leave her too much alone. She feels it."

That's a new one. Perhaps my face shows it, for Gawain looks faintly defensive. "Well, she does. Any woman would. People talk."

Evidently.

"And if you're seen to ignore her... Others may try and make something of it. They think, 'yon lass is lonely', and..."

"And?"

He looks uncomfortable. "Well, they try things."

With sour Luned? This is getting interesting. "What kind of things, Gavin?"

"*You* know." He stares again. My spine starts itching. "Paying court. Making advances. You should stop it."

"I haven't seen it start."

"Exactly. Because you neglect her. You let people get away with too much. Yon Lamorak..."

"Gavin..."

He rides over me, firmly. "Yon Lamorak's been making sheep's eyes at her. She told me so herself."

All the de Galis family are handsome, even quiet Aglovale. Percevale, the middle one, looks like the picture of St George in my mother's book of hours. "Lucky Luned. Perhaps it'll take her mind off Gareth."

"*Ga*heris!" Gawain's voice is too loud. Half the room turns to look at us, and I blush. "This is no joking matter."

No, Gavin.

"The family honour..."

Yes, Gavin.

"You must put your foot down, and stop letting people push you around! "

Overnight, it rains. The ground is caramel-sticky, clinging to boot soles, and miring the horses' feet. The sort of texture that makes the squires uneasy and crimps Kay's long face with a smile. It's warm, too, in that particular way that always makes me feel I should wash more often. I feel thick and disjointed, my hands too swollen to be ready on my sword. Lamorak's wasting his time. Crossing the first court, I skid three times, cursing, and drop my shield.

"Warm, wet and whingeing." The voice belongs to my brother Agravaine. Better and better. "I'm surprised at you. It's perfect weather for ducks." There's less than no point rising to him: it only makes him worse. I just shrug, and keep walking. Gawain's doing, probably. Sent him along to watch me. Guard the family honour.

Maybe *he* can spar with Lamorak. Then at least someone would get something out of this. Me, with luck. Picture Agravaine face down in this mud... Our mother has always said I'm too hard on him... I make myself smile. "Hmm. It's a pity I missed out on the webbed feet." He grins back at me, mocking.

Lamorak is waiting by the postern. The snake eyes are downcast. Well, anyone would have a thick head on the amount he drank last night. When I hail him, he jerks upright. "You're late, Gaheris." And then, frowning, "Oh, hello, Sir Agravaine."

"He's come to see the slaughter. Someone has to take the pieces back."

Agravaine cuts me off. "No, I've come to see fair play. One can't be too careful with some people."

"You'd know, I suppose," Lamorak says, smiling.

This morning is getting worse by the minute. Getting through the postern, I catch my lanyard on the latch and wind up dropping my shield again. Picking it up, I catch Agravaine in the side with the end of my scabbard.

"You are *such* a fool. Why didn't you bring Evan?"

"He's hungover. Anyway, I hardly need him for this. We're not even armoured."

"You should've been a priest. Good works and lame..."

"Ducks."

Agravaine catches my eye, trying to frown. I hold his gaze a few moments, then mouth *quack*. We both break up, laughing.

Lamorak has got ahead of us, and is already on the practice field, doing fives. He's quick, whipping the blade round, and stopping it with precision. Quicker than me. I may just have reach on him, if I can only keep my footing. I must remember not to hit him too hard, if I can hit him at all, unarmoured as we are. My strength is my only real gift in combat. For the rest... Having Agravaine for an audience is likely to guarantee I wind up flat on my back, even without the mud.

Agravaine is watching Lamorak. After a moment, he turns to me, and his face wears its calculating look. "You're sure you can do this, Heris?"

The buckle on my sword-belt is recalcitrant. "Umm?"

"I could take him for you. There are no witnesses, after all."

"Ouch!" The buckle springs open rather suddenly, and jabs me in the thumb. "What was that, Agrin?"

"I could fight him in your stead."

"I suppose it would be better from his point of view." I look at him, puzzled. "Shall I ask him?"

It's Agravaine's turn to look perplexed.

"Well, he did ask me originally..."

"So what?"

"So, he may prefer..."

"Heris, what does it matter which of us does it? All right, I am the older, but on that argument, it should be Gavin; and as long as father's finally avenged..."

"Avenged?" Sometimes I speak louder than I intend. Lamorak turns to look at us, enquiring, and moves to approach. I wave him back with a hand. "Would you care to explain that?"

Something, some light, drains from Agravaine's face. "My God. Gavin was right, then."

"Right about what?"

"About you and him." Agravaine gestures at Lamorak. "You're just letting him exploit you. And to think I thought... How did I come to be related to someone so stupid?"

"Ask Mother."

"Keep your tongue off her!" For a moment we stand, glaring at each other like over-heated boars. Then he sighs. "You have this golden opportunity... Everyone knows how Lamorak pesters you, and how inexperienced he is. An accident..." I never set out to fight with my brothers. It just happens. My hand is formed into a fist before I realise it. Agravaine watches me, supercilious, superior. "It could still happen, Heris. Maybe you are good enough to kill him. Or bright enough to let me do it for you."

I hit him. I may be heavy, and stupid, and slow, but I'm still bigger than Agravaine. He goes down in a heap at my feet, and lies there gasping. "Get up and say that again."

"And let you knock me down?"

"Why not?"

"Because you're not worth it." He pulls himself backwards on his elbows, and stands up a few feet away. "You'll regret this, Heris."

"Going to tell Mother?"

"I might."

"How brave. The haut Sir Agravaine, hiding behind a woman's skirts."

This time, he charges me. I get his legs in a scissor grip, and we both go down. Over his shoulder, I get a brief glimpse of Lamorak, gawping. Then Agravaine bites me, and I get distracted. It takes a few muddy minutes, but finally I'm kneeling astride him, with his right arm locked behind his back. "Apologise."

His face is half in the mud. Even so, he gasps out "Drop dead."

I'm not feeling obliging. Somewhere off to one side, a voice asks "What's happening", and Lamorak answers "I have no idea." Someone else, disappointed, says "Oh, it's only the Orkneys again."

Lovely, an audience. "Apologise, Agrin."

"No... Heris, you'll break my arm!"

"Good. Maybe you'll learn some manners."

"From you?" He manages to laugh. "I doubt you could do it. *You* can't even bed your wife."

He's my brother... Somehow, I keep my spare hand from his throat.

From behind me, Lamorak says "You filthy liar!", and Agravaine laughs the more. I breathe in, deeply. I must keep Lamorak out of this...

He's standing right behind me. I gesture for him to move back, then rise to a crouch, holding Agravaine at arm's length. "If I let you go, will you get up and walk away?" He lies there, still laughing. "Will you, Agrin?"

"Yes."

"All right... No, Lamorak, stand clear..." I step aside myself, still holding on. Agravaine cheats. "I'm letting go… now."

I'm not quite quick enough. As I let go, Agravaine rolls, and kicks me above the knee. He's laughing as he walks away. "Brother Gaheris. What an idiot."

Lamorak pulls me to my feet again. I'm resigned, but he's white-faced, and trembling. "Why do you let him talk to you like that?"

I'm going to limp for an hour or two. Still Agravaine's black eye will last for days. "He's my brother. Forget it."

"But he treats you like… like…" Lamorak stops, stuck for a word. "And Sir Gawain, last night…"

"Older brothers" privilege."

"You don't act like that with Sir Gareth."

"Gareth doesn't need it."

"And you do?"

"Probably."

For a moment, Lamorak glares, angry less with Agravaine than with me. Then without another word, he turns and walks away.

It's late – midnight or after – when the knock comes at my door.

Evan lies in heavy sleep across the hearth: I too should be sleeping, but I can't. An hour-long lecture from Gawain, followed by reproaches from Gareth and a tearful interlude with Luned have cut up my rest. It's with resignation that I roll off the bed, and answer the door. If I'm *really* lucky, it's Agravaine, back for another round.

Lamorak stands outside, swaying. His clothes are stained, and his face is bruised and blotchy. Blood runs down over one hand, and drips on the floor. He links at me, owl-like. There's enough alcohol on his breath to floor a donkey. He takes a pace forward, then stops. "Did I wake you?"

"No." I don't know what to say, caught here framed in my own doorway. His hair is falling into his eyes: he pushes it back, smearing blood across his face. The effect is grotesque.

"Can I come in?"

He'll wake Evan. "No, Lamorak. It's late."

"But I want to." He looks perplexed. "Please, Gaheris." "No."

His face crumples, child-like. Tears spill over from the snake eyes. He's drunk and he's maudlin. Holy Saints. I could wake Evan myself, and have him fetch Aglovale… "You don't like me. No one does. No one wants me round here."

"Lamorak…"

"You don't want me." His voice is rising: someone is going to be disturbed, and Gaheris of Orkney will take the blame again. "All right, you can come in. But only for a minute or two."

Evan is bound to wake up: I can't let him see Lamorak in this condition… I steer Lamorak into the window embrasure, then go and shake Evan awake. It won't be the first time. There's a girl, from the laundry, who visits me sometimes. Evan looks up blearily, and I pull him to his feet. "Go and sleep in the dormitory. I've got a visitor." As I speak, I'm bundling his bedding into his arms. "Go on. Come back in the morning."

Luckily for me, he's more than half-asleep still, and doesn't bother me with questions. I shut the door behind him, and turn back to Lamorak.

"So. What's the matter?" He's sitting on the window sill, looking woebegone. I shall have to do something about that hand. There are bandages somewhere… "What did you do to yourself, anyway? You haven't been fighting?"

"No…" He doesn't sound certain.

"Did you break something? Fall over?" He shakes his head to both. I find clean linen at the bottom of a chest, and start pouring water into a basin. "What, then? You do remember?"

"Yes." He's barely audible. The water's cold, but it'll have to do.

"Want to tell me?" It's too dark in here for cleaning wounds. I light the candles. "Come and sit down over here."

He's trailing blood everywhere. Something else to take care of. He sits down on the edge of my bed, and looks at me, plaintively. The blood is from a deep cut in his right forearm. It's dirty now, but it was made by something clean; a knife, perhaps, rather than a stake, or a potsherd. He winces as I start to wash it. "Well then?"

"Percevale…"

"*Percevale* did this?"

"No." For a moment, Lamorak sounds almost scornful. Then "He doesn't care enough. He said…"

"Yes?"

"He said it's all my fault."

Families. Sometimes I wonder what would happen if they were simply abolished. "What's all your fault?"

"This morning. You fighting with Sir Agravaine."

"He's daft, then. Agravaine and I are always falling out about something. We've been doing it all our lives."

"Yes, but…" He rubs his uninjured hand across his face. "It was because I… Percevale thinks… Lady Luned…"

It takes me a moment or two to work out what he's trying to say. I put a hand on his shoulder, and look into the snake eyes. "It had nothing to do with any compliments you may have paid to Luned. Agravaine and I don't need a reason to argue. We just get under one another's skin. Don't you ever fall out with your brothers?" Was I ever this young? It doesn't seem likely. When I was sixteen we were at war, and Gawain and I were fighting for Arthur against the five kings. Fighting against our own father, Lot, who died in that war at the hand of one of our allies. So Orkney: to fight each other over one thing, then close ranks after the event. Agravaine stayed out of that one, left on Orkney to guard our mother and two youngest brothers. He wasn't there when Lot fell, at Pellinore's hand, or Balin's or God alone knows who. But he remembered, and worked on Gawain, until the latter had no choice but to seek vengeance.

Agrin never forgives or lets go.

No point in telling Lamorak about that. He's too young to remember my father at all, or much about his own, and his older brothers are peaceful men.

I wish Gawain had let Pellinor alone, all the same.

"My brothers and I…. Aglovale's too old, and Percevale's too… Percevale."

Well, when it comes to it, I seldom quarrel with Gareth. "I expect it's the red hair that does it, then. All my family have terrible tempers. Especially when it's raining." That makes him smile. "So. About this cut?"

He looks uncomfortable. "I did it."

"You cut yourself? Why, in God's name?"

"To even things out. I hurt you, this morning." His eyes begin to fill. He's less sober than I'd begun to hope. I've finished cleaning the cut, and am tying off the bandage. "I'm sorry, Gaheris."

"There's nothing to be sorry for." I pour some more water into a cup, and hand it to him. "Now, drink that. It'll help clear your head."

Obediently, he drinks. I start to clean his blood from my floor. He says, softly "My family isn't like yours. We're not... close."

"There's something to be said for that."

"It's lonely." There's silence: in the hearth, a log falls. "What's it like, having brothers like yours?"

"Very noisy, usually."

"I wish I was one of you."

"Do you?" I look across at him. "You might not like it. Our mother... "

He interrupts me. "Gareth. I wish I was Gareth."

"The second-best knight in the world? It's a fair ambition."

"No." Again, he's scornful. "I could be close to you. And no one would mind."

I don't like where this is heading. It happens sometimes that one of the squires or knights' candidate gets to following one of the senior knights. Lancelot, most often, or Bedwyr. Never me. I don't know what to do with this. I say, "Gareth and I aren't so close. I was away to serve Arthur while he was still in the nursery, like you and Aglovale. You should be going back to your room, now, Lamorak."

He ignores me. He's pulled his legs up onto my bed and is sitting with his chin on his knees. "You remember the Chester court? Eight years ago?"

"Not specifically."

"It was midsummer. Mother brought to court for the first time. I was eight years old." His eyes are far away, seeing something outside the room. "It was... I don't know. Another world. There was a tourney. You took the prize."

Now I remember. "Lancelot was away, and Gareth still home in Lothian, and Gawain was so hungover he couldn't ride straight. It was no big achievement. I was just lucky."

"It was everything." Lamorak's voice is fierce. "You're so fair to everyone but yourself!"

"We all get our moment, I suppose."

"Don't…" His voice cracks suddenly, and he hides his face on his knees. Muffled, he says, "You don't understand."

"No." I put the basin back down on its stand, and go to sit beside him. "When I was your age, I worshipped my brother Gawain. He seemed… I don't know, he was so…"

"It's not like that." I'm startled by his vehemence. Startled, and a little afraid. After a moment, he raises his head again, and smiles. It's weak, but a smile, all the same. "I think I drink too much."

"It's possible."

"Will it always be like this?"

"What?"

"I don't know. Life."

"Who knows? You might ask Bishop Dyfrig."

"Yes… Gaheris, may I ask you something? A… boon."

I'm going to regret this. Gawain will lecture and Agravaine will shout. I should say no, but he's giving me the spaniel face again. "I don't know. What is it?"

"At Christmas, I'm to be knighted. Will you stand sponsor for me?"

"That's your brother's place."

"Aglovale won't mind."

"I wouldn't be so sure of that."

"Please, Gaheris."

"It's not that simple. Protocol…"

"I could petition the king."

"No, Lamorak, listen…"

"And you'll train with me? I mean to be the third best knight in the world, after Lancelot and you."

"You mean Gareth."

"Do I?"

Two

It's a fortnight or so later that Kay starts one of his 'improving' conversations after dinner. It's one of those fascinating issues: the ideal of knighthood. What makes a knight, and why. What qualities he should display. Which of the current knights show which qualities, and which, if any, reach the ideal. The queen has retired, but the king my uncle remains at table, listening. I'm not really paying attention: I nurse my ale, and stare into the fire. I'm warm, well-fed, and comfortable. Agravaine has let me alone for the past five days entire. Lamorak hasn't wept on me once. Even the weather's improved: the only cloud is my mother's imminent arrival. We've drawn lots for that, and it's Gawain who's to be the sacrificial host. To Agrin's irritation, and Gareth and my silent relief.

That's not one of the knightly virtues Kay suggests, filial devotion. Saints be thanked. I've enough shortcomings already. His trainees toss the words between them, each anxious to shine, and win the king's approval. There are six of them, due to be knighted at Christmas: quiet Astamore; merry Patrise; Gereint, who's a distant cousin of mine; Amran, oldest of Bedwyr's sons; Osian the poet; and Lamorak. He's unusually quiet, for once, watching his companions.

A handful of the older knights remain, though not all are listening. Bedwyr sits in a corner, smiling as his son, blushing, defends the role of loyalty in a knight's code. Beside him, Lancelot leans on the mantle. Percevale has already held forth for fifteen minutes or more on the need for piety. Lucan the butler cut him off, with a comment on hospitality which made the trainees laugh, and Kay turn his eyes to heaven. The room is blessedly clear of Orkneys, unless one counts my first cousin Ywain, who looks to be asleep.

"But what's more important," asks Osian, "loyalty to one's liege, or to God?"

"It's the same thing," says Amran, shocked. "The king is God's anointed!"

"But if your liege is a duke, say, not the king?" Kay suggests.

"Well, a duke is the king's servant, so…"

"And if he goes into rebellion?"

"You stand by your king!"

"Not your liege-lord? Even though you've sworn a holy oath to uphold him?"

"If he's betrayed his own oath…" Amran looks at his father for help: Bedwyr smiles, and opens his hands. "Well, God can see into all men's hearts, which might…"

"It becomes a matter of conscience," I say quickly. Amran looks relieved. Arthur glances across at me, and smiles. "You have to do what you feel is right."

Kay catches my eye, wickedly. "Whatever the cost? Even at the expense of betraying a kinsman?"

So Gawain chose our uncle over our father. I was his squire back then and I followed him for love and honour. Before I can do more than pull a wry face at Kay, Percevale says firmly "God is the highest liege a man may have."

"That's why a knight absolutely has to…"

"What about courtesy?" puts in Kay, who isn't famed for possessing it. Percevale subsides with a grin, and the discussion veers off on this new tangent.

I top up my ale, and go back to staring at the fire. Perhaps this is why we do it all, for these quiet evenings. Patrise has taken firm hold of the conversation, and is about demonstrating, point by point, that Lancelot is the highest flower attainable by chivalry, and a paragon of all knightly virtues, to boot. Gereint keeps trying to interrupt him with an obscure comment about Tristan, of all people. I'm fervently grateful for the absence of Agravaine. He'd be unlikely to be able to resist the chance to drop hints about loyalty to queens.

"… and Sir Lancelot's honourable, too. His word…"

"Yes, but about Tristan…"

"Shut up, Gereint. Everyone knows that Sir Lancelot's word is as good as a Bible oath. He…"

"This is complete hypocrisy!" The voice is Lamorak's. Lancelot straightens ups, and looks at him speculatively. "You're all sitting here, talking as if he isn't here, praising him to the stars, and he hasn't even blushed!"

"Lamorak..." Kay begins.

Lamorak ignores him. "If he's so good, and noble, and... and so all-round perfect, then..."

"*Lamorak...* "

"No, Kay, let him talk," Lancelot says quietly. I wish Gawain was here, suddenly, or that Ywain would wake up.

"Well, you'd think he'd at least have the grace to look embarrassed!"

Lancelot looks startled. He was, I suspect, expecting something else. Kay chokes on his drink, and has to be thumped on the back by Lucan. There's a silence. Lamorak hesitates, then takes a deep breath. "I'll tell you what makes a true knight."

"Oh, will you?" says Kay, gasping.

"We've been talking round it, all evening." Lamorak sounds defensive. "Courtesy, and altruism, and being merciful, and loyal, and all that... But it's not just having those qualities, is it? It's *how* you have them." Percevale has been frowning; abruptly his face clears, and he looks at his brother with a curious intensity. "The way you make it sound, a knight spends all his time thinking about himself. Doing all those fine things just to show off how noble and knightly he is. Like a competition, or something. Instead of doing them... naturally. Doing them because they're right, and because it serves other people, not to show off, or to beat someone, or to be best all the time."

"Humility, you mean?" says Bedwyr.

"Yes. That's it. And if you start thinking about how things look, or how good you are compared with others, wanting to be top, then you haven't got it, have you? And it doesn't matter if you *are* the best warrior, or the most courteous, or anything, because you're doing it all for the wrong reason. You're doing it for yourself. And, in the same way, it wouldn't matter if you're *not* the best warrior, or whatever, as long as you're doing what you do for the right reasons. Because you believe in the ideal, not in yourself."

There's another silence. Then Percevale says "But God grants skill to His chosen. When a knight acts for Him, then He rewards His servant with excellence, for God's greater glory. And since only God can confer excellence, then…"

"No!" Lamorak glares at his brother. "That's just arrogance. Assuming God favours you just because you happen to be good at thumping people! Assuming someone's better spiritually simply because of feats of arms!"

"Amen to that," Lancelot says, softly.

My uncle the king looks at Lamorak, thoughtfully. "That's a very high ideal of knighthood. But is it possible? Do you think a man can be so selfless?"

"He can try, sire." Lamorak hesitates, then looks at me. Suddenly, I've got a very bad feeling about this.

"And I know someone who does. Without thinking about how it looks, or how good he is, or making comparisons. Just being… who he is."

I'm quite close to the door. Perhaps I can leave without attracting too much attention… Behind me, Kay says "Well, Lamorak, enlighten us. Who is this paragon?"

I *wish* I was faster on my feet. I still don't have my hand on the latch as Lamorak says, scornfully, "Gaheris, of course."

Of course.

"He's kind, and courteous, and always ready to help others – like you, Amran – and he never makes an issue out of his own abilities, but praises other people, and he doesn't try to be top, or to show other people up, and you all make fun of him, and tease him, and he doesn't even mind…"

All eyes have turned to me. My face feels as hot as the fire, and my pulse is pounding. If the floor would only open up. Lamorak pursues his theme relentlessly, "And he's loyal, and honourable, and…"

My mouth is too dry to interrupt. Some-one says *"Gaheris?"* and some-one else answers "Surely not..."

I find my voice, at last. "Lamorak means Gareth. Don't you? It was a slip of the tongue."

"No." Lamorak begins, but I talk over him, blessing Orkney volume. "Gareth, now. I'm his brother, and maybe shouldn't say it, but you'd go a long way to meet his equal – saving your presence, Lancelot. We all know how brave he is, though he'll never admit it, and..." Lamorak is staring at me as though I've just stabbed him, but I don't stop talking until Gereint butts in, and finally makes his point about Tristan.

I stop him, later, as the conversation breaks up. The snake eyes are anxious. "I'm sorry, I'm sorry."

"I've survived worse things. Cheer up."

"I didn't mean to embarrass you. It's just..."

"Forget it."

"But I *didn't* mean Sir Gareth."

"No. But you're still wrong about me, you know. Regardless of... strength of arms, or whatever, I'm no paragon."

"Gaheris..."

"No, listen to me. I have a God-awful temper, and I'm easily as stubborn as Gawain. I'm unfaithful to my marriage vows. I forget fast days, and sometimes I avoid confession for weeks at a time. I have all the Orkney virtues; pride, and vengefulness, and... and damned arrogance about my family. And I do mind when people make fun of me: you saw me fight Agravaine."

Lamorak looks unconvinced. "You always put yourself down."

"I thought you considered that a virtue!"

"I didn't mean..." Lamorak begins, then gives up, and just laughs.

I'm about to follow him from the room, but the king stops me.

"Heris? May I be avuncular and interfering?"

"I've done something stupid again!"

"What? No." He looks faintly rueful. "You shouldn't be so apologetic, you know. Come and sit down over here, and talk to me." I sit. "It's something I've done. I've been meaning to mention it for ages, but somehow..." He shrugs. "You've a knack for blending into the background."

"Handy, in my family."

He considers. "Yes, I suppose so. Agravaine's poor eye!"

"I'm sorry about that. I got carried away."

"Yes, well, I expect he asked for it." I must show faint surprise, for he smiles, and adds "I do know a thing or two about the dynamics of your family."

"Yes, sire. Uncle."

"Anyway… It's about Luned."

Gawain must have been at work. I stare at my feet, and try not to shuffle. "I'm sorry, sire. I do try to make her happy, but…"

"Dear Gaheris. I do wish you'd let me finish."

"I'm sorry."

"She is unhappy, isn't she? Are you?"

"Well, I… It's not as though I had a special lady or anything, before, or…"

"It wasn't fair, was it?" I look up, puzzled. "Poor Luned. I thought it would be for the best, at the time, giving her some status, and you didn't seem to mind, but…" He sighs. "It wasn't, though. I'm very sorry, Heris."

Kings aren't supposed to apologise, even to their nephews. "It's all right, really. I mean, the queen likes her, and…"

He laughs. "Oh, Gaheris! Always trying to make the best of it!" He shakes his head, and looks sober. "The fact is, I should never have forced you into marrying each other. Luned was in love with Gareth, and I rushed her. I should have let her stay here as one of Gwen's maidens for a while, let her settle down, and get over it a bit. Instead… And now she feels hard-done by, and entrenched about Gareth, and she blames you, which is most unfair since it's really *my* fault."

Not Gawain, then. Luned must have been talking to the queen. "I'm sorry. I do try to be nice to her."

"I know you do, but…" He pauses, frowning. "This is going to be the interfering bit, I'm afraid."

"I don't mind."

"No." Again he looks thoughtful. "It's just I've noticed the way you behave with her… If I didn't know better, I'd think she was in the last stages of some terrible illness. Do you think you could treat her a little bit more like an ordinary person?"

"I just worry I'm going to upset her."

"I know you do. But the result is, I don't think she's ever really got to know you."

"I'm sorry."

"Oh, Heris…!" He looks reproachful. "I feel mean, asking. But…

Do you think you could court her a little? As if she's just another of the Queen's ladies? Let her see herself as something other than the girl Gareth rejected?"

I hadn't thought of it like that. "Yes, sire. I could try, anyway. She may not like it, though."

He smiles at me. "You've a good heart, Gaheris. Lamorak de Galis was right about that."

"Oh, Lamorak...! He was just talking. He didn't intend anything."

Arthur's expression is quizzical. But, "I wonder?" Is all he says.

"Oh, that's beautiful!"

I'm standing watching the youngsters tilt: Kay's notion of a present to them, a whole day of games. On the field, Lamorak has unhorsed Astamore with a clever double feint. The manoeuvre attracts a ripple of applause. Lamorak looks up and grins. The snake eyes are shining. Meeting mine, briefly, he gives me a high sign, and I shake my head at him. I'm not really expecting a response to my comment, but: "It *was* splendid."

Lancelot, of all people, has come to lean on the railing beside me. His face is thoughtful. My brothers Gawain and Gareth are close friends of this man. They can spend hours together, talking and joking. For myself, I'm foundered in nerves by his reputation. Out in the field, Lamorak and Astamore are squaring up again. I keep my eyes on them. Lancelot says softly, "He has that look to him... that shining quality..."

Like Gareth. Like Lancelot himself. I can't quite keep the pride from my voice, answering. "He is good, isn't he? He wants to be the third-best knight in the world, after you and Gareth."

"Why aim so low?" Lancelot says, and sighs. "He's a credit to you." Surprise makes me look at him.

"To Kay and Aglovale, surely?"

He shakes his head. "Oh, Gaheris... How many hours a week have you worked with him?" I say nothing, picking at a splinter on the rail. "Everyone's noticed. Half the trainees are jealous, and Kay's on at the king to have you made his deputy."

"Lamorak's a natural. I'm just someone to practise on."

"Heaven give me strength! I'm beginning to see why you Orkneys are always fighting each other... Lamorak has aptitude, I grant you, but that's not enough on its own. You've got him to slow down, to think with his head as well as his reflexes."

"I doubt it. Thinking's not my strong suit. Kay..."

"Agrees with me." There's a small silence. On the field, Lamorak has Astamore down again, and is dismounting to fight on foot. Quietly, Lancelot says "I've been thinking about what he said about you."

"Kay?" Waste of time, I'd have thought, unless you happen to be fond of poultry. Still, Lancelot's an odd one. "I took no offence: it was fair comment. My foot-work..."

"I was talking about Lamorak."

Oh.

"The other evening..."

"He didn't mean it. It was just..."

"What he most assuredly did not mean was your brother Gareth."

"Oh, but..."

Lancelot cuts me off firmly. "That boy idolises you. You're his pattern... his *preux chevalier.*"

"I can't think why. He can aim much higher."

"For heaven's sake, Gaheris!" He sounds so exactly like Gawain that I turn to stare at him. So do several other people. For a moment he looks at me in pure exasperation, then he shakes his head. "Now you've got me doing it! Don't you ever have a single, positive thought about yourself?"

"I'm as selfish as the next man."

"Hah!" He pulls a face. "As long as you're standing next to Percevale, or Bors. Lamorak has you almost exactly right. We could all learn a thing or two from your humility."

"That's nonsense." I clench my hands on the rail, and look down. I want to be almost anywhere else.

"What did he say? Courteous, considerate, careful in your

dealings with all…"

"I've had more than my share of blood-feuds."

"All of them started by one or other of your incendiary brothers."

"Just stop it!" I don't believe I've just said that, to Lancelot, of all people… "Saints, I'm sorry. I didn't mean…"

"Shut up." I fall silent, but it's a moment or two before I remember to close my mouth. "Lamorak was right. Knighthood isn't just a matter of skill at arms – though you're no fool in that department, either – (no, don't interrupt me). It's a… a question of attitude. A man can be the greatest warrior in the world, and still be nothing, if he forgets his honour, or betrays his duty. And God help him who does that…" His voice trails off. For a moment his face is bleak. He's talking more to himself than me. Then he looks up and says briskly, "The only thing Lamorak missed about you is your damnable naivety. And God knows, if it was a question of Gareth, or Percevale, they'd call it innocence… You're hating this, aren't you?" I say nothing. "I should know better than to lecture you."

"No, I…" I make myself look across at him. "It doesn't sound like me."

"No, I don't suppose it would." Lancelot smiles. "Forgive me?"

"Nothing to forgive." A burst of applause tells me Lamorak has won his round. I hesitate, then "Lancelot, I wonder – could I ask a favour of you?"

"Of course."

"It's not for me, really, it's for him; for Lamorak." Lancelot looks enquiring. "He's got this silly idea about his knighting… He wants to petition the king. Of course, it's Aglovale's place, but for some reason he wants me instead, to sponsor him. And I thought, if you're willing, if you were to offer yourself, then no one would make anything *political* of it, and it would be an honour for Lamorak…"

"He'll refuse."

"Of course he won't. To be sponsored by Lancelot du Lac! I mind our Gareth…"

"Some of them might like the idea, but not your Lamorak." Unexpectedly, he puts a hand on my shoulder. "Gaheris, he wants *you*. Not his brother, or the seneschal, or the soi-disant best knight.

It's an honour. You should agree."

"Gawain…"

"Gawain's a reasonable man. Who knows, maybe this is just the thing finally to put an end to that blasted feud. Unless you don't want to?"

I look at Lamorak, garnering congratulations from the other trainees. "My brothers won't like it."

"Confound your bloody brothers!" says Lancelot.

Oh, no.

Oh, no. Three pairs of accusing eyes line up against me, along the wall of my room. All right, two accusing and one baffled, if you make allowances for Gareth. But all the same, my own room is going a bit far. I close the door behind me. "This is nice. Is it my birthday?"

Dear Gareth looks even more perplexed. "I don't think so. Gavin said he wanted a conference, so…"

"My room being smaller than his, darker than yours, and messier than Agrin's, you decided it was the obvious location?"

"Stop trying to confuse Gari." Gawain frowns. "Surely you know why we're here?"

"I daresay I could make a wild guess."

"There's no need to take that tone," Agravaine says. His black eye has healed, more's the pity.

"Oh?"

"I could teach you a better one."

"And earn another black eye?"

Agravaine takes a step forward. Gawain puts out a hand to halt him. "Heris, sit you down. Agrin, stop the insults."

I hesitate. Gareth adds, "Please, Heris?"

Sometimes I think the young and the innocent make the best manipulators.

Gawain waits till I'm seated, then, "We have need of your opinion."

"If," says Agravaine, "you know what one of those is." Gareth kicks him. He frowns, but falls silent.

"Well then, Heris?"

"It might help if you told me *what* you what my opinion on. If it's Agrin, there, for instance…"

"You can stop it, too," Gawain says. I shrug. "It's about Lamorak de Galis."

"Oh, Gavin, not again."

Gawain grins at me. "Lance told me what he said of you. That's a compliment for any man."

"Granted the wit to see it," puts in Agravaine, and Gareth kicks him again.

Gawain ignores the interchange. "Happen, too, I watched the infants' tourney. Lamorak's a fair man with his arms."

"Well?"

"Well, our uncle tells me he's bespoke you as sponsor."

Here we go. "Yes, but I told him…"

"Now, then. It befits a man to hold by his kin, and it's not always a fine thing, choosing another over a brother. But that said, our Gari chose Lance over me, and he's no less our brother for it. Then, too, the king would like it, all of us to be brothers in the fellowship."

"To which Lamorak has not been elected," says Agravaine, "Nor may he live to be."

"Stop your mouth, Agrin, or I'll stop it for you. It comes to this, Heris. I'll not say I'm keen on these sons of Pellinor, but if you want to do it, I'll not stop you. What do you say?"

There's a strong temptation in me to ask him why he needs my opinion on what is, after all, one of his pronouncements. However, Agravaine is making enough trouble for now. So, "You're speaking for yourself, or for the family?"

"The family," Gawain says, over loud sounds of derision from Agravaine. "Leastways, Gari feels as I do, and Agrin *did* say, earlier, that he'd no mind to stop you, umm…"

"From making a public fool of myself?"

"As long as it's quite clear to all parties that I've no part in your folly," says Agravaine, and bows. "But as to Mother, and Medraut…"

"Medraut's not sixteen, yet," says Gawain, as though that settles it.

"And Mother?" Agrin has a point there. Our mother may not have loved our father, but she has a highly-developed sense of property.

Gawain's about to pronounce on this, when there's a knock at my door. Evan, probably. Answering it, I get as far as "What...?" before Lamorak bounces past me, talking a blue streak.

"I was good, wasn't I? I saw you watching, and Sir Lancelot said so, after, though I'd rather have your opinion than his. And he said I could fight on his side at the New Year's tourney, if I liked, but I said I'd rather be on yours, and, oh, Gaheris..."

It's nice to be popular... About this point I manage to break in, by dint of raising my voice rather more than I like to. "Good evening, Lamorak. Will you come in, and greet my brothers."

He stops, then, and looks about him. Gareth smiles. Agravaine is staring at the floor. Gawain just looks at him. "Oh." Lamorak shuffles. "Good even, my lords of Orkney."

"Good even, Lamorak." Gareth is amused. Agravaine simply mutters.

Gawain nods. "Lancelot's no mean judge of fighting men. I might even agree with him. You did well today."

Lamorak looks momentarily nonplussed. Then he remembers his manners, and bows. "Thank you, Prince Gawain." At once he forgets them again. "Oh, but, Gaheris..."

"What did Kay say?" I ask.

That deflates him a little. "That a shield is to be used for parrying, not for waving at people with. But, Gaheris..."

He reminds me of Gareth at this age. Myself, too, I daresay. "You'll do, I expect." Lamorak looks downcast. "You were good."

"Oh, thank you!" For a moment, I'm afraid he's going to hug me. But he controls himself, and merely bounces a little. "And about the big tourney?"

"You're not a knight, yet," says Agravaine, silken-smooth. "What makes you think you can ride with the Orkneys?"

Lamorak looks anxious. Gently, Gareth says "It's a great honour, being asked by Lancelot."

Gawain is watching, thoughtful. "Well, lad? Do you hold yourself good enough to be one of us?"

"But, Gavin, if Lance…"

"Be quiet, Gari. Let the lad speak."

Lamorak draws in a deep breath. Then he looks straight at Gawain. "No, my lord Prince. But the honour of it!"

It's an answer calculated to appeal to Gawain's vanity, and Gawain's smart enough to spot it. Hastily, I say, "Wait, though. Gawain's not fighting. *Will* there be an Orkney side this year?"

Agravaine sighs. "My God. It's true: one must pin something to a lance, and run you through with it before you notice anything." Beside me, I feel Lamorak tense. "Of course there's an Orkney side."

My brother the second-best knight in the world goes faintly pink. "As it happens, our uncle has asked me to be the other leader. But Lance and I thought, for this year, we might pick teams in a less family-oriented way."

"Stupid idea."

"Do be quiet, Agrin, please. For myself, I'd be happy to have Lamorak, if he likes. But I think Lance is meaning to ask Heris."

"Well, lad," says Gawain, looking wicked, "will you go with Gaheris, or do you prefer the honour of riding with Agravaine and Gareth?" Lamorak looks stricken. Suddenly, Gawain laughs. "Let be: I'm teasing. Ride with whoever you please, though happen I was leading this year, I'd choose you, anyway." The light is back in Lamorak's face. "Aye, and my brother will stand sponsor for you, if you wish it still."

He might have asked me… Lamorak makes his very best bow to Gawain, then turns. "Gaheris?"

"What about Aglovale?"

"He doesn't mind. I asked him."

"You could have Lancelot."

"Gaheris!"

I look round at my assembled family. Gareth is still smiling. Agravaine has turned his back. Gawain stares back at me for a long moment, then, all unexpected, winks. "All right, then, Lamorak, but…"

This time, he does hug me.

Three

The next fortnight is a chaos of activity for everyone from the queen down. Rooms that haven't been looked at for eight months are turned out and shaken. Private quarters are commandeered wholesale, and most of us regular residents find ourselves stacked up dozens deep. As two brothers married to two sisters, Gareth and I are packed in together, with one and a half rooms for ourselves, our wives, and brother Agravaine, whose wife Laurel is a cousin of Luned's. We're spared Gawain only by Llinos's pregnancy, which leads the queen to take pity on her, and spare her his snoring. The knights-elect are even worse off: usually they're two to a room, but now all six are squashed into one dormitory along with the junior squires and even some of the pages. Lamorak bewails the impossibility of ever finding any of his particular possessions again. I tell him it's character-forming (one of Agravaine's bouquets), and find it necessary to throw him before he hits me.

The first three times I try courting Luned, she behaves as though I'm in the last stages of insanity. The fourth time, she asks me what I'm up to. The fifth, she hits me, but more in exasperation than in anger; and I make a number of interesting discoveries, not least that there are one or two situations to which brother Gareth's perfect manners just aren't adequate.

Mother arrives, with my appalling youngest brother Medraut in tow, and demands of the king that he start his knightly novitiate immediately. Medraut himself responds by forming an instant passion for Laurel, which distracts Agravaine nicely. Luckily for her other sons, Mother is co-opted to help with the castle-keeping, and more or less leaves us alone. Even with her occupied, though, it's safest to spend as much time as possible as at the far end of the grounds. Some blessed conjunction of circumstances keeps Mother from discovering my exact involvement with this year's knightings, and for once Kay plays right into my hands by anticipating royal consent, and installing me as deputy.

I find I quite enjoy dropping – and being dropped by – trainees into the mud. Llinos wails at the amount of dirt I trail into our overcrowded quarters, and Agravaine congratulates me on having at last found my natural element. In honour of Mother, I refrain from blacking either of his eyes. Lamorak complains, a little, at having to share my attention, but his heart isn't really in it. There's too much going on.

It's my favourite of all the courts, Christmas. The speaking silence of the midnight mass, with all of us lined up in the cathedral, row upon row, united, at peace. And after it, the revelry, with ranks and quarrels put aside, and pages running riot, and Kay uncertain whether to laugh or curse as the conventions fall down around our ears. And the music, and the dancing, and the sudden sweet flirtations… And at New Year the great tourney, with rebated weapons and laughing conflict. It's everything, all folded into a ten-day, and played through at speed. Nothing spoils it, not even Mother. I've not missed a one, since I first came to Caerleon as Gawain's squire.

Until this year. The day before Christmas eve, I misjudge a parry, and catch Lamorak's sword between my shield and my forearm. We're both off-balance: his full weight comes down on me when we fall. I hit my head hard enough to knock myself out, and break my collar-bone and two ribs. He gets away with a few bruises. It's an accident, clear enough, though Agravaine growls, and Aglovale de Galis takes to looking anxious. Lamorak acts as if he's expecting to be tried for murder, and I get to miss most of the festivities. The only consolation is that at least I get a room to myself, on the direction of the court physician. Too much to myself, it turns out, for no one has time to amuse the wounded at this season.

St Stephen's, Kay comes by to see me. The vigil of the new knights will be the next night, with the investiture the day after. It's already been established that I'm to play no part in it. A maimed sponsor is an ill-omen. Kay sits down on my bed, hard, and glares. "You're a bloody trouble-maker, Heris."

"I'm sorry."

"Hmm. Of all the stupid, incompetent…"

"I know, I know. Agravaine already told me."

"Did he? Well, for the first time in his useless life he seems to have a point."

"I"ll tell him you said so."

"You do that." He looks at me, considering. "Maybe not. Your Agravaine's got nasty, vengeful habits, and I'm getting too old for all that."

There's not a grey hair in his head. I look at him quizzically for a moment or two, and we both laugh. This hurts. I wind up clutching my side, and gasping. Kay says "Oh, dear," in a tone of the utmost insincerity.

"Just wait… till I can use… my arm again!"

"I'll look forward to it." His face gets serious. "About Lamorak de Galis. "

I haven't seen Lamorak for four days, since Amran and Osian helped me off the field. "What about him? Is he all right?"

"It depends," says Kay, in his worst dark tone, "if you mean all right for normal people, or all right for Lamorak. Whatever *that* is. He spent half of yesterday howling on your brother Gareth."

My family haven't been telling me things. "Oh, Lord."

"Quite. He wants to wait until Easter. He's a screaming failure. He has no honour. He wants to die. You hate him. You'd think he'd just murdered his mother, not fallen on an Orkney! Although now I come to think about it…"

"No blood-feud jokes!"

"Oh, if I must. Though it would make *my* life a whole lot easier if one of you would just tidy him away."

"Kay!"

"All right, all right. I didn't mean it."

"Good. "

"Anyway, I thought I'd come and inspect you, and see if you were even remotely *compos mentis.*" Again he looks thoughtful. "Although it's hard enough to tell with you even when you don't have doctors dosing you to the eyeballs."

"Oh, thank you."

"You're welcome. So, are you up to it?"

"To what?"

"Holy Mother! Lamorak."

"It's unlucky..."

"I didn't mean that, you idiot. I meant, are you up to talking to him? He's been trying to get to see you for days, and your brothers won't let him, (and very sensible, too), but now he's started on me..." He shrugs. "I don't want Lancelot complaining to Arthur that I'm being nasty to the poor little trainees again."

"As if you would be!"

"Watch it! Well, can I wheel him in?"

"He's here?"

"Outside the door."

I'm not feeling at my best, if truth be told. The collar-bone isn't too bad, now it's strapped up, but the doctor keeps making me drink foul concoctions that make my head swim, and my ribs ache. I'd love to find an alternative to breathing... Exactly like Kay, to present me with a *fait accompli*. "Is he sober?"

"Yes, of course." I catch his eye, and stare. "Well, he's sober-ish. For heaven's sake, man, it's Christmas!"

"Not so I'd noticed."

"Poor thing! Next time I'll bring you a piece of holly."

"*Too* kind."

In the brief pause, Kay suddenly grins at me, and produces a half bottle of wine from the floor at his feet. "Just don't tell the doctor where you got it."

He's not such a bad sort, Kay. "I won't. Thanks."

He holds it just out of reach. "And Lamorak?"

I must remember not to laugh. "All right. Let him in."

"I just knew you'd say that. Anyone ever tell you you're a soft touch, Heris?"

"All the time!"

He laughs, and goes to the door. As I find a suitable – and handy – spot for my wine, I can hear him lecturing. "Right. Prince Gaheris will see you. But no dramatics, no vapours, and no tantrums. D'you hear me?" I can't hear Lamorak's answer, but Kay tuts, and says "You'd better mean that, or I'll tell Sir Agravaine where you are."

Prince Gaheris. It's been a while since anyone called me that. Even Agravaine tends to forget his title. Come to it, Lamorak's as much a prince as I am. More, maybe: Nordgwalia's a bigger place than Lothian. Kay ushers Lamorak in, scowling. "Here you are, then. Now, behave yourself."

Lamorak shuffles, and stares at his feet. "Yes, lord seneschal." He might be twelve, not nearly seventeen. Kay snorts, and exits, shutting the door. There's a long silence.

In the end I break it. "Happy Christmas, then, Lamorak."

He looks up at that, and the snake eyes are tearful. Oh, not again... I smile at him, and say briskly, "Surely Kay isn't that bad?" He gives a soft wail, and drops to his knees at the foot of the bed, burying his face in the blanket. Fabulous.

Evan has propped me up with a few pillows, but all the same, it isn't easy to crane my neck to the required angle. "For heaven's sake, Lamorak... Whatever is the matter?"

He gulps, and says something indistinct in which Kay, Aglovale, dishonour and the castle moat are all muddled up together. It makes about as much sense as one of Mother's pronouncements on politics. "Lamorak, do stop it, please, and *talk* to me." No answer. "Will you at least move down this end? You're hurting my shoulder."

At that, he looks up. "Oh, Christ," he says, more distinctly. "I can't do anything right, can I?"

Why must the young be so fragile? I say, firmly, "Don't be daft," and pat the bed with my good hand. "Now, come here and tell me about it. "

He blows his nose on his sleeve, and obeys. "I'm... I'm sorry, Sir Gaheris."

"*Sir* Gaheris? What's this? Respect?"

"No... Yes... I messed up again, didn't I?"

"I don't know. What have you done?"

"What have I done?" He looks at me, appalled. "What haven't I?"

"Killed someone? Insulted a lady? Perjured yourself?"

"No, but..."

"Well, then. Dear Lord, Lamorak, you have got to learn to stop over-reacting to the least thing, or you'll draw yourself more trouble than you can handle." The snake eyes are doubtful, looking at me. "All this, because a middle-aged knight made an idiot's parry?"

"You're not middle-aged."

I'm twenty eight. "Well, maybe not. But I *am* an idiot." He opens his mouth to contradict. "Any junior squire knows not to parry like that. I was stupid, and now I'm paying for it. But you haven't 'messed up', or crippled me, or dishonoured yourself. It was an accident."

"But..."

"Not everything you do will be glorious, or tragic. Sometimes things just happen." No need to tell him now how much accidents may cost. He'll find out. "You don't need to dramatize everything."

"That's what Sir Kay said."

"Well, he's right."

"Yes..." He hesitates. "They wouldn't let me see you, and Sir Agravaine said... If you died, he..."

I'm going to give Agravaine considerably more than a black eye. I have to keep the anger from my voice, answering. "Well, I'm not intending to die. This time."

"No." Abruptly, the snake eyes overflow again. "Oh, Gaheris." He lifts my good hand and hugs it to him. "Kay said you weren't... and Sir Gareth... but..."

"I've done myself more harm falling off my horse. Oh, Lamorak, do stop it."

He sniffs, hard. "I'm sorry."

"That's better. I'm sorry, too. But it's done, and must be lived with." I manage to get my hand back, by dint of some wriggling. "I'm afraid I've let you down."

He straightens up somewhat, and seems to be making an effort. "I wanted to wait for Easter, but no one agreed."

"Quite right, too."

"Do you really think so?"

"Of course."

"But..."

"Why delay something so major for the sake of a two-hour

lecture while you're sitting in your bath?"

That makes him laugh. Then he says "But a sponsor… It's more than that, surely?"

"No. How do you think all the people who get knighted in the field manage?"

"I hadn't thought about it."

"Well, then." I gaze at the foot of the bed, thinking. "It's… it's a formality, really. Like checking you've got your shield before riding out. To remind you what you're taking on." Remember Gawain, looking momentous… "Aglovale's a fine man; he'll make a grand sponsor."

"I'd rather have you." Lamorak sounds wistful. "What were you going to say to me?"

"I'm not sure… Try to be fair, to yourself and others. Keep your word, to king and country. Remember to parry with your shield, not your elbow." He smiles. "That sort of thing. What Gawain said to me, more or less (except the bit about parrying)." Strange how some things stay with you. I can still remember the narrow room, the feel of cooling water, Gawain's face in the firelight…

"What did he say?" Lamorak asks. He's watching me with an odd intensity, as if he's waiting for something.

"That's a long time ago." All that time as Gavin's squire. We were closer, then. Before all this blood-letting began. Perhaps I'm silent a long time, for Lamorak begins to look worried.

"Are you in pain?"

"I'll do." He still looks concerned. "I was trying to remember, that's all." He relaxes a little. "Well, then…" When I try, I still have the accent of my childhood, that we all have in stress, and Gawain more than most. "Something like this: 'Love your king – and God – and your own kin. Stick by what you know to be right, and don't go chasing follies. Keep your sword clean, and your honour with it, and never forget whose arms you bear. Be polite to women – all women, not just ladies, mind – and watch your tongue with your elders and betters. Happen you'll disagree, betimes, but see you keep quiet – and that means you must mind Agrin, as well as me, and don't go pointing out mistakes we can see by ourselves. Don't take an insult; but don't go looking for them, neither. And never refuse an adventure, or a fair request – although mind you don't go making yourself a martyr to all comers, for you will go letting others put on you. And see you wash regularly, and don't go doing all the damn fool things I did!" By the end of this, Lamorak's laughing helplessly.

"Did he really say that – about washing?"

"Aye, man, happen he did."

He laughs some more. "And you were going to say that to me?"

"Well, maybe not the bits about washing, and listening to Agrin – to Agravaine. And there might have been a thing or two I'd add for you yourself, as Gavin did, when he told me to stand up for myself." I sigh. "There's a lesson in that, if you like, for he's still saying I don't and telling me I should."

Again that intensity in Lamorak's face. "Do you think he's right?"

"Who knows?" Shrugging is nearly as bad as laughing. "It's just his way of telling me to do right – and to have right done by me."

"I hadn't thought of it that way." Lamorak looks thoughtful. "What would you say just for me, then?"

"Aglovale…"

"I want to know!"

There's such urgency in his voice that I jump. "Why does it matter so much?" He gazes at me for a long moment, then looks away, shaking his head.

"I can't explain. I just… I can't tell you." I can hear his breathing, quick and ragged. There's something here I don't understand.

"You feel things too much. You need more… I don't know, more sense of *proportion*. You care too much."

"Do I?" He laughs mirthlessly.

"Well, maybe you don't. I don't know. All I know is that you're very different to me."

"Am I?"

"I think so. I'm not very good at understanding people." Lamorak is silent. Suddenly there's a tension between us, and I can't see why.

With sudden ferocity, he says "I don't want you to understand!" And then, "No, I do want it!" He draws in a long breath, and turns round. "Tell me: what do you think of me?"

I can't help smiling. "That you have an incorrigible habit of fishing for compliments." He bites his lip. "Dear heaven, Lamorak! You're a very promising young knight."

I expect him to seize on the compliment, in his usual fashion. Instead, he looks down and shuts his eyes. His face is bleak. I'm afraid for him, suddenly. There's a shadow across the light that Lancelot spoke of, a darkness. "Lamorak?" He makes no answer. I'm not equipped to deal with this... I need Gareth... He's right, I don't understand.

It's Gawain who breaks the spell, opening the door and entering. I jump. "Rescue squad," he says, cheerfully. "Kay said you'd need it." Lamorak beside me swallows hard, and rubs a hand across his eyes. Gawain looks at us. He's slightly drunk, which emphasises the accent. "Christ, man. Will you look at the pair of you! There's someone dead, is it? You willna learn, Heris. You will go letting yourself be put on."

Beside me, Lamorak gives a laugh that turns quite suddenly into a sob.

I persuade the doctors to let me out of bed for the tourney. They don't argue too hard: maybe even they are softened by the Christmas spirit. My brothers are delighted. Now Gawain can fight, and I (oh, joy!) can field Mother. She's on form. As I settle myself under the royal canopy, she's already in full flow, talking and eyeing up the young men. Agravaine holds she's beautiful. I'll grant she has a fine way of grabbing attention. I'm a poor substitute for Gawain; she's already made that plain. One can, I suppose, be thankful for these small mercies.

Her daughters-in-law cluster round her. I'm not really listening, but the giggles suggest that the conversation is typically scandalous. To my left, my aunt catches my eye, and smiles sympathetically. "Poor Gaheris. Are you feeling very left out?"

"Not really." I smile back. "Look at the company I'm getting to keep. "

She pulls a face. "Quite. I'm relying on you, though. You'll have to help me judge, since Arthur has abandoned me." My uncle has, for once, exercised privilege, and taken the field with Gareth's side.

"I'd be honoured."

"Bless you, Heris; you're a treasure." She looks at Mother, briefly. "And a welcome relief from gossip." Her expression is just a little wicked. "So. Who do you think will win?"

I have to think about that. It's pretty even this year, though Lancelot may have gained some advantage in replacing me with Gawain. "I don't really know."

"Diplomat! Who'll take single honours, then, since both Gareth and Lance have exempted themselves."

"Gawain, of course." She laughs. "Well, maybe Palomides."

"Agravaine," puts in Mother determinedly, "is not to be discounted lightly. He looks very good to me." He would. He's wearing her favour. "You always underrate him, Gaheris." I shuffle my feet and do my best to avoid her gaze. She goes on, "Some of my sons are a credit to me, anyway."

"Yes, Mother." She glares. I've forgotten again, not to call her Mother in public. It reflects badly on her age. "I'm sorry."

"Well, that's normal."

"Agravaine is certainly looking handsome," my aunt says, hastily. "I'm not surprised you're proud of him. And you, too, Laurel."

Mother preens. Laurel, overshadowed, says nothing. Llinos says loyally, "Well, I think Gareth looks marvellous", and everyone smiles.

"I have such attractive children," Mother says, complacent. "Do at least try and keep out of my light, Gaheris."

Gawain has ridden his horse two circuits of the field: now, he reins in before us, and bows. Lamorak follows him, hovering. He looks nervous. Under cover of Gawain's salutations, I catch his eye, and smile.

He's white. "Good day."

"And to you. Don't look so worried. It's only a friendly competition. It's been years since anyone died."

He gives me a dusty look. "I think I'm going to be sick."

"You shouldn't drink so much."

He looks startled. "No… Gaheris?"

"Lamorak?"

"I was wondering… Since it's my fault… That you're not out here, so I…"

"I thought we'd agreed not to apportion blame."

"No, please… Would you let me carry the Rose-Knot for you?"

The Rose-Knot is my device: Lamorak as yet has only his blank shield. Gawain has already asked me the same question, and received the same reply. "I don't think so."

"Oh, but…"

"It isn't necessary. Or appropriate."

"But I wanted…" He looks at me, snake eyes pleading.

I have to be gentle. "It's a kind thought. But I'll have other days, and this is your very first tourney. You should act in your own name."

"Are you sure?"

"Yes."

"Oh." He hesitates. Gawain has already made his farewells, and is riding back to be mustered in by Lancelot. Lamorak says "Then…"

"Yes?"

"With your permission… If I might address Lady Luned…" She turns, hearing her name, and Mother looks round with her. "My lady, I'm at least partly responsible for depriving you of seeing your lord win glory for you today. As some slight recompense, would you honour me with your token instead, so that I may try to redress the wrong?"

It's a pretty speech: the smile that accompanies it is devastating.

Luned, turning to me, misses it, giving Mother the full benefit. Lamorak waits a moment, then adds, "Please?"

"Why, how charming," Mother says. "And so proper. Be kind to him, Luned. I would."

Luned still hesitates. Lamorak says, "It would be in Prince Gaheris' name, of course. I mean no impropriety."

"Charming," repeats Mother.

He looks so vulnerable… It's a very smooth act. Luned is

wavering: her hand twists in her veil. I look at sly Lamorak, and shake my head. Then I smile at my wife, and say, "I wouldn't mind, if it's your wish."

"Oh, you must," Mother says, and smiles at Lamorak. "I'd give you my token, were Agravaine not already wearing it."

He bows. "I'm honoured, your majesty."

He's a twicer... Luned has unfastened the veil. Leaning forward, she offers it to him. "Here, then."

Taking it from her, he makes an issue out of kissing her hand. "Thank you, gracious lady." Another bow, then a look at me. "Gaheris..."

"They're nearly mustered. Go on, now."

"Yes..."

"That's a very pretty child," Mother says, as he rides away. "And so gallant. Not like you: you were a late starter." I keep quiet. "Whoever is he?"

"Lamorak de Galis. Pellinor's youngest."

"Is he, now," says Mother, and her eyes linger on Lamorak.

He doesn't disgrace Luned's token. Gawain, too, upholds a private promise, and gives Agravaine a hard fall. Palomides carries the palm. The new knights all give good accounts of themselves, and all escape injury, so no one must be left behind when they leave, two days later, for their year's errantry.

They always go at dawn. In the cold and damp, it's usually only close kin who rise to see them off. Even so, despite my shoulder, I prevail on Evan to wake me, and make it down. Bedwyr grins at me, and Ywain raises a brow.

He's there for Gereint. I greet them, and spend a few minutes discussing his intended route. Beside me, Mador de La Porte is lecturing Patrise and Astamore. Lamorak is all but invisible between his brothers.

"You're early," says a voice in my ear. Kay. "Learning the ropes? Very diligent."

"Something like that."

"Hmm." He's looking at Lamorak. "Worthy. Most worthy."

"My best quality."

"Really?" He pulls a face, and we both laugh.

"Ouch. Well, maybe my second-best." Aglovale has turned to speak to Osian: over his shoulder, I see Lamorak looking round. The snake eyes are anxious. Then he meets my gaze, and, quite suddenly, his face clears. No smile, but some other thing... Think of Llinos, seeing Gareth safe home...

No.

Percevale, too, has noticed me. Being Percevale, he bows, and offer me an arm. Once accepted, he conducts me to Lamorak, and leaves us alone. There's a small silence.

"They should patent him... Are you ready to go?"

"Not really." Lamorak grimaces. "Travelling in mid-winter."

"New Year's the right time for making beginnings."

"Is it?" He looks pensive. "Is it right to begin with a parting?" I've no immediate answer to that. It's not an angle I'd ever considered. "Well, it's not really a parting. You'll be coming back soon enough." Most of them, anyway. Almost every year, there's one or two...

Don't think of that.

He smiles, twisted. "So I will." I've heard Agravaine sound more sincere. "There's something to look forward to."

He should be excited. Not this tension. Behind us, I hear Patrise's quick Irish voice bubble and laugh. Amran is grinning as he listens to Bedwyr. Suddenly Lamorak takes hold of my good arm and stares straight at me. "Oh, Gaheris, I can't."

"Don't be daft."

"But if I go... I won't..."

"I thought you were going to be the third-best knight in the world."

"Oh, that! What's that, compared to being without..." He trails off, but I've a glimmer of a notion as to his problem.

"If she loves you, she'll wait."

"What?"

"Whoever it is you can't do without." He looks unconvinced.

"She'll still be here when you get back. If that's what's bothering you."

"Sort of." I can't make sense of his expression. "And if… she… doesn't wait?"

"Then she doesn't deserve you."

"Oh, God, you would say that!" His laugh is a little hysterical. "Though I expect you're right."

"I'm quoting Gawain, so I must be."

"I've never thanked you, have I? For all your time and help."

"It's nothing." I don't like to be thanked. Pink doesn't mix with sandy hair and freckles. "Forget it."

"Never." His intensity unnerves me. "I'd count that dishonour."

"It really isn't that important. So, do you have everything you need to take with you?"

"Yes, almost." He releases my arm. I step back. "Plus a lot of advice from Percevale that I really don't need."

"I can imagine. I recall Agravaine giving our Gareth a half-hour lecture on pavilion etiquette alone."

"He didn't mention that one." Lamorak looks wicked. "Shall I ask him?"

"Percevale? Saints, no!" I think. "Aglovale, though…"

"Indeed?" The snake eyes narrow. Twisting round, he taps his brother on the shoulder. "Loval, what's all this I hear about your lady- killing exploits?"

"What?" Aglovale looks stunned.

"I have *very* good authority. My lord prince Gaheris tells me…" My lord prince Gaheris is doing his damnedest to look innocent.

Aglovale makes his excuses to Osian, and joins us. "*My* lady-killing exploits? That's a good one, Liam, after what you've got up to round here. And as for you, Gaheris…"

"I was just making polite conversation."

"Oh, well, that explains it." Aglovale de Galis is an odd one. Even Agravaine has never been able to pick a fight with him. Now he favours me with an amused glance. "Gaheris is an expert."

"No, I'm not. I'm married."

"A *married* expert…"

"All right, all right. I'm sorry. I was only trying to explain to

Lamorak about pavilions."

"The first rule is *never* to get into a bed in one unless you're quite sure it's empty first."

"Or looking for trouble."

"Or for Lancelot." Our *parfait gentil knight* has made a fool of himself that way a time or two: Aglovale and I catch each other's eyes, and laugh. Lamorak looks cross. Aglovale pats his shoulder. "All right, little brother. The grown-up knights will stop behaving like children." Lamorak doesn't look convinced. "I'm sorry, Liam." Behind him, several of the others are already mounted. Patrise is adjusting a stirrup. "All set?" Aglovale asks.

"I think so." Lamorak sounds nervous. "At least..." Abruptly, he stops, and hugs his brother.

Aglovale aims a mock punch at him. "Off with you, then. I want my breakfast. Give 'em hell, all those recreant knights... Have you said goodbye to Piers?"

I step back some more, and try to wave to Gereint. He doesn't see me.

It's only as he's about to leave that I realise I've said no farewells to Lamorak. He looks the part; the compleat knight-errant. He'll be fine. The cold is hurting my shoulder. I watch a moment or two more, then turn to go. There's a great turmoil of hoof-beats and goodbyes: I'm on the stair before I notice my name being called.

Lamorak has ridden his horse to the foot of the flight: we're almost on eye-level. "Gaheris?"

"Yes?"

"You didn't say goodbye."

"Goodbye, then."

"Yes." He bites his lip. "I will see you? Next year?"

"God willing. Maybe even in the summer, if our paths cross."

"I hadn't thought of that." His face lights up. "The summer, then."

"Perhaps."

"I can hope." He hesitates. "Gaheris?"

"Yes?"

"I wanted... He reaches a hand out. I come down a step or two to clasp it. "Will I make it?"

55

"Who knows? I think so." The others have all left. "If you ever set out in the first place, that is."

"Well, I have to." Again, that pause. "Could I... would you...?"

"What?"

"It's just that..." Quite suddenly, he leans down from his horse, and tugs one of my gloves out from where it's tucked through my belt. The other falls to the ground. "Can I have this?"

I'm not comfortable. It makes me irritable. "What for?"

"Please, Gaheris."

"I'm not sure I..."

"It's to remind me."

"What about?"

"Of... of the right way to parry. Shield, not elbow."

This is ridiculous. He has on his spaniel look. "Oh, all right. But it's silly." He smiles. I add, "God speed you."

"Thank you. You're not cross?"

"Only a little."

"I'm sorry, then. I'll see you. In the summer." He turns his horse's head towards the gate.

"That's not certain," I call after him, but he doesn't seem to hear.

Kay has to pick up my other glove for me, from where it lies on the ground.

Four

It's not a long winter, nor a cold one. My bones heal clean, and I'm kept busy by my new duties. Brother Medraut proves to be the worst aspect of these. He's the most apt of the new squires, but his tongue would cut stone. I'm torn between fraternal pride, and a pure desire to wring his neck. Llinos's child is a girl, and Gareth insists on calling her 'Lancella', for his hero. The rest of us laugh at him, except Agravaine, who wanted her named for Mother. The latter stays with us until Easter, which is a delight for some, and a burden for many. I'm not the only one breathing the easier for her departure in early spring.

Intermittently, there's word of our new knights. Someone bumps into one of them, or they send tidings back. All alive, all doing well. The first of the overthrown foes to come and pledge himself to Arthur is sent by Gereint, to Gawain's delight, but one comes from Lamorak not long after. From then on, he seems to send one almost every other week. They all bring the same message: "Sir Lamorak de Galis has vanquished me, and sent me hence to swear eternal allegiance to his lord King Arthur. Oh, and I've a message from him for Prince Gaheris of Orkney."

After the third or fourth, Kay gets to calling them "Lamorak's love letters", and I'm obliged to give him a fall on the wettest part of the tourney-field.

I'm too busy to ride out that summer, and it's Christmas before I see Lamorak again. He rides in on Christmas Eve, with Palomides' brother Safere, and Astamore. They're the last, save for Amran, and they're made much of. It's hard to tell which of the girls clustered around Lamorak is the special one.

He's grown a beard, and has the remains of a bruise along one cheek bone. He's taller, too, standing nearly on eye-level with me.

Not that I see so much of him: there are a lot of people bidding for his time, and I have my hands full with the trainees. He is most often with Safere, and sometimes Tristan, who's honouring us with his company this year. Every so often, I feel myself watched, and look up, to find eyes on me. Occasionally, it's Lamorak; more frequently it's Safere, which perturbs me a little. I don't know why.

Agravaine finds this funny, for some reason.

Mother chooses to spend the festival with Aunt Morgan, which only adds to the pleasures of the season. Medraut takes himself off to visit her, with cousin Ywain. Kay and I open a book on how many quarrels they're likely to have. The rest of us Orkneys combine with a number of the other Northerners for the New Year tourney, and astonish everyone except Gawain by taking the day. He wins the solo prize, too, after disarming Lancelot and wrong-footing Bedwyr. Even Agravaine is laughing as the hall is decked with Orkney pennants: Gavin's Pentangle, Agrin's Sunburst, Gari's Lion-and-Lamb, and my own Rose-Knot. He has Bors to his credit, and a set of bruises to remind him. My own bruises bear testimony to a show of determined aggression by Sagremore and Safere. The latter refuses to shake hands, after, and stays away from the feast. Agravaine finds that funny, too.

It's two mornings later that I find Lamorak lying in wait for me in the south vestibule. He puts a hand on my arm, and stops me. "Come riding with me, Gaheris?"

The snake eyes are bright and guileless. "Good morning, Lamorak."

"Yes, yes. Will you?"

"I have things to do. Duties. Later, maybe."

He takes his hand away, abruptly dignified. "Forget it. I am sorry to have troubled you, Prince Gaheris."

It's far too early in the day for moods. "Have it your way, then."

"Oh, I wish!"

"What?"

"All I wanted was a chance to ask you in private just why you've been avoiding me. But if you're too ungenerous to grant even that…!"

"I beg your pardon?"

"You know what I mean!"

"No, I don't." We're beginning to attract attention. "Do calm down, Lamorak." I hold a hand out to him: he ignores it.

"You're deliberately trying to humiliate me!"

The Orkney temper is not always an asset. I have to struggle to keep my voice level, answering. "No. I assure you I am not doing that."

"You're a liar."

If Agravaine said it, I'd hit him. Lamorak isn't my brother. Ten or twelve witnesses have heard the insult... As lightly as I may, I say it. "No, I don't think so," and I start to walk away. I'm shaking. Now would not be the best time for a display of Orkney temper. All the same, I don't understand, entirely, what is happening.

"Don't walk away from me," Lamorak calls after me. I keep going. I don't trust myself to answer him. Behind me, voices are starting to murmur, and Lamorak shouts my name again. Gareth would have handled it right. Gareth would never find himself in the middle of a public quarrel... Half the court has heard me called a liar, and seen me take it... I slam a fist a few times into a convenient hay-bale, and swear. Gaheris the incompetent does it again. If Agravaine needed an excuse to warm up that old feud, he has it now.

Wonderful.

My hand hurts.

It takes me a few minutes to get myself back in control. Then I grit my teeth, and go back inside in search of Lamorak. I find him the refectory, glaring into a goblet. Safere is with him. So are a number of other people, including (lovely) Tristan. All I need is *his* indiscretion... Safere looks up, and his eyes narrow.

I'm unarmed. Perhaps it's for the best. When I stop in front of the table, Safere makes a gesture to wave me away, but I ignore him. "My lord Prince Lamorak."

He doesn't answer. Tristan gives me one of his rueful grins, and says, "Rotten timing, Gaheris."

"Quite probably." Tristan raises an eyebrow. I raise my voice, and repeat myself. "Prince Lamorak."

Of all my family, I have the least public grace. When I still receive no response, it's in me to give up and walk away. Then Safere smiles at me. Mother should practice that much malice.

Here goes nothing. "Prince Lamorak. I have offended against you. I was wrong. Therefore, I render you my unconditional apology; and I pray you will do me the honour of accepting it." My voice should have carried to the furthest point of the room. Agrin's going to love this. Safere's smile vanishes, and he regards me thoughtfully.

Lamorak still doesn't answer. I bow, then, and prepare to go.

Safere's light voice stops me. "Admirably tactful, but quite unnecessary, in the circumstances. Very surprising." He leans back on his bench, and draws a finger along his jaw. "Little snake is sulking. Little snake knows he doesn't deserve apologies when he's childish." His eyes flick up and down me. "So perfectly charming."

He manages what I could not: Lamorak looks up. He's scowling. "Shut up. Saf. This is none of your business."

"Indeed not? Shall relief overwhelm me?" There is in Safere's voice all the compassion of wire rope. He turns back to me. "I shall not pretend I like you, king's son of Orkney; but I grant you this much. You are doubly fair. There are those who are not."

Well, I don't like Safere, insofar as I know him at all, either. And I've never been any good at riddles. I mutter something non-committal, and begin to back off. Lamorak goes on glaring at Safere for a few moments, then rises, and follows me. "Gaher... My lord prince... "

"Yes?"

"He's right. Safere. I'm at fault. I..." He hesitates, looking round him, then raises his voice. "Please accept my apology."

I'm wary. He's too much trouble, this morning... But half the hall is still watching us, so I bow, and offer a hand. "Of course. What is all this, Lamorak?"

He looks over his shoulder. "It's just that... Are you really avoiding me?"

"Don't start that again."

"No, I'm sorry. It's..." Again the pause. "Can you really not spare me a few minutes?"

Here we go again. Well, I suppose Kay can do without me for

one morning. "All right. But no dramatics."

"No… Can we go out of here?"

I shrug, and we make our way out in self-conscious silence to the stable. It's only as we're riding along the track from the postern that Lamorak sighs, and says "It's the one reliable thing, isn't it? I make trouble for you. And I never intend to."

"I don't suppose I think you do."

"Is that why you put up with it?"

"No." He looks concerned. I say, "It's simply that I don't like scenes. I'm lazy."

"I see." He sounds disappointed. "Is that why you've been avoiding me?"

"I thought we agreed… Oh, all right. I hadn't noticed that I *was* avoiding you. What makes you think I am?"

"I came back, and… You didn't seem pleased to see me, and you were always busy, and…"

"Well, I am busy these days." It isn't a satisfactory answer. "I don't know, Lamorak. It wasn't deliberate. But you have your own place, now. And I suppose I saw you with Tristan, and so forth, and we've never got along… It's lots of little things. People grow up, Lamorak."

"Even me?" He smiles. "Is that a hint?" I don't say anything. He goes on, "Well, it's fair comment, I suppose. When I was away… It never occurred to me that things would be changing here, too. And when you didn't show up in the summer, I thought… "

He stops, and shakes his head.

I look across at him curiously. "That was never a promise. As it turned out, I didn't have time to leave court. I didn't even get out to any of my own holdings. I assumed you'd realise that."

"You hadn't forgotten, then?"

"No."

"Safere thought you had. And Margawse – I mean, your lady mother – said that Sir Agravaine… That is…" He has twisted his reins around his fingers; he won't look at me. "She thought it possible that Sir Agravaine had told you certain… details that weren't to my credit. "

Mother is a trouble-maker. Pellinor must once have turned her down. "Agravaine says a lot of things about a lot of people. Usually

I ignore him."

"But did he say anything about me and… Well, anything…?"

I frown; I can't remember anything that struck me as being above Agrin's usual level of malice. Nearly everyone young and promising is an effeminate fool in my dear brother's eyes. "Nothing I specifically remember, no."

"I see." He looks at his fingers trapped in his reins, and laughs. "I'm idiotic, then."

"You said it." Something occurs to me. "You saw my mother?"

"Yes, I…" He stops, and to my astonishment, I realise he's blushing. "I was a guest of hers at Belmotte for a while. She was very kind to me."

Oh, was she? Well, that explains the apparent disappearance of his special lady here. Trust Mother. He's far too young for her. And if one of my brothers gets to hear about it… "I wouldn't build too much on her kindness, if I was you. She's, umm, kind to a lot of people."

He shuffles. "I enjoyed her company."

I shouldn't listen to this. "Hmm. Just don't tell any of my brothers."

"No." He looks up at that. "I do know that much."

"I should hope so."

He's looking thoughtful. "I did like being with her, you know. She made me feel… less isolated."

I'll bet. I favour him with my best sardonic look. "Well, it's your funeral."

"I hope not!"

"Be careful, then." Blast the woman. Let's just hope that winter court will take his mind off her. We ride on in silence in a few moments, then I raise an issue that's been on *my* mind. "Lamorak, do you happen to know why Safere doesn't like me? I barely know him."

"I didn't know he didn't."

I don't quite believe that. "He said so not an hour ago."

"Oh, that." Lamorak looks awkward. "Well, you overthrew him at the tourney… "

"If I held a grudge against everyone who ever defeated me, I'd have no one to talk to!"

"I don't know why, then. Why do you expect me to?"

"No special reason. I thought he was a friend of yours."

"He's all right." He sounds defensive. He won't look at me.

"I didn't say he wasn't. What's the matter?"

"Nothing." He pauses, then takes a deep breath. "I think I just... I've been on my own so much, and now it seems so crowded here." I understand that one: I smile at him reassuringly. He continues, "And the whole time I was away, I missed being here so much. And now it's all different."

"Not completely."

He smiles. "No. Not completely."

Amran doesn't come back.

Ever after, the time that follows is known in family memory as 'Gaheris' good year'. Perhaps it's all the practice. Perhaps it's just a change in my luck. Whichever, for a while the old awkwardness falls from me, and I find I have an aptitude I formerly lacked. It's interesting, though I'm not wholly sure I like it. The winter is quiet enough, apart from Mother's visit. Lamorak hangs around her rather more than is strictly wise, and I have to caution him before Agravaine notices and takes umbrage. He's already cross enough with Lamorak: the latter has trounced him twice in tourneys, and picked three fights with Medraut. The cause of this turns out to be insults to me. I can't take Lamorak in the field, but I still weigh more than he does: it takes me three-quarters of an hour and a lot of bruises, but eventually I have him convinced to leave my family quarrels alone. In the summer, Kay and I get grace to ride errant, and wind up tangling with a fair cross section of the Cornish knights. Somewhat to my discomfort, the local sub-king, Marcus, takes it into his head to pull Lancelot's stunt of riding incognito, and I give him a hard fall. Luckily, he thinks it funny. I rather wish Lancelot had never started that fashion. It can get embarrassing.

Three weeks later, I resort to it myself. We've seen several of our companions, but heard nothing of Lamorak. He left somewhat later than we did, waiting for his brothers, and intending to ride west. But in mid-August, Kay and I come on two pavilions pitched in a largish clearing next to a ford. It's a good spot for casual sport: indeed as we round the hill-crest, we can see two knights practising in full kit. One of the shields – a snake curled about a stylised rose – is unfamiliar to me. The other is Safere's. Oh, joy. I've fought him three times since Christmas, and won every time, but his hostility unnerves me. Worse, he was travelling with Tristan, the last I heard. Tristan doesn't like the Orkneys. It's not his shield, granted; but he's one who makes a habit of disguise.

Well, there's no way out of it. And Kay beside me is cheerfully preparing himself for a friendly bout. If anything involving Safere can be said to be friendly...

I look across at him hopefully. "Umm..."

"Let me guess. You want to swap shields?"

"If you don't mind. It's just that Safere... But I think the other one's Tristan... Of course, if you feel more glory..."

Kay shields his eyes with his hand. "No. He's too slim to be Tristan. I think it's Andred. You know, that bloody cousin of Marcus'? He has a different device every time I see him. So, *do* you want to swap?"

He's looking at me quizzically. I shuffle a bit, and say "Yes."

"The things I do for you!"

"I know. I do appreciate you."

"Oh, really?" He raises a brow. Then he passes me his black tower shield.

I hand him the Rose-Knot. "Thanks, Kay. You're a good friend."

"Tell that to my contusions. Safere has a spite against you, Sir Duck."

"Quack." Kay pulls a face. "I had noticed."

"You and the rest of the court." He pauses to pull down his visor. "Shall we?"

"Lead on, foster uncle!"

Our direction of approach gives us a slight advantage: because of the rise, the knights encamped below don't see us until we're almost upon them. There's a brief instant of chaos, then Evan yells

"Give passage to my lords!", and Safere's Aidan yells back "Not without they fight mine, if they have the courage for it!"

I'm still trying to place the serpent-rose from the style of his riding, when his lance point impacts neatly with my shield, and punts me off my horse.

Well, I've been expecting to come back to the ground sooner or later... I pick myself up, duck out of Kay's path, and draw my sword, as the serpent-rose comes back round for another go. He's fast, but he's not a master horseman... he has a slight problem managing reins, shield and lance. I wait till I think he's about to strike, then duck, and come up under his shield arm, tipping him neatly to the grass. Then I stand aside, and wait for him to stand up.

This proves to be a mistake. On foot, he's better than I am.

Sometimes, I think altruism is not a survival characteristic. I wind up desperately trying to hold my guard against a flurry of fast and rather accurate attacks. Holy saints be thanked this is only for fun... I'm certain by now that whoever he is, he's not Andred. There's a suspicion building at the back of my mind... Parrying in quarte, I find I'm being backed almost into the other combat, and have to step aside hastily. The grass is wet. I keep my footing, but behind me, some-one curses, and goes down.

Abruptly, the serpent-rose is wide open. He's not even looking at me. Before I've quite finished debating whether it would be fair or not to hit him, he pushes past me.

There's an "Ouf" from behind me. Then Safere says, conversationally "You little bastard."

"He fell. Accidental advantage. You were going to follow up on it. That's not fair."

I know that voice... I turn, and start to fumble with my helm.

The familiar voice goes on, "This was meant to be in fun!"

"Who for?" Safere sounds scornful. "Not, me, most certainly."

"You have no sense of honour..."

There's a pause, then Safere throws his shield to the ground and stalks away.

Kay has climbed to his feet. Wrenching open his visor, he glares at me. "You and your damned feuds."

"I'm sorry."

"Hrmph." Then he looks at the serpent-rose. The latter has raised his visor, and is looking at us in some irritation. "Lamorak de Galis. I might have known."

"Sir Kay!" Lamorak sounds embarrassed. He glances over his shoulder towards Safere's retreating back. "I thought..."

I've finally got my helm off. "I'm here," I say, apologetically. "We swapped."

"*You* fought me?"

"Well, yes."

"Deliberately?"

"No. Yes... Well, I didn't know who you were..."

"You *fought* me..."

"Saint Michael and all the archangels!" Kay has no time for amateur dramatics. "Gaheris had simply had enough of fighting your homicidal Moorish friend – and I'm beginning to see his point, too. If you didn't want to fight us, you should have said so; if you youngsters would stop changing your devices at the drop of a hat, this kind of muddle wouldn't happen." Lamorak stares at him, warily. "I'd say you owe Safere an apology."

"But he..." Lamorak looks at me, and stops. Then he bows, and goes across to Safere's tent.

Kay and I exchange glances. After a moment, he shakes his head, and says "Don't ask."

So I don't. About ten minutes later, Lamorak comes back, smiling, and invites us to stay the night and share their accommodation. I'm uncertain, but somehow I find myself cajoled into co-operation. Before I'm really ready to agree to it, I'm bathed, changed, and sitting in a nicely appointed pavilion drinking a wine that has been chilled to near perfection by the convenient river. The squires are pitching a third tent, and Kay is swimming.

Safere still seems to be sulking.

Lamorak is sprawled on a pile of cushions, looking Moorish enough himself. He's picked up a fine tan, and there's a new scar down his left forearm. He's wearing a ring that looks vaguely familiar.

"Well, you've certainly made yourselves comfortable."

"It *is* nice, isn't it? We get a fair amount of action, being on the road. And it's handy for… this and that."

My aunt Elaine has a castle not half a day's ride from here. Suddenly I've a context for the ring, too: what was it Gawain said about Mother's summer itinerary…?

"Oh, Lamorak. You're not still playing up to my mother?"

"I like her."

"So you said. But…"

"And your aunt has an excellent library. Safere…"

I don't want to hear Safere's opinions on books. "I think you should stop seeing her."

"Why?"

"Because…" I cast around for the right words. "Well, because your father may have killed mine – no, don't butt in – and my brother Gawain certainly killed your father, and…"

"Aglovale…"

"Be quiet. And because my mother isn't entirely… wholesome. She dabbles in things that aren't very healthy. *And…*" And I fix him with my best Gawain-style glare, "Most importantly, if they ever get to hear about it, my brothers Agravaine and Medraut would probably try to kill you."

"If they could."

"If they could. By foul means when fair failed. And if you were to kill one of them, you'd have Gawain to answer to, and he isn't a pushover. And after Gawain, Gareth and me."

"Would you care?"

"If you killed Gavin? Certainly."

"If he – or any of them – killed me."

"Of course I would. The last thing I want is the revival of that stupid feud."

Lamorak looks down. "The feud. That's all?"

"Don't fish." He swallows. "All right. Yes, I would mind if they killed you." He looks up, eyes shining. "I wish you'd be a little more sensible, that's all."

"I can't." he smiles. "It's in my family, you know. Aglovale got all that: the rest of us are unbalanced."

"Don't be ridiculous."

"No, I mean it. Percevale and I – and Dornar, too – we're none of us quite… normal."

"Tor was normal enough."

"Tor was only half a Pellinor. My parents were cousins, you know."

"My father was a homicidal maniac, and my mother's a witch. I don't think that makes *me* crazy."

"Ah, but you're like Aglovale." Lamorak looks at me oddly. "Everything about you has such clarity. Like flawless glass."

"Oh, aye. Completely transparent!" I laugh.

Lamorak starts to protest that he didn't mean it quite like that, but halfway through gives up and starts laughing too. And somehow I lose sight of persuading him to give up Mother.

Late that night, as I'm falling asleep, Kay says suddenly "Heris?"

"Umm?"

"I think you should stay away from Lamorak."

"Why? Because of Safere?"

He sighs, in the darkness. Then I hear him shrug. "No. Because of Lamorak."

Five

The rest of the year is normal enough. Tristan breaks the monotony somewhat by starting a new scandal: in between running for his life, he still finds time to discuss knightly rankings with all and sundry. He tells Gauter, who's an old Cornish gossip, that he'd place me in the top five, higher than any of my brothers. And Gauter tells Dinadan, who tells Ywain, who tells Gawain, who passes it on to me in high delight.

"I knew you had it in you. Don't say I never told you so."

"Oh, absolutely, Gavin."

Praise from Tristan is another good reason for avoiding knocking Cornish kings into the dust.

That Christmas, Medraut gets his knighthood, and heads out on his year's errantry. This would be nice and peaceful for the rest of us, only Mother elects to visit. About a month later, the king chooses a handful of new companions of the Round Table. This includes Lamorak, who's been hanging around court since late November, getting under my feet, and generally impeding the healing of his wrist, which Ector de Maris has kindly cracked for him. Luckily, Luned, forgiving his earlier gallantries, decides he reminds her of her brother, and finds plenty of occupation for him; winding wool and so forth.

Kay snorts darkly, but refuses to expand on his warning.

I can't see the harm in our friendship, though I do notice an odd look or so from Agravaine's friends. Not even Agrin actually says anything, however: injured or not, Lamorak has become a force to be respected.

It's a dark February evening when we all come together in the great hall, each companion in his own place, silent and with the tapers unlit before us. Only Lancelot, as champion, stands apart, ready to give and receive the three blows. White-clad, the candidates must pass him, and come before the king, to swear the oath and take the flame. After, they must circle the hall one by one, lighting the tapers of those assembled, and exchanging the kiss of peace. Taper by taper, until the whole room is a circle of fire.

That's my favourite bit. (That, and the dancing that follows, when the ladies come in.) The lights seem to leap from hand to hand, like a spirit, or an idea given life. Agravaine says I have it wrong, and that the whole is far more complex. But that's what I've seen since the first time, when I was the lighter of candles.

Anyhow, it takes different people different ways. Some are solemn as monks. Some are close to laughter. I mind our Gareth wept; and not the only one. Percevale fainted. And Gaheris? Gaheris of Orkney totally forgot the need for silence, and exclaimed "Oh, Gavin, look!", as he completed the circle at the king's left hand.

We're spared any excesses this time. Lamorak comes round the last of all; and as he rises from where the king has spoken to him, he looks round into the gloom, snake-eyes bright. He can't possibly see any of us properly, here in the darkness, but I smile anyway. Gareth beside me puts a hand on my arm.

That look to him… that shining quality… I'm thinking of Lancelot's words as Lamorak comes round us all, and I'm suddenly cold. To shine, he will have to live. On his hand that is illuminated, lighting the tapers, gleams my mother's ring. If Agravaine should notice, when Lamorak gets to him…

Little fool. There's such joy in his face, as he reaches me, that my heart stops still. He's too damnably young. My hands are shaking so much that I drop my taper, and have to fumble for it in the dark, fingers mixing with Lamorak's. We're forbidden to speak. I can do little about his confusion, as I tug the ring free, only frown. Lamorak looks into my eyes for an instant, then he's past me, and Gareth's taper is springing into life.

I'm in need of a drink. I'm profoundly thankful when the doors open and the rest of the court floods in. Gareth is looking at me curiously. "Are you all right, Heris?"

"What? Oh, yes. Hot wax." What if Agrin noticed…? I'm looking round for him, but there are too many people.

"Oh, that explains it, then." Gareth isn't really paying attention: he's trying to spot Llinos. "Better put something on it. Butter, isn't it, for burns?"

"I thought that was cats."

He turns. "For burns? Alive or dead?"

"No, no. Butter for cats. To stop them wandering." Some-one has put a full glass in front of me: I drain it gratefully. Lamorak is nowhere in sight, either, but I can see Percevale steering purposefully towards me. All this and now religion. "Gari?"

"Hmm?"

"Do something for me?"

"Of course." He's sighted Llinos, and was beginning to wave to her.

Now his courtesy takes over. "What?"

"Field Percevale for me? I'm not feeling up to it."

He looks down at me, then, concerned. "You do look pale. Shall I call Evan to you?"

"No, I'm just tired." He looks doubtful. "And lazy." He pulls a face. He's kind, Gareth. "Thanks, little brother."

He smiles. "You're welcome."

I don't find Lamorak, but after a couple of hours, I nearly walk into Safere, in a corner by the kitchen door. We've mostly avoided each other since the summer, and he doesn't look pleased to see me. I apologise, shuffling, then: "My lord Sir Safere?"

"What?"

"I was wondering if you… That is, Lamorak…"

"Yes?" He smiles at me nastily. He's rather drunk.

"I was looking for him."

"His heart will beat the faster for it."

"Yes, well, I wondered if you…"

"Little snake," says Safere, glittering with spite, "may be anywhere. Perhaps he is drowning his sorrows. He is too slight to withstand your disapprobation."

"I thought you might... What?"

He puts a hand on my shoulder, and leans on me. "Do you read Greek, Prince Gaheris?"

"No." I rather want to get away from him. He looks up at me from beneath his lashes. "Lamorak does..."

"Well, I expect he had a better tutor. But, really, Safere..."

"Do you want to know what he calls you?" He really is very drunk. I start to pull away, and he tightens his grip. "He talks about you all the time. In bed, even. Especially in bed."

"Let me go, please."

"I thought you wanted to know where little snake is laired? Beautiful Gaheris?"

"No. Not particularly. It can wait." His touch repels me. It takes much of my self-control not to push him away. "Please let go of me."

"His favourite topic. Beautiful Gaheris."

I don't want to hear this. For a slight man, he's surprisingly strong. If I have to force myself free, I may break his arm. He looks up at me, and begins to laugh. "I disgust you, don't I? The little sodomite. Alas, then, for Lamorak."

"I don't have any opinion of you."

"No? Why, then, do you shake so?"

I'm not shaking, I can't be shaking. "Claustrophobia." In this room full of people, surely someone will come to my aid. "I don't like dark corners."

"Or tight ones." Safere is still smiling. "Little snake has conceived an unholy passion for you. That's why he beds with your mother. "

"You're drunk." Oh, God, where's Agravaine.? If he's in earshot of any of this...

"Perhaps that is where he is even now. Substituting one Orkney for another."

I feel sick. Over Safere's shoulder, I can make out the broad silhouette of Gawain, the bright sheen of Gareth's hair. No Agravaine. No Lamorak. No Mother. Holy saints. Across the crowd, my eyes meet Lancelot's, and he looks puzzled. I can't afford to attract too much attention. Come on, Lance… Something in my face must speak to him, for he bows to his companions, and begins to make his way towards me. Now pray… "Safere?"

"Yes, my dear lord prince?"

"Is that where Lamorak is? In my mother's room?"

"That is possible." He leans against me, loosening his grip. At last. I get my hand around his wrist, and twist. He gasps.

"Stop playing games. Where's Lamorak?"

"You are hurting me."

"For heaven's sake, Safere, this is important." Lancelot has nearly reached us. "Where is he? I swear to God, I'll break your arm."

Safere looks up, and all the haziness is gone from his eyes. "You astonish me. You really mean it, don't you?"

"Just try me."

"What in God's name…?" Lancelot has arrived, and is staring at us in some disbelief. "Gaheris, I don't think…"

"Where's my mother?" I ask him.

"What?" Lancelot frowns at me. "Are you all right, Safere?"

"He's fine. Where's the queen of Orkney?"

"I don't see…"

"Lancelot!"

"Very well." He looks at me as at a loose wolf. "She excused herself about an hour ago, feeling unwell."

Oh, God… Safere shifts a little, and I tighten my hold on him.

"And Agrin? My brother Agravaine?"

"Still talking to Bors and Bleobaris, as far as I know. What *is* this?"

"Does he know about Mother?"

"How should I know?"

"Think!"

"How much have you had to drink, Gaheris?"

"Less than you, almost certainly." He looks unconvinced. "Lancelot, this could be a matter of life and death. If Agrin hears that our mother is ill, he'll go to her room."

"So?" Lancelot looks at Safere, then back at me. "What is all this about?"

"Love." says Safere, sweetly, and smiles. "Or, perhaps, mere lust."

"What?"

"Charming Gaheris is perturbed over an *affajre de coeur.* He is trying to prevent a hypothetical murder. And all for the sake of a fine pair of yellow eyes."

I still can't see any sign of Agravaine. I may already be too late...

Lancelot folds his arms. "All right. Explain it to me very slowly. And, Gaheris?"

"Yes?"

"Let Safere go."

"But..."

"Just do it." Reluctantly, I release Safere's arm. He rubs it resentfully, but doesn't walk away. Lancelot continues, "Now, then?"

"It's Lamorak. He's been carrying on with my mother. I think he's up there with her now. And if Agravaine finds out, or goes up to see her, thinking she's ill... "

"I can imagine. A lover *and* a de Galis." Lancelot frowns. "Not very discreet of them. But I'm sure we can prevent Agravaine from surprising them, this time, at least."

"If he hasn't already done so."

"Calm down, Heris."

"But I haven't seen him all evening."

"He's over under the gallery, next to Bleobaris. He's been there for the last hour to my certain knowledge: I can still see him clearly. And I'm quite sure it's him."

Oh, thank you, God. I shall light three candles... "If you could make sure he stays down here for the next half hour or so, I'll deal with Lamorak and Mother."

"Is that wise?"

"You know my family."

"Well, I suppose so, but..."

"Forgive me; I intrude upon your deliberations, but..." Safere bows, smiling. There's something unpleasant about it. "Your precautions are admirably considerate, but quite unnecessary. Little snake is probably no longer with your mother."

"What?" I'm ready to hit him: Lancelot stays my hand. "You said that."

"I said that there was a possibility." Safere props himself on the wall. "For which you abused me quite outrageously."

I'm surprised no one's done it before... I have to stay calm. "Well, I'm sorry, then. But Lamorak..."

Safere shrugs. "Quite the centre of the world. Little snake *was* with your mother. But someone golden and perfect made a show of ritual disapproval earlier this evening, and tipped the balance of his indecisive mind. Little snake finally concluded it was in his long term interest to bid the sweet queen adieu."

"Lamorak went to break off his liaison with my mother?"

"That was what I said, yes."

"When? Where is he now?"

Safere studies his fingertips. "Desolated though I am, I must confess I have no idea. It is upwards of an hour since he left to perform the delicate deed."

Lancelot has been standing in apparent thought. Now he meets my eyes, and says, "I heard an odd story about your mother and Macsen of Rheged...?"

"It's true." My heart is racing. The room has turned cold. Mother is a worse loser than Agrin... "Lancelot?"

"Yes?"

"Keep Agravaine down here. Gawain too, if possible. I'm going up."

"Wouldn't I be more... diplomatic?" Lancelot asks.

"This is an Orkney matter." Lancelot bows. I say, "Safere?"

"Beautiful Gaheris?"

"I know you don't like me, but for Lamorak's sake, get a horse saddled and waiting by the south gate, just in case..." For the first time, there's a flicker of concern on his face. I'm probably over-reacting, but my mother can be as blood-thirsty as the rest of my family, and she hates to be rejected.

It's hard, keeping to a walk as I make my way out of the hall, and once I'm through it, I give up and start to run. I take the stairs two at a time. The antechamber of my mother's room is completely deserted. Her door stands closed. No sounds come from behind it. There's a faint, sweet smell, like incense.

I don't knock. The door, mercifully, isn't locked. It opens quietly, at a touch.

Oh, sweet Jesu.

The candle-light is merciless. There's blood staining the rushes and the hangings of the bed. The coverlet is torn, and hangs mostly onto the floor. The air is heavy with blood and scent. Nothing looks quite real. Lamorak is crouched in the hearth, his arms wrapped tightly around him, His clothing is torn and stained. There's no sign at all of Mother. When I touch him, he pulls back as if burnt. There's a gash across his left cheek, and another along the line of his collar-bone. His eyes are unfocussed. He's trembling. I've seen men like this, after battle… The whole thing is like a distorted rerun of that night three years ago, when he asked me to knight him.

I have to find out what's happened here. I fetch water from the antechamber, and lock the door. He doesn't move.

"Lamorak?" When there's no answer, I take him by the shoulder, and shake gently. "Lamorak, wake up." He's limp in my hands. "Lamorak." I shake harder, and this time, he moans, pressing a hand to his side.

I pull it away. Well, that explains the blood. Oh, sweet Jesu. "Lamorak, talk to me." Holding on to him with one hand, I begin to wash the blood away. "Tell me what happened." His eyes are beginning to focus. I smile at him, and say gently, "You're safe, now. It's over. Just tell me what happened to you."

He licks his lips. "Gaheris."

"Who else?"

"Always sorting me out."

"Someone has to."

He smiles a little, at that. "Sorry."

"I know." My bathing hits a sensitive spot, and he winces.

"What happened?"

The smile goes. "I tried to tell her it was over. After tonight..."

"The business with the ring. I understand."

"She..." He swallows. "Gaheris..."

"Still here."

"Yes. She cried, and I tried to... to comfort her. But she... there was a knife. She stabbed me."

The man who wrote that hell hath no fury was understating his case. He'd clearly never met Mother. Lamorak is shaking, and I put an arm around him. He clutches at me, gasping. "Slowly. It's over."

"No. Oh, Gaheris..."

"Not even the king's half-sister can get away with attempted murder. She won't hurt you again."

"You don't understand. Gaheris, I'm frightened."

"No need." I'll fix the others, somehow. He's been punished enough. And to hell with Safere.

"Gaheris."

"What is it?"

"Your brothers... "

"I'll deal with them."

"No." he pulls away suddenly. The snake eyes are wild. "You don't understand."

"What?"

He swallows again, hard, and points to the bed. "Under the quilt... I didn't mean..."

I can just about reach from here: I flick the coverlet aside with one hand, confused. Then everything stands still.

Oh, holy God.

It's Mother. She lies in a graceless heap. Her neck is bent the wrong way. I don't understand why, but suddenly I'm crying, and it's Lamorak who turns comforter. His hand catches mine. His fingers are cold. "Gaheris. My heart."

"Don't."

He leans away. "It was an accident. I swear to God. I only meant to push her away, but she lost her balance, and..."

"Yes." I swallow. "Perhaps she's only unconscious."

"No. I... checked."

"What a God-forsaken mess..." I rub a hand across my eyes, and start trying to think. "Who knew about you and Mother?"

"Several people. I... wore her favour in Cornwall."

"Tristan?"

"Yes."

Wonderful. He has all the discretion of a magpie. "We've got to get you away from here. Do you think you can ride?"

"Perhaps." He looks across at me. "Gaheris..."

"No, listen. My brothers would come after you for openly being her lover, let alone..." My throat is closed. I have to stop, to swallow, to regain control. "So I tell them I've already dealt with you. But you have to stay away."

"I don't understand. It was an accident."

"I believe you. Gareth would. Gawain might. But Agravaine and Medraut... They will try and kill you."

"As you warned me." His voice is bleak. "Do you know, I don't care. "

"Yes, you do. Just now; you're in shock. You have to protect yourself. You have to leave; now. Say you're on a quest, or a pilgrimage, or something. And, with luck, they'll never suspect you were here."

"But..." he glances across at the body, and turns pale.

"We have to explain the blood, too... Well, I have the Orkney temper. I expect I did it. Agrin would believe that, anyway. He never did like me much."

"What?" He's weeping, silently, without his old drama. "Gaheris, no. You can't. I won't let you."

"*Listen.*"

"They'll kill you instead."

"I'm one of them, Lamorak. Kin. Even Agrin respects that."

"But..."

"Can you think of anything better?"

"No... I can't think." He reaches out to me: I take his hand. "Why should anyone believe you?"

"Why not? A family quarrel – a tragic accident. We're famous for those, the Orkneys. And Mother has never been particularly fond of me."

"But..."

Oh, God. "Lamorak, think. This is a question of your life. Your life, or my honour. There's no contest."

"I can't let you do this."

"Why? Do you want to die?"

He stares at me in silence for long moments. Then he says "Yes. If that's the price of your name."

"Don't be ridiculous. This is no time for..."

He interrupts me. "I'm not. It's the one thing I could never tell you. How I feel about you."

"Lamorak, I..."

"No, you listen." Suddenly, he looks older. "I could never find a way to say it... I owe her that, at least." He looks at the body again, and shivers. "Gaheris – dear Gaheris – I don't know what you've made of me, all these years, but I don't think of you as my mentor, or my companion-at-arms, or even my hero. It's quite simple. I love you."

Safere said... It makes no sense. Not of me. It's on the tip of my tongue to deny it, but Lamorak shakes his head. "I mean it, Heris. My Gaheris. I'm in love with you. I always have been. And I daresay you now despise me." The last word is almost inaudible: he looks down, and hides his face in his hands.

I get to my feet. There's a lot of people I love; my family, friends... No one I love in this sense, no one I love as Gawain did Rhanillt, as Lancelot loves... his lady. As Lamorak loves...

No.

I have to get him out of here. He's crying again, as if his heart is breaking. Agravaine will try to kill him if any of this gets out. I can at least give him a head start. I owe him that much.

I don't want to think about this. I have to explain the death, the blood... It's all his, there's not a mark on her. I have to explain the violence of it... His blood is on my clothing, too, and my hands, and I am whole. Why would she seek to stab *me*? What could I have done to her? Or she to me... The idea forms as I look again at Lamorak. Safere's word for himself, what was it... An insult to any man... All my family are crazy; my father was a maniac, and my mother's a witch...

Agravaine's no fool. If Lamorak stays here wounded, he'll put the pieces together. I go back to Lamorak, and put my hands on his shoulders. He won't look at me. "Can you stand?" No answer. "Listen, Lamorak; I don't despise you. I'm even quite fond of you. But right now, I'm trying to save your life, and you have to help me. Lean on me... that's it..."

Somehow I get him downstairs, and outside, to where Safere's waiting with two horses. Our eyes meet as we hoist Lamorak onto to one of them, and Safere says "I'm going with him."

"I'm glad." I say. "Take him a long way and keep him there."

"I will." He doesn't ask for details. I'm grateful for that.

Lamorak looks back at me as they start to move away, and his lips form my name. I shake my head at him, cautioning silence, and he looks down.

Then I go back to the tower, and I cut off my mother's head.

It doesn't work, of course. My mother's *affaire* with Lamorak is better renowned than I'd hoped; and too many people draw conclusions from his departure. Some go so far as to accuse him of the murder: one more act in our feuders' tragedy. And even those who happily credit me with the killing refuse to belief he's not involved in some way. The favoured story, in the end, has me finding them abed, and slaughtering Margawse in jealous outrage.

No one hazards any comments as to the object of my jealousy, in my hearing, at least. The king of necessity holds an enquiry: his jury of my peers acquit me, finally, complaining of inconclusive evidence. No death, no exile; only the enduring cloud of penance and suspicion. It seems that no one is willing to be quite sure. Sometimes, I catch my uncle watching me, and in his face are pity, and concern. Perhaps Lancelot has told him something. Perhaps he knows me more than I had thought.

I wish I was a better liar.

Not even Agravaine seems to think it worth the trouble of

trying to kill me. He avoids me, muttering darkly about Lamorak; and corresponds with Medraut.

Kay stands by me. He doesn't even say, "I told you so."

I discover I'm missing Lamorak. There's no word of him for the longest time, although through Segwarides I learn that Safere, at least, is in Gaul. And after half a year or so, most people cease to speak of it.

Then a red-disguised knight shows up at the royal tourney at Surluse. He carries a blank shield, and keeps his visor down. It's a game Lancelot has played a hundred times, only Lancelot's here under his own arms. And Lancelot never wore one of my gloves pinned to his shoulder as a token. Perhaps even with that, he might have got away with it, only Medraut recognises his squire. And then again, perhaps he was expecting it. I have no way of knowing. I know only that my brothers, having once located him, will not readily let him go. Not even Gawain, though he at least speaks of fair combat, and even of royal arbitration.

Nothing I say can change it. The knowledge, the bitterness, is fixed. Lamorak de Galis dishonoured our mother. Lamorak de Galis forced Gaheris" hand. Lamorak de Galis must pay.

I don't even get a chance to warn him: Agravaine dogs my every step. Lamorak leaves the tourney with the prize in his hand, and a price on his head. He leaves quite alone.

It's as though he's courting his death.

Gawain wakes me at dawn, the day after. "Agravaine's for following Lamorak. You must come, Heris."

"I can't."

"Aye. But you must, all the same."

"No... Can't you let it be? Leave him alone?"

"Perhaps I could. But Agrin, now, and Medraut... That's why you must come. To see it done fairly."

"Gavin, I can't."

His face is kind. "You're not understanding me. Agrin blames you, as well as Lamorak. If you don't come willing, he's for tying you, and bringing you perforce."

"Gavin... "

"Will you swear to me, on your oath of knight-hood, that Lamorak had no part in our mother's death?"

"That's not fair."

He puts a hand on my shoulder. "Can you swear it?"

Her fault, not his... "Will you let him be, and make sure Agrin and Medraut do, too?" He looks down. "Why, Gavin?"

"Happen it's the only way they can admit they loved her."

"And you?"

He sighs." I am the Eldest." He knows it's no answer. There are none, except the old tangle of Orkney pride. Orkney folly. "But you must come."

"I can't hurt him."

"Aye."

"And I don't think I can watch."

"You must."

I dress, arm myself, and mount in silence. In silence I ride, alongside Gawain, into the forest of Surluse. Don't look at Agrin. Don't listen. Don't think.

I have never known a deeper shame. I cannot bear myself. I cannot bring myself to understand. I cannot even, any longer, hope.

Safere is safely in Gaul. Lamorak must have escaped him and run mad, to come back here.

He hasn't even tried to run. We find him in a wide clearing some eight miles from Surluse, pavilion pitching in plain sight, serpent-rose flying. He waits before it, fully-armoured save for his helm. As we ride in, he scans us anxiously. Then he sees me, and his face clears. He smiles. I meet his gaze, but cannot hold it for more than a moment. If I were a better man, a stronger one, we would never have come to this.

Gawain rides forward, and salutes him. "I must challenge you. Will you accept?"

"I will."

"Aye. Well, then..." Gawain sighs. "We'll fight here. But only you and me. And whichever wins, may give or refuse mercy as he will; and whatever happens then, that's an end to it, on my honour.

No reprisals. Do you agree?"

"Willingly."

Gawain glares at Agravaine and Medraut. "Do you mind me? I will not have you breaking my word."

"As ever, Gavin." Agravaine says. Medraut simply bows. I can't speak. My eyes are locked on Lamorak. He's so calm. He seems so much older.

The squires help them ready themselves. My hands are damp on my reins. I can't bear this. The hoof-beats on the turf are like thunder, like battle drums. I can't watch the cut and thrust of sword blows. Lamorak is better than Gavin.

Gavin is my brother.

I'm not watching. I tell myself that, over and over. I am not looking at Medraut as he circles behind Lamorak, a crossbow in his hands. Agravaine seizes my arm, a knife in his hand to ensure I don't shout out a warning. I call out anyway, and my voice is lost in the volley of blows. Medraut's hands are white on the trigger. The bolt is silent as it arcs through the air. I press forward and Agrin's knife is a scarlet pain across my forearm. Time stops.

Then I'm on my knees on the grass, and my hands are bloody, and my face is wet. Lamorak has dragged his helm off, and is lying half against me. We've been here before, but this time there's death in it. Blood trickles from the corner of his mouth, as he tries to speak to me. Somewhere, some world away, I can hear Agravaine laughing.

"Beautiful Gaheris..." There's a smile for me, though the snake eyes are already dimming. I still can't speak. My hand finds his, and grips it, tightly. There's no answering pressure.

I'm sorry.

"Well," says Agrin, sweetly, "And how do you feel now about murdering Mother?"

Nothing. I feel nothing. Gavin says roughly "Be silent, Agrin, or I'll make you."

I look up, at Agrin, at Medraut. "You'll never live this down. Gavin had given his word."

"Aye," says Gawain, and his voice now is smooth as silk. "You swore to me. It was to be a fair fight."

"You might," says Medraut, silkily, "have lost."

"What of it? You've shamed me. This is a bad day's work. This taints us all forever." Gawain turns his back and stalks away. I have heard that that tone from him only once before in my life, and then it was death for anyone who came in his way.

Medraut just shrugs. He was still a child when Rhanillt died and Gawain lost his centre. Agravaine smiles, and rests a hand on my shoulder. "You see, Heris? You should have let me kill him all those years ago."

I push him away, leaving bloody marks on his surcoat with my bloody hands. "I wish you'd tried. Perhaps he'd have killed *you*. Because, God help me, I can't, and I wish I could."

Not even Gawain tries to stop me, as I mount up and ride away. Nor does he speak up that evening, when in front of all I take up my sword, and lay it at the feet of Aglovale de Galis.

Coda

High on a tower, high on a hill, two men are standing. One is square-built, iron-haired, solidly mature. The other, the younger, is made imposing only by his height. His countenance is unremarkable. The most common expression in his eyes is puzzlement. They wear that aspect now, puzzled; and a little sad, as they gaze out beyond the battlements, out into the mist, and the distance. He's the air of a bit- player, an extra, one who has no need to understand the lines, the acts, that fall to him.

Perhaps that's for the best.

The elder, the remarkable, is watching his face. His own is unreadable. In a quiet voice, he says, now, "I remember a squire, once, who contradicted his king, and rightly. Do you mind it?"

"I do, sire."

"There are two good knights lost for the sake of one. What changed, Heris?"

"I don't know, sire. Uncle. Perhaps I never really said it. Perhaps it just grew in the telling."

"You will leave yourself with nothing." The king puts his elbows on the parapet, and gazes out at his land. "We all will, if we turn on ourselves from within."

"You have other knights. Better knights than me."

"I have many unique men. I did not seat you all at a round table to be quantified by some external scale of ability." His voice drops. "Have I lost two more good knights, Gaheris, for the sake of one vain woman?"

"You have already lost one."

"Yes. Poor Lamorak."

"He came to die so gently. As though he wanted it."

"Yes. Poor Gaheris, too." The king is pensive. "What will you do now? Will you leave us?"

"I don't know. It shall be as you wish it, sire."

"Will it?" The king sighs. "Will you forgive your brothers, and forget the past, for the sake of one aging man?"

"No, sire." From the tower, one may see five counties, if the day is clear. "But I will do it anyway."

"Why, then, Gaheris?"

I turn my back to the wall. "Because Agrin would like it so, if I didn't."

Across five counties, the rain starts to fall.

PART TWO:
ROSE KNOT

Prelude

I suppose that it started with Essyllt. Or then again, perhaps not. Perhaps, like so much else, it started with Lamorak de Galis. It would be easy to blame Lamorak. He's dead and gone, with no one at hand to speak up for him. But they say it's unlucky to speak ill of the dead. And from what little I know of Lamorak, he's unlikely to have thought beyond the immediate effect of his action. Perhaps I should learn to wish that he had never met that monk. Perhaps then I could tell myself that none of this would ever have come to pass.

It takes a particular kind of mind to lie to oneself. My sister Luned would have no difficulty at all. But I just don't have the heart. It would have happened, most of it, come what may. There's a shadow which follows my husband's kin: Lamorak was no more than another eclipse, brought down in the darkness we do not name.

I am Llinos of Kinkenadron, wife to Sir Gareth of Orkney, and this is my testament. Read it as you will. It is my truth. I seek no forgiveness, I offer no revelation. It began for me on a cool autumn evening at Camelot. It began with my cousin-by-marriage, the Queen of Cornwall, lovely Essyllt.

One

"Well," Essyllt said, "I wouldn't put up with it." She pressed the last pin into the net which held up her hair, and picked up her silver-bound mirror. "I'd do something about it right away: be sure of that." She paused a moment, gazing at her reflection. Then her brows drew together. "Do you think I'll do?"

In the warm light of the candles, her beauty was quite startling. The heavy mass of apricot hair was woven with pearls no whiter than her skin and her spring-green gown held her like a lover. The very sight of her made me smile. "Of course you will."

"Really?" She hesitated. "I'm trusting you, Llinos, so you have to tell me truthfully." She put down the mirror, and turned. "You must be completely honest. I can handle it. At least, I think I can... There are so many beauties here, what with the queen of Logres, and Lady Enide, and Laudine, and you, of course, so I... Well, go ahead, tell me." She straightened her shoulders, the defendant before the judge, and looked straight in the eyes. "Go on."

I had to control an impulse to laugh. "You're beautiful. As usual."

"Oh, praise heaven!" Essyllt rolled her eyes in deliciously comic relief. "I'm always on such pins whenever I come here, between one thing and another. Marcus frets me, and makes me forget half my baggage, and then Guenever... I know she doesn't mean it, but somehow she always manages to make me feel as if I dye my hair." Crossing the small room, she sat down beside me, and kissed my cheek. "I do miss having you amongst my ladies, love. I wish that husband of yours would let you come back to Cornwall."

"Gareth likes to be near his uncle."

"Yes, I know." She leant over, and took my embroidery out of my hands. "You're so pretty, and you know how to make everyone so comfortable, so of course he wants to keep you with him. But I want to be selfish and keep you too."

"Not so pretty after the baby." I looked from her trim waist to my own. "I'm growing sadly dumpy."

"No, you're not, love. You just let people neglect you." She looked wicked. "I've a good mind to steal you, and take you home with me to be pampered. That Gareth of yours is neglecting you shamefully. And so I shall tell him, if I get half the chance."

"He's busy, that's all."

"Well, he has no right to be." Abruptly she leapt to her feet. "I'm going to make you beautiful for him. Or for someone else, if he's too busy to look."

"Essyllt!"

"No, you're not shocked. I can tell when you're pretending. I'm in the mood for sorting people out. Now, tell me: *is* there someone who's caught your eye?"

"I love Gareth."

"I know, lovey – and so does half Logres, after those silly chastity tests – but it won't hurt to stir him up a bit." She lowered her lashes, and looked coy. "A little jealousy can work wonders in affairs of the heart."

"I don't know…"

"Well, I do." She pulled me to my feet, and looked me up and down.

"Do let me, Llinos. It'll be fun, I promise." Her voice was pleading. I tried to shake my head at her, but found myself laughing instead. She smiled. "I knew you would." Drawing me over to her dressing chest, she picked up a brush, and began to take down my hair. "Look at all this. Mine will never behave, or stay tidy. We'll show it off, and we'll take you out of at least one of those petticoats. You don't need them with the fires in the hall, anyway. Then we'll see who is and isn't looking."

Her hands moved quickly skilfully, braiding my front hair, leaving the remainder to fall loose down my back, like a maiden's.

91

"What colour were you wearing when you first met your Gareth? I know you remember, so don't try to tell me you don't."

"I won't, then. It was white. But…"

"White it shall be. I have just the gown. Context is very important. I only have to wear a little rosewater around Tris, and…" She broke off, laughing. "It works like magic."

"Essyllt, you're so careless." It was easy to be fond of her; easy to love her, too. But she worried me. She had no discretion. "After that incident with the monk and the chastity test."

She sighed. "I know, lovey. I do try, but somehow I can never remember to be really cautious." Her face brightened. "And I avoided the test well enough, didn't I, and no harm done. If Lamorak de Galis had any real sense of honour, he would never have let that monk take that horrid thing anywhere. But I suppose one can't expect anything better from a man of his kind." She was frowning. That made me nervous.

I said "Lamorak's very young. And…" I hesitated. Then: "I'm sure he meant no dishonour to you. I think he was just trying to get back at Tristan." ·

It was quite the wrong thing to say. Her lovely eyes narrowed. She said "And just what is Tris supposed to have done to him?"

Insulted my brother-in-law. But that was not a matter to raise with indiscreet Essyllt. I shrugged, and said "'I've no idea. Some joust or other, I expect."

"Tris *is* very skilled at jousting." Essyllt seemed ready enough to let the matter lie. She smiled at me, and added, "You mustn't worry. I'll be all right. Truly, Marcus doesn't care over-much what I do, so long as he can spend time with Andred. I don't know what I'd do if he behaved like some of the courtiers here: your Agravaine, for instance. I believe he takes those tests *seriously*. His poor wife!" Her blue eyes danced. "Perhaps I should light a candle in gratitude for a complacent husband."

"Oh, Essyllt!" Despite myself, I was laughing. "It really isn't funny."

"I know it! All those hypocrite men testing us with magical robes and cups, and looking supercilious. And hardly a one of

them with even a shadow of a claim to the moral high ground."
She twisted a silver pin into my hair, and looked pensive. "And a
good thing, too."

She sounded as if she might be plotting something. I said
carefully, "Why?"

Her expression became demure. "Well, Tris is in France – and
playing up to half the women at Claudas' court, if I know him –
and Marcus isn't interested. I have to amuse myself somehow while
I'm here."

"You're incorrigible."

"I'm made like that, I can't help it." Again, that wicked light in
her eyes. "Maybe I should lead that horrid Lamorak on. Serve him
right if I broke his heart."

I thought about Lamorak de Galis, with his yellow snake's eyes,
and smooth manners. A good man in the lists, my husband said,
but wild. Other rumours around the court linked him with my
mother-in-law, the treacherous queen of Orkney. Essyllt would be
no match for Margawse. I said "I don't think that would be a good
idea."

"Oh?" Essyllt looked intrigued. And then "Don't tell me the
stories are true? I thought that was just more of Andred's
nonsense." My concern must have shown, for she added,
"Lamorak's supposed to have some dark unrequited. passion.
Something utterly mysterious and perverted."

All of those were words I could find quite apt for my mother-
in-law. But then there was that happy word unrequited. It was
probable that even Agravaine would overlook an unfulfilled love
for his mother. I looked down, hastily, and said "I don't know
about that. I just meant that Lamorak is flighty. I don't believe he
cares for much at all, apart from knighthood." Sometimes, it can be
a burden, being a step-Orkney. So many sore places to avoid.

"Oh, another one." Essyllt was dismissive. "Well, it runs in his
family, I suppose. His brother Percevale is an absolute prig." She
put her hands on my shoulders. "Still, there's no shortage of more
interesting men here, anyway." She kissed my cheek.

That made me laugh again. "Oh, Essyllt!"

"No, you can't possibly understand. You're loyal, and sensible, and good, and married to lovely Gareth, who adores you (when he remembers). Whereas I'm just incurably frivolous." Her tone was unexpectedly serious.

I half-turned, and caught her hand. "You're not unhappy?"

"What?" She shook her head. "No, lovey, I'm just restless. I need to find someone to play with: I'm tired of being grown up and responsible, and Tris is getting so possessive. I'm counting on you to help me find a playmate."

"Me?"

"Who else? You know everyone here, and they all love you. You can put me on to the good ones." She took her hand away, and went to her clothes' press. Opening it, she began to rummage. "That dress should be in here: I know I packed it. So, tell me about that delicious brother-in-law of yours."

"Which one? I have four, in case you hadn't noticed."

"Who could miss them? The Orkneys, such glorious specimens of manhood! It makes me quite dizzy to think about it." She re-emerged from the closet, clutching a cream over-gown, and a pair of matching sleeves. "I'm sure this will fit. Let me help you." She spun me round, and started on the lacing of my bodice. "Anyway, what do you make of my chances with your delectable kinsman?"

"You still haven't told me which one. If it's Gawain…"

She paused, holding one of my skirt tags in her hand. "Ah, Gawain. Beautiful, attainable, and fickle as a breeze. He's a dream, of course, but who can hold him? No, I meant the big one."

"The big one?" For a moment, I couldn't think who she meant. Then "Gaheris?" I looked back at her over my shoulder. "Not Gaheris?"

"Don't look so surprised. Why not?"

"Well, I…"

"It's not as if your sister has any real use for him. (Do you know who it is she's involved with at present? I'd love to know.) And I only want to borrow him." She looked wicked. "You know, I think he's almost bigger than Tristan." Her tone was light, but her expression lent ready scandal to her meaning. "What do you think?" I looked unconvinced. She continued "Does he have some terrible secret?"

"Not that I know of." I hesitated, then turned properly, and faced her. "I wish you wouldn't."

She sighed. "Don't disapprove of me, Llinos, please."

"I don't. It's just… Well, Heris is shy, and…"

"Still waters run deep."

"I daresay, but the fact is he doesn't get on with your Tristan, and I'd hate for the two of them to fight. Heris would lose, and then the rest of the clan would get all riled up on his behalf, and… "

"Yes, I see." Essyllt was briefly serious. "The Orkneys never forget." She shrugged. "Well, it was just an idea. Luned threw such a wobbly about him after the mantle test last month that I thought there must be something…"

My sister Luned has never been good at hiding her feelings. I waited for Essyllt to finish pulling the cream gown up over my shoulders. Then I said, "That was Agravaine's fault, really. He made such a huge scene about Laurel failing the test that Luned felt slighted. Heris is her husband, after all, yet he didn't say a word. She said he didn't even value her enough to be angry, he just looked resigned."

"Oh, poor Luned!" Essyllt caught my eye, and giggled. "'That *is* rather deflating."

"I know, but she'd have been even more upset if he'd beaten her, as Agravaine did Laurel."

"I'm beginning to feel sorry for the delightful Gaheris."

"Essyllt…"

"I know, I know, I'll leave him alone, I promise. But I do think we should try turning the tables on Agravaine and his ilk. In fact, I'm beginning to have rather a good idea about that…" She gave a final tug on my laces, and began to tie them. "'There. I've always said front-lacing gowns are the most flattering. Look at yourself." She picked up the mirror, and held it where I could see. The dress was a little on the tight side. It did interesting things for my bust. Essyllt said "You look lovely. "

I reached over, and kissed her. "'Thank you."

95

"You're welcome." She smiled. "I shall speak to Brangwen about my idea… Shall we go down and stun the courtiers?" Her arm slipped about my waist. "I'll only be a little naughty, I promise. Now, tell me what you think of Kay."

"Beautifully brusque. But he isn't here: he went with the king to London."

Essyllt pretended to pout. "Everything's against; me! I suppose it will just have to be Gawain, then." She sighed, and placed a hand over her heart. "Oh, the burden of it!"

"You'll survive," I said, smiling.

"I know, love," she said. "And knowing Prince Gawain, I'll enjoy it."

I could be melodramatic, and say that that was the last night on which I remember seeing my husband and his brothers all together in harmony, but I don't know if it would be true. Distance lends everything a gloss. More likely there were the same petty frictions and jealousies which in the end tore us all down. I remember coming to the foot of the stair with Essyllt to find them all grouped together at one end of the hall, neat and uncomfortable in their finery. "Holy Virgin!" said Essyllt into my ear. "The people of the hills. Don't they ever intimidate you? One forgets there are so many."

Malicious tongues credit my mother-in-law with finding a different father for each of her children. Perhaps it was true: I've never known. Certainly, no one could have told it by looking at her sons. They all looked like her, with that rich brown hair that is red under strong sun, long, big bones, and dark eyes. Gawain is the darkest, and many think him the handsomest, too, with his spare frame and sleepy, slow smile. He has a quick temper and a kind heart, and he notices everything. That night, he stood in the centre as always, looking down the hall towards the queen, whom he was officially escorting. Agravaine stood to his left, a little shorter than Gawain, and a little broader, with hair the exact same russet shade as his mother's. He was laughing, showing his fine teeth. My Gareth beside him was laughing too, the fairest and slightest of all the family. His hair needed cutting: he'd been on at me for weeks to trim it, but I'd resisted. It hung to his shoulder blades, a little untidy, two shades lighter than Agravaine's. Medraut was to Gawain's right, composed and still. He's as dark as Gawain, and not done, quite, with growing. He stood almost as tall as Gaheris, who's the tallest man at court, saving only Kay. Gaheris himself stood, as ever, at the back, mainly in shadow, as if he would disguise his size. Alone among the brothers, he has grey eyes, not brown. I'd thought perhaps he had them of Lot of Orkney, but my cousin Marcus, who's old enough to know, told me Gaheris was the image of his maternal grandsire, Duke Gorlois. That Cornish blood runs strong, swamping all other humours which come in its way. I've a little of it myself, and both Luned and I are as dark as Medraut and Gawain. The bishop had frowned, marrying Gareth to me. Cousins in the third degree, too close for comfort and refusing from love to await the Roman dispensation. But I'd have wed Gareth anyway, whatever the church required: over the broom if necessary. I stood there by the stair, watching him, content and complete, and Essyllt laughed, looking at me. Then Gawain noticed us, and prodded Gareth.

No, it was an evening like any other, arranged by the queen for the amusement of herself and her guests. A light supper, and then the covers were drawn, and the musicians came in for the dancing. Medraut kissed my fingers behind a pillar, and whispered "Why didn't you keep a sister or cousin for me, Llinos?", and, a little drunk, I only smiled, and kissed his cheek. I'd lost Essyllt long before, whisked into the circle by someone or other. I was dizzy and breathless, and when the music ended, sought refuge on one of the long benches. Gareth was leading out the queen: across the room, we caught each other's eyes, and smiled. Beyond him, I saw Luned, flirting with two or three of the younger knights.

From my left a voice said, "You look hot, Lady Llinos. May I fetch you something?" I turned. It was Lamorak de Galis. His left arm was in a sling; looking at me, he bowed and added, "I can't dance, as you see, but I can make myself useful fetching and carrying." He smiled. "It's important to be useful, don't you think?"

"Very probably."

"Gaheris says I'm dreadfully underfoot." His smile turned rueful, and he drew up a stool. "May I? Or shall I bring you wine?"

"If I drink any more I'll be paying for it all tomorrow." I rather liked Lamorak, what little I knew of him. I could afford to: I had Gareth. I was immune to others' charms. I smiled at him.

He sat. "How lovely you look," he said, easily. "Sir Gareth is lucky." He had probably said very similar things to more or less every other woman present. I looked at him steadily, and after a moment he looked down. He said, "You know, I can talk nonsense by the hour. But not to you. You're very serious, Lady Llinos."

Sensible, Essyllt had said, but it amounted to the same thing. I watched her for an instant, dancing with Gawain. Her eyes were very bright. He was smiling. Accomplished, the pair of them, in the art of dalliance, ready to play and walk away. Lamorak followed my gaze. He said "Now that lady isn't serious at all."

"Only in her displeasure." I turned back to him. "It isn't for me to mention it, but…"

Lamorak held up a hand. "No. I called you serious. I deserve it." He was trying to make me smile. He really was very young, and something about him was vulnerable. Too young by far for Margawse, who can cow even Kay with a look. Lamorak was smiling, but it didn't reach his eyes. He said, "It's that business with the monk, isn't it? It was a terrible thing I did. I wouldn't blame her if she sent her men after my head." He looked down. "I could say I wasn't thinking, but it wouldn't be true. I'd had an argument – a dreadful one – with Tristan, and I felt like killing him. When the monk appeared with his magical test of female constancy, all I saw was a chance to humiliate Tris. I didn't even think about what it might mean for Queen Essyllt… I'm glad she avoided it. I should never have sent the monk in the first place." He paused and drew a breath. "Gaheris says I should apologise."

"Gaheris is right." But something in Lamorak's voice troubled me. His face was averted. I said, "Is something wrong?"

"Good heavens, no!" He laughed without turning. "Just cowardice. I'm terrified of the Queen of Cornwall. Impressive, don't you think, in a fighting man? Do you think she'll poison me?"

"She's more likely to try and break your heart." Lamorak's head snapped up, and he stared at me, startled. I was fairly surprised at myself. "Essyllt doesn't bear grudges, not really. But you insulted her, and she doesn't know why."

"I do everything wrong." He shook his head. "Gaheris says I forget to think." I was silent. He rubbed a hand along his bandaged arm. "I suppose it won't help if I tell her the truth?"

"I don't know."

He looked away again. "She's very beautiful," he said, and sighed. "But she can't break my heart." He was not watching Essyllt. His face was sad. He was staring at the other side of the hall, at my sister Luned, and her coterie, and beyond, at the tall shape of my brother-in-law Gaheris, standing silent in the shadows.

Two

Sometime after midnight, Gareth lifted his head from my shoulder, and said "I saw you talking to Lamorak de Galis."

I was warm, and content, and more than part asleep. My husband had been very taken with my borrowed dress. I opened my eyes a little, and said "Hmm?"

"He worries me." Gareth said.

"Why?" He was silent. I added "You're not jealous?"

"What?" He looked startled. "No, sweetling. I trust you." He kissed my brow. "It's just Lamorak... He attracts trouble." He hesitated. "Heris says he'll grow out of it... What is it?"

"Lamorak. You reminded me – he kept saying that, too: 'Gaheris says'."

"I don't like it," Gareth said. "I keep thinking something bad will happen."

A little over two months later, my mother-in-law died by violence. No one seemed clear as to the how or the why, although it was Gaheris who stood trial for the deed. The Orkneys quarrelled bitterly, before dividing along familiar lines. Gawain and Gaheris. Agravaine and Medraut. Gareth trapped helplessly between them, unable to mediate, miserable, confused. Lamorak de Galis had vanished from court the night of the murder, and no one knew the reason for that, either. "Perhaps," Luned said, maliciously, before the whole court, "he's trying to protect *your* good name, Heris." Gaheris, quieter than ever, could not meet her eyes. He would not defend himself, not even at the request of the king. He would not talk about it at all, except to repeat over and over, "It was my fault."

It could not be proved either way. The trial ended nothing; Agravaine muttered darkly about Lamorak. And within a half a year, Lamorak too was dead.

I barely registered the fact. A month before, Gareth and I had lost our baby, our only child. There was no tragedy to touch it. I fled the court, home to Kinkenadron, where no one murmured or looked; and Gareth stayed behind. Those days are not, even now, to be spoken of. I could not bear myself, for living when my child did not. The world held no solace: not even Gareth understood. He had duties at court, business, family quarrels. I had nothing. We could not even comfort each other. When Gareth came west to the domain, we found we had nothing to say. Each time he left, I wept, yet I could neither talk to him nor follow him. And the intervals between his visits and letters grew longer.

Not wholly his fault. He at least made attempts to come to me. I made none whatsoever to go to him. I was lonely, there in Kinkenadron, yet I lacked the energy to mend the condition. Queen Guenever sought me to return to court for Christmas, and I pleaded off. In February, Medraut came to the domain alone, and stayed a night or two. He'd grown a beard, and was beginning to fill out to match his height. I barely listened to his fund of witty, clever stories of the court. It was nothing to me, who loved whom, who lived and who died, aside from my one child. "How pale you are," said Medraut, taking my hand. "More fool Gareth, leaving you here alone."

"I like it." And I would have withdrawn my hand, but he was the stronger.

He said, carefully, "There is a terrible pain in this family. Gareth... There has been something said, between Gareth and Gaheris. You should come back to court, Llinos."

But I did not heed him. The Orkneys were forever at odds with each other. I would not recall that Gareth, over all, forbore to quarrel with his brothers. Heris, at least, had the Orkney temper. It would pass, all earthly things passed. I remained alone at

Kinkenadron until it was almost spring. Almost a year since the loss of my little girl. Mid-March brought another letter from the queen: no request, now, but a command. I must attend her at Easter, she would brook no excuse. She had sent my half-brother to fetch me: I must be escorted, we must travel the long way round. A shadow lay on Surluse forest in late days; there were strange stories, rumours of fell creatures and worse. Some claimed a ghost knight had been seen riding there. The queen would expose me to no dangers. Dutifully, I packed my chests, and Gringamore and I made the long journey back to Camelot.

I felt rather like a ghost myself. I had nothing to say to my companions, to the queen, to her ladies. At night I lay away from Gareth, my face to the wall.

I had entirely forgotten Essyllt and her half-laughing schemes of vengeance. I lived now in another world. I think I did not even look up fully when the green-clad damsel came before the queen.

She bore a rosewood box: with a deep reverence, she laid it at Guenever's feet. "A gift, madame, from the queen of Cornwall."

Guenever smiled, and took the box. The lid was plain. She opened it, and frowned. Within lay a silver-bound hunting horn.

"It is magical, my lady," the damsel said. "A species of game. The horn may be sounded only by he who has remained faithful to his lady for the past year and a day."

Slowly, the queen said "This tests male fidelity?"

"Yes, my lady."

There was a small silence. Someone giggled. Guenever smiled. Her fingers drummed on the edge of the box. "Well, she said, softly, "trust Essyllt." She looked across at Andrivete, Kay's wife and head of her household. "I think," she said, "that we must hold a special supper party."

It did not occur to me that the plan could in anyway affect me. A game, no more, and one which seemed to touch on nothing of any importance. The queen laid her plans quickly, and swore us all to secrecy. It was almost May: Easter had come late this year. What season could be more appropriate? We would ride out for the Maying, and end the celebration with a small, exclusive supper in the Queen's large chamber. The men should be told nothing: the ladies would lead them blind into the test, as the knights themselves had formerly led their ladies. "And about time, too!" said my soft-voiced cousin Laurel. She wore only high-necked gowns, to hide the scarring on her shoulders. Agravaine was an unforgiving husband. "Let those hypocrites suffer, for once." She looked down. "I expect Agravaine will beat me for not warning him, but it will be worth it to see him fail."

"You're so sure he's unfaithful?" asked Alis, the new bride, a little shocked. "It's worth risking his anger?"

"Who knows?" said Luned. She smiled. "We might all be in for a few surprises."

Mayday was bright and clear. There was laughter as we rode through the cool green woods. Laurel had talked me into colours: the first time for a year. There was no wind. It might almost have been summer, there amidst the trees. Someone started up a song. The voices rose clear, if not always true, verses traded back and forth between men and women. Gareth looked at me as he sang, and I wished suddenly that we were alone. He looked tired: something was troubling him, and I had taken no account of it. How long since we had exchanged more than formalities? Six months? Ten? I turned my horse's head towards him, but the queen suddenly spurred on into the wood and I had to follow. The men pursued us, laughing, as we collected the May blossoms. Later, we gathered on the river bank for refreshment and more music. When I looked around for Gareth, he was nowhere to be seen. I remembered again that my child was dead, and for me the sun went in.

Gaheris settled on the bank beside me, a cup of ale in either hand. There was a dark mark all along one of his cheekbones, like dirt, or a bruise. He saw me looking, and said "I was careless in the practice yard. Kay always says I lumber like a camel." And then, "You're not singing."

"Neither are you," I pointed out.

He grinned. "If my life depended on my carrying a tune, I'd be sending for a coffin-maker."

"I don't feel like singing."

"No. Poor Llinos." He looked at me a moment, then added, "It's good you're back with us. Gareth was miserable without you."

"Then where is he now?" I said, and looked down.

"Someone's horse cast a shoe. You know Gareth: he always has to help those in trouble." Gaheris put the ale down, leant back on his elbows, and crossed his ankles. "He'll be along soon, I daresay. Or you might ask Gavin to go and look for him."

"Not you?"

He avoided my eyes, gazing up at the sky. "I'm too lazy today."

"You know, Heris," I said, slowly, "Medraut came to see me at Kinkenadron." Gaheris was silent. "He told me that you'd quarrelled, you and Gareth."

"Mouse has a loose tongue." He stopped, then sat up. "He didn't need to trouble you with that. It was nothing."

But Gareth was unhappy… Medraut was right, I should have returned sooner. I looked across at Gaheris. "Has something happened?"

"No," he said. Then he flushed, and went on, "Just me making a fool of myself. The usual. It doesn't matter, now you're with us again."

The sun was low when we returned to the castle: there was a terrible flurry to wash and tidy up for the queen's supper. My sister Luned snapped as the maid tried to brush out her hair, then quite suddenly dissolved into tears. I sent the girl away, and tried to comfort her, but she would have none of it. "You don't understand," she said furiously. "You never could."

We went down together in silence. As we gathered in the solar, Andrivete looked at the queen. "You don't have to go through with this."

Guenever bit her lip. Then she shook her head. "And have Essyllt say ever after that I was afraid to play the men at their own game? No. It will be done."

"There will be trouble from it," Andrivete said.

"As there was trouble over Dame Morgan's mantle?" Guenever said. She looked across at Laurel, who lowered her eyes. "Let there be."

The hall was bright with candles, and fragrant with the May. Over the courses, the guests grew merry. Gareth and I shared one dish, and his hands were warm on mine. The light seemed to be everywhere, filling my eyes. The shadow was beginning, perhaps, to go its way. To my left, Gawain paid meticulous, insincere court to the queen, who laughed at him. Across the table, Luned stared into her lap, and kept her face averted from her neighbours. The king was at Winchester with Lancelot and the bishops. It occurred to me that Guenever would not have played this trick had the king been present.

"Llinos," Gawain said suddenly, "I appeal to you. Her majesty calls me a frippery thing: please defend me."

Gareth peered at him over my shoulder. "Not frippery, surely? The amount you eat, Gavin, you're too big to be a trimming."

Gawain bowed to him. "Attacked on both sides," he said, ruefully. "I'm the eldest, Gari. Have you no respect?"

"Over dinner?" said Gareth. "No."

"You see," said the queen, "false coin will out." Gawain put his elbows on the table, and laughed.

Guenever smiled. Then she clapped her hands, and the servants came in to draw the covers. As they went out, she rose and called her ladies to her. We stood at her shoulders on the dais under the unicorn tapestry. She waited for silence, gesturing to the men to remain seated. Then she spoke. "Gentlemen, today is Mayday, and, as you know, Mayday is ruled only by a queen. You have chosen me. Are you ready to obey my commands?" Some laughter, a murmur of amused consent. At a signal, a page brought out the rosewood box. Guenever continued, "I have an entertainment for you. A challenge, of a kind." She opened the box, and removed the horn. "Only he who has been faithful to his lady for the past year and a day may sound this horn. Come, gentlemen: let us hear your fidelity." Another murmur. "You agreed, did you not, that I had the right to command? Well, I command this to be done." She handed the horn to the page. "Take this to my knights, and let them essay this test."

I looked out into the chamber. The signs of discomfort were clear. Agravaine stared fixedly at his plate, red with embarrassment or, more likely, anger. Kay had his arms folded; his eyes narrowed as he watched the queen. Sagremore looked frankly terrified. Medraut was smiling; rising, he bowed and said, "Your majesty, if we have no lady?"

"Then you have nothing to fear," Guenever said. He shrugged and resumed his place.

The page reached the table and halted, looking up at the queen. She nodded, and he passed the horn to the first man. I looked sidelong at the other ladies. Andrivete frowned. Luned clutched her hands in her skirts, and muttered *sotto voce*. Alis was smiling. It seemed to me, abruptly, that we were taking a very great chance. Essyllt was thoughtless: she never looked beyond the moment. Andrivete was right: there was mischief in this. Too late, now, to stop it.

The horn passed from hand to hand. Young Alisander blushed as he sounded a note, high and true. Beside me, Alis clapped her hands in delight. Patrise next to him failed, and two more beyond him. Agravaine failed, and scowled at Laurel. Medraut drew one clear note and looked at us, laughing. "Does this mean," he said, "that I'm in love, and don't know it?" But after him, five successive failures. One of the ladies began, softly, to weep. Then a success, and another. Sagremore failed. The horn reached Kay, who held it for a moment, weighing it in his palms. He looked at Andrivete. "I can see, wife, that I'm going to have to increase your dress allowance." Laughter sprinkled the hall as he blew the horn, and played, albeit flat, the first few notes of 'Cuckolds All Awry'. Next to him was Gaheris, who did not look at the dais as the horn came to him. The note again was true. "You," said Luned, furiously, "you do this just to spite me. Do you think this makes you better than me?" He shook his head, and his eyes slid quickly from her face. After him came four more failures, a success, and another failure. It arrived at Gawain. He rose, and looked at the queen. "Is it worth my even trying?" He was laughing, but there was an air to him that bespoke disapproval.

"No exceptions, Sir Gawain," said the queen.

"Ah, well." He shrugged, and inhaled with exaggerated vigour. The horn made for him not the faintest sound. He shook his head, and handed it to Gareth.

Medraut said, "Unnecessary, surely. Is this not the very pelican of fidelity?" Gareth stopped and turned to look at him, the motion hiding his expression from me.

"Pelican?" someone said. And someone else answered "Thought that was for maternal devotion. He means swan."

"I said no exceptions," said the queen.

Gareth turned again, and looked up. Medraut had come to stand at his shoulder. Gawain moved to the very edge of the dais. I could almost touch him. Gareth raised the horn, hesitated, and looked at me. For a moment, it seemed he might speak. Then he closed his eyes, and blew.

There was no sound. For the longest moment I was waiting, expecting the note to rise. He was drawing his breath, that was all, in a second it would be over... No one moved, no one seemed even to breathe. Then Gareth lowered the horn. He opened his eyes, and looked at me again. Then he put his face into his hands.

There was a hand under my elbow. All around me, the ladies retreated. I could not look at their faces. Their hems rustled, brushing the rush matting; mud on one, a tiny tear in another...

odd, what is noticed, what is forgotten. The hand slid up to my shoulder, and turned me with gentle ease.

"Llinos," Gawain said, softly, "Come and look at the rose garden."

Three

"You knew," I said to him, on the terrace. A cool night had come in to follow the warm day: there were no clouds, and the moon was crisp and clear overhead. Gawain had draped his mantle over my shoulders: he held my hand in his as we sat on the low wall. "You knew. That's why you sent Medraut to me in Cornwall."

"I didn't know." With his free hand, Gawain brushed a speck of ash from his knee. "I suspected." He hesitated. "But I sent no one. I had no proof. And I have faith in Gareth."

"It's my fault, I stayed away…"

He shook his head. "It sounds shallow, but these things happen." A pause. "Gareth loves you."

I stared into the shadowy garden. "I shouldn't have come back."

I don't know precisely how long we stayed outside. Not long; no more, perhaps, than half an hour. I felt still, inside myself: my thoughts refused to move on from moment to moment. I was not ready to feel. It seemed that nothing would ever again reach me.

The corridors were empty when we went in. But lights burned under doors, and there was a continual murmur of voices. Most were hushed: in the painted chamber, they were raised. We could make out the words from the foot of the stair. The Orkneys. Always the Orkneys.

"…nonsense about pelicans!" That was Agravaine. He sounded disgusted.

"Believe it or not, Agrin, I was trying to help." Medraut, sounding irritated.

My Gareth's voice, then, softer, but still not low. "We know that, Mouse, but…"

"Will you stop calling me that!" Medraut snapped. Gawain and I were almost at the top of the stair. Through the open door, I could see Agravaine in the centre of the room, hands on hips, glaring. Medraut stood by the hearth, one elbow on the mantel; beyond him, Laurel hovered, twisting her veil. Gareth was out of my line of sight.

Agravaine drew in a long breath. "Yon test was false."

"Oh, aye." Medraut laughed without mirth. His eyes met mine briefly, as Gawain and I came into the room. Then they flickered to his eldest brother. "I'm sure Gavin will agree that he's the very zenith of virtue."

Gawain handed me to a chair. I could see the rest of them, now. Luned sat in the south window, spine rigid, face set. Gareth beside her avoided my gaze. Gaheris stood a little apart from the others, back to the room, staring through the other window into the night. Gawain found himself a corner of a chest, and sat down. Then he said "Like you, Mouse, I have no one to whom to be true."

"Don't call me that!" Medraut said again. And then "Not even a memory, Gavin?"

There was a nasty silence. No one ever talked about Gawain's long-dead Rhanillt; it was one of the family's unwritten rules. Medraut looked down. "I'm sorry. I didn't mean that."

"The Orkney talent," Gawain said. "Saying what we do not mean."

"I'd just like to know," Medraut said, "why you're all picking on me, when it was Gari who failed."

"We have no proof the test was true," Agravaine said stubbornly, drowning out an attempt to speak by Gareth, who shook his head and fell silent. "It was no more than women's meddling." Agravaine's eye fell on Laurel. "Aye, and a better test of female honesty than male. A true wife would not have let her husband go unwarned into such folly."

Laurel stared at her feet. "The queen made us swear…"

"The queen! Did God appoint the queen head over you, or your husband?" Agravaine took a step forward. "No, madam, this is more of your disobedience."

Laurel gave a little gasp. From the window, Gaheris said, "Let be, Agrin. Don't make this worse."

"You!" Agravaine was scornful. "You can't rule your own wife! Don't tell me how to treat mine."

"Our mother," Gawain said, "did not raise any of us to strike or bully a woman. Don't blame Laurel for your own bad temper."

Another silence. Then Luned said, lightly, "Well, your mother didn't do a very good job, did she?" Agravaine scowled. She smiled at him. "Just look what my husband did to *her.*"

Gaheris turned. He was white. "Is this my fault, now?"

"You shamed me before everyone," Luned said. "There's not a soul in this court believes there's more than air to our marriage. But you mock me with your sham fidelity."

"No, I..."

"Do you think that this will shrive you? Will these petty virtues wipe out what you've done?" Luned was trembling. "I live every day with your dishonour." Gareth reached out and put a hand on her arm. She ignored him. "Matricide and destroyer of good knights!"

Gaheris choked. He put a hand to his mouth, looking across at Gawain. Very carefully, Gawain said, "I am sorry for your pain, Luned, but it does no good to rehearse these matters."

"Why not?" Gareth said, suddenly. We all stared at him. "We never do talk about that, do we? Why is that, Gavin?" His voice was sharp, tight: still he would not meet my eyes. There was something here... Medraut had tried to warn me. *There has been something said, between Gareth and Gaheris.* Gareth swallowed. "Go on, Gavin, tell me."

"It hardly seems relevant..." Gawain said, but his voice was uncertain.

"The truth is," Agravaine said, "that Heris is your favourite. However clumsy he is, however stupid or vicious, you allow him anything."

111

Gawain looked up. "No, Agrin, I…"

"Listen to you!" Gareth interrupted him. "I want to talk about this now. I want to talk about Lamorak de Galis."

"What for?" said Agravaine. "Lamorak was no part of us. Son of our enemy, and despoiler of our mother. It's her death we should be thinking about."

Gareth ignored him, looking at Gawain. "Here you all are, gathered to rehearse my faults. But you called no family council over Heris."

"I called none over you." Gawain spoke softly, but in his voice was the leading edge of anger. "I took your wife from the sight of your shame, and I hoped to find you alone to receive her again." Laurel took a step forward, as if she would speak, then stopped at a glance from Agravaine. I pulled Gawain's cloak tighter about my shoulders, as though it might keep out the words.

Gareth released Luned's arm. I had almost never seen him angry. One thought of gentleness, of grace, in connection with him; easy enough to forget that he, too, was Margawse's son. Easy, until you caught sight of the tilt of his jaw, the line of his brow, the dark colouring in his eyes. An Orkney, every bit as much as the rest of them. He inhaled raggedly, and said, "Thank you, Gavin. May I point out to you yet another difference?" Gawain's eyes narrowed. I put out my hand, and Laurel took it. Gareth continued, "You interfere quite happily in my marriage. Yet you do nothing at all about Heris's."

I said, quickly, "It wasn't interference," but no one paid any attention. There was a pause.

Then Gaheris said "If it helps, Gari, he's been nagging me for years."

"I don't believe you," Gareth said. "I don't see him sheltering your wife from your shame."

Gaheris looked down. Laurel said "But Heris didn't fail… If the test was true, he's loyal."

"I wish," Gaheris said, rather sharply, "you'd all stop talking about my character as if I wasn't here." He spread a hand out in front of him, and stared down at it. He looked cornered. "If you've something to say to me, Gari, say it, and have done."

"Loyalty," Gareth said, and stopped. For the first time since the test, he turned towards me. His face was quite blank, as if he was beyond any feeling save anger or confusion. A glance of a few seconds, no longer, then he looked away.

Into the silence, Luned said "Tell us about loyalty, Heris. How can you pretend to be loyal to me, when you couldn't keep faith with those for whom you actually cared? You broke faith with Lamorak. Why not with me?"

"I have no idea." Gaheris said. I tightened my hold on Laurel's hand. "I wasn't thinking." He sighed. "A year and a day… Chance. Does that help?"

"And Lamorak?" Gareth said. "He adored you. He named you his sponsor. He followed you everywhere, and you betrayed him." Gaheris let his head fall. Gareth said "You killed him."

"No!" Gawain, finally, had lost his temper. He came to his feet, glaring. "That's a lie. You will take it back, right now. Heris had no part in that death."

"Lamorak trusted him," Gareth said, simply.

"Aye," Gaheris looked up. "He trusted me, and it got him killed. You think I don't know that?" He came into the centre of the room. "I offered his brothers my life in return." He put a hand to his belt "The offer stands, Gari. I've a knife here, right now. You can use it, for Lamorak. Or," and he turned to Agravaine, "Agrin may, for mother." Agravaine stared at him, blankly. Gaheris swallowed, looked down at me. "I'm sorry, Llinos. All my fault. As usual."

No one moved. After a moment, Gaheris passed a hand across his eyes, looked down, and walked out. He didn't slam the door behind him.

Laurel had started crying. I could think of nothing to say to her.

Agravaine, surprisingly, seemed more puzzled than angry. Gareth stared at the floor. There was a long silence. Then Medraut stepped away from the hearth, and let a hand fall onto my shoulder. "Are you all right, Llinos?" I couldn't answer him. My mouth was too dry. He shook his head, then looked across at my sister.

"Well," he said, lightly, "are you happy, now? Have you got everything you wanted?" Luned flushed. "There's loyalty for you," he continued, "or don't you count it necessary, between sisters?"

Somehow, Medraut bundled them all out of the room, even Laurel, who wanted to stay. Luned had pulled down her veil: I think she wept behind it. Gawain kissed my cheek before leaving. "I should have known," he said, "I should have taken you to some more private place, and brought Gareth to you."

But Gareth would not speak to me. In the doorway, he paused, and looked back. "Llinos…" He shook his head, and fled. I had left him too long alone. I had lost him. I still couldn't feel it. I had lived so long with pain that I could not comprehend this new one. Medraut escorted me to my own room, and then, like Laurel, tried to linger. I sent him away. He sighed, ruefully, but he obeyed.

I couldn't sleep. I didn't even undress for bed. I sat in the window, chin on my knees, waiting for the dawn. Around me was only silence. I let the candles burn out, remained there in the dark. I sat there all night, but Gareth did not come.

Four

A little after dawn, someone knocked on the door. It was Luned. She didn't look as if she had slept, either. She said "Is he here? I need to speak to him."

"Gareth? No."

I thought she would leave, then, but she hesitated, playing with the loose ends of her hair. She said "What do you want me to say? That I loved him first? It would be true." I said nothing. She wound her hair around her fingers, one way, another. I could remember that habit right back into our childhood. She said "You don't know what it's like, being married to Gaheris."

"Is that an excuse?"

"You're angry… I suppose that's fair. No one thinks you've done anything wrong. It's me that's the shrew, again. I've been so lonely." She looked away down the corridor. "I don't suppose you even want to hear this. Gaheris either ignores me or placates me. I don't love him. I never have, but…"

"Would you rather he abused you, as Agravaine does Laurel?"

"I don't know." She spoke slowly. "You can't imagine what it's like. Nothing I do touches him. Not even when I…" She stopped, then finished, "Not until now."

I could not be angry: the emotion was gone with the rest, buried under the grief. Yet something made me say "Is that why you did this to me? To get a reaction from Gaheris?"

"No." She looked back at me. "Not even I would do that. But Gareth saw, don't you see? He saw how unhappy I was, and he came to save me. And I didn't think about you at all, because you just didn't seem to need him any more."

I could hear the castle coming to life as I closed the door behind her. Someone else would come, all too soon. Laurel, or Andrivete, or kind Gawain. I had fled from their sympathy before. I could not bear to stay for it now: it would burn me. I gathered a few things into saddle bags. I'd leave orders that the rest be sent to me later. I'd be safe at Kinkenadron. I'd always been safe there. Only Gareth had ever broken through those walls. I'd held them secure two years against Ironside, the Red Knight of the Red Launds. I could hold them again. At home, I would know each and every one of my boundaries, and no one would hurt me again. I changed hurriedly into travelling clothes, and when my maid Alison came in, sent her to gather her own few necessities, while I fetched a day's rations. In less than an hour, we were ready. We were silent as we rode out of the stable yard and down towards the river. We would need no escort, not on the king's roads, along which it was said a maiden with a bag of gold might travel quite securely from one end of the kingdom to the other. It was better this way.

Alison and I were almost four miles from Camelot when we heard the sound of horses coming up fast behind us. Couriers, no doubt. Obedient to the regulation, we drew over to one side, and waited. Yes, there they were, two horsemen coming at the gallop down the hill. They wore no livery, though one had an indistinct badge on his shoulder. The morning air turned the leader's hair amber: for a breathless moment, I thought it might be Gareth.

Gareth was not so tall. I looked down, as the hoof-beats approached us, slowing to a walk. The horsemen reined in alongside us, and Alison bowed from the saddle. I turned. The leader pushed his hair back from his face with a large hand, and looked at me apologetically. The shoulder badge was his personal device, five long-stemmed flowers entwined in a pentangle: the rose knot. The same device was painted on the shield strapped to the saddle of the sleepy-eyed squire. I looked from one to the other. "Is something wrong? Is it Gareth?"

"No." Gaheris rested a hand on his saddle-bow. He wore travel gear: there were bags slung across his horse's rump. He shrugged.

"Gavin sent me. To see you home." His expression was quizzical. "I think he wants me out of the way."

"Just you?" I said.

"Well, of course." Gaheris was puzzled.

It made no difference either way. I pressed my knees to my horse's sides, moving it to a walk. "So," I said, "let's go."

The weather was unkind. Day after day of clear skies and bright sun. All along the roads, trees blossomed; around their boles clustered the flowers of early spring. The nights were warm and balmy. We stayed in the houses of domain lords, as was the right of the king's knights, or with the dignitaries of the small towns. The officials talked to us of politics and taxes, trade and fashion and sheep. Everywhere I looked there were children: in the gardens of cottages, on village greens, in the houses and streets of the towns. And, too often, there were lovers of all kinds and conditions. It tore at me to see them. I felt very alone. We did not speak of what had passed, Gaheris and I. At first we exchanged only commonplaces, when we spoke at all.

After four days of travel, the settlements began to be further apart, the landscape wilder. On the western horizon, the dark smudge of Surluse forest grew. At a small manor, Gaheris bargained for a pack-horse, and a tent that was almost a pavilion. We would not venture into the forest, but we must pass close by it; we might not always be sure of lodging. Oh, to be sure, we might have avoided it wholly, turning north to take the Bristol pack-horse route. I had travelled that way in March, but it added ten days or more to the journey, and I longed to be home.

Our chosen route lay off the main roads: a track, even a path, unpaved, never pioneered by the distant Romans. It wound lazily, apt to the shape of the land, along shallow vales, skirting spurs, following the contours of hills. There were no orchards here, no nascent fields of corn. The ground grew stiff grass and gorse, and sheep wandered across it. Hawthorn and scattered birch marked the leading edge of the forest; at night the wind brought the scent of bark and mulch. We camped by the path's side, close to rivulets, or in the lee of low hills. Gaheris and his squire, Evan, pitched the tent for Alison and me. They lay out under the sky. "What if it rains?" said Alison.

"We get wet," said Gaheris.

"His mail rusts, and I have to clean it," Evan finished gloomily.

But it did not rain. On the second day, we reached the border of the forest proper. Wide-spaced trees paced us, beech and ash and oak. There was grass and bracken beneath them: here, there was still sufficient soil and light. Deer and rabbit tracks wandered in and out; the sun patterned the leaves. Surluse seemed green and cool and inviting. All of us knew better than to wander in. We must skirt it for four more days, then turn south-west, towards the coast. The forest was content to ignore us; nothing came from it, apart from birds, and rabbits, and the occasional deer. Evan's skin turned brown from the sun, and Alison fussed with veils. Gaheris, as every year, began to freckle.

We forded two largish streams, and several minor ones. Gaheris kept a count, though I was uncertain why: the path was well-marked, and there were no junctions. Away from the vavasours and gentry, we began to talk to each other more. Alison flirted gently with Evan, or gossiped about the court. I heard about Evan's sister, who'd gone to a convent, not to take the veil but to learn surgery. "My mother would have approved," said Gaheris, then fell very silent.

Tacitly, we agreed not to discuss the condition of the family and the trouble we were in. Instead, I told over my plans for the home farm at Kinkenadron, or planned still room projects with Alison. I'd managed the household since my thirteenth year, when my father's sister left us to be married. My mother was long dead, and both Luned and I had grown up accustomed to help our aunt: the transition had seemed natural. When our father died, I took over management of the lands as well. I enjoyed it, and, moreover, found I had a gift for stewardship. It was only in martial matters that I had no grounding. I could neither lead nor muster men, and my illegitimate half-brother lacked both the age and the position to act in my stead. Yet with all this, Kinkenadron was no soft target. My ancestors had built it for strength, and I ran it to endure. When Ironside had besieged us, he had been unable to breach our walls, or starve us, or wrest away control. With our own water supply, and careful management, we'd been able to hold out until Luned brought us succour from Arthur's court.

Until Gareth arrived... How astonished he'd been to learn I was my own steward. But he was Margawse's son: he did not think such behaviour unfit. By marriage-law, my lands were now his, but he had not sought to overturn my dominion. I had thought it charmed him to have such a wife. He had always said as much.

And yet... Luned had accused me of not needing him. Perhaps I had been wrong all along. Perhaps I had been mistaken in believing he liked my independence. I had no answers, but I pondered as I rode.

Gaheris seldom ventured new topics of conversation, although he seemed willing enough to contribute to discussions of root vegetables and dyeing and bottling plums. He was surprisingly well-informed. When I asked, he shrugged. "It's the king, I suppose."

"The king?"

"The daily audiences. Either Kay or I have to attend him. The petitioners talk a lot about sheep and such."

"Yes, I suppose so."

"And then, Gavin..." He shook his head, abruptly, and stopped.

Family. It always came back to that, casting shadows over everything.

The third day beside the forest dawned cold and overcast. Evan squinted up at the sky and forecast rain with an air worthy of a septuagenarian, reducing the rest of us to laughter. We struck camp with greater than usual speed, and did not linger to break our fast. We had camped in a shallow coombe: the forest skirted us on more than half its circumference. The morning was very still: no birds sang. The path led up one side, narrow and flinty, then along a slight ridge, before beginning the slow incline downwards to the last ford. It was a river we must cross, rather than a stream, and one with a name for unreliability. It was, moreover, a boundary. Beyond it, the land no longer answered directly to Arthur, but rather to the rule of one of his sub-kings, my cousin Marcus, king of Cornwall. There had been talk, from time to time, of building a bridge, yet nothing ever came of it. The border was ancient; even in these peaceful days there was a hesitance about compromising it.

We wound our way downhill in silence. Around mid-morning it started to drizzle, and I wrapped my cloak around me tightly. The horizon closed in: the hills were low and ragged. Beside us, the forest was dank and still. The change in weather had made Alison cross. She muttered to herself from time to time, frowning. Evan blew on his fingers, and made vain attempts to keep his face half dry. Gaheris kept looking into the wood. After a few miles he called a halt, and took his shield from Evan.

"What is it?" I asked. "Did you see something?"

"No." He hesitated. "I'm just jumpy."

It was a little before noon that it happened. The day had brightened, somewhat, and the drizzle had died away. Evan began whistling, tunelessly, between his teeth as he led the small party downhill. We had just crossed over another rivulet, which now ran parallel to us, bordering the forest. To the other side the land had become quite steep, and we were obliged to ride in single file. The path turned a corner. Evan headed round it, leading the pack-horse. Alison behind him. I had turned to ask Gaheris how much further we had to go, and wasn't paying especial attention to the path.

There was a sudden sharp crack, like ice, breaking. Gaheris yelled "Ware!" and spurred forward. I looked round wildly. Nothing, nothing... I'd dropped my reins. I leant forward, scrambling for them. Something struck me sharply on the back of the hand. I looked up. The hillside was moving.

No.

Earth and stone and even a bush or two, sliding downhill. I could feel the thrum of it underfoot. Pebbles bounced and tumbled past me. The larger rocks were slow, but gathering momentum. My horse twitched and shivered. The back of my hand stung. I made another grab for the reins.

Gaheris cannoned into the back of me. My horse shied. I made a wild grab for its mane. The horse threw up its head and leapt toward the water. Without the reins, I had no hope of halting it. I clung on. Water sprayed up around us. The horse started to canter. Up the far bank in a scrambling leap, and into the forest. Branches whipped past, snarling my hair and tearing my clothes. I lost my cloak. My eyes streamed and stung. Distantly, Gaheris yelled my name. I had no breath to answer. I hung on, and prayed the horse would stop. I could barely see where we were headed. We hurdled over a low clump of bushes: I banged my face on the horse's neck, and my nose started bleeding. I dared not raise a hand to staunch it. Gaheris' voice was gone. I could hear only wind, and hoof-beats. I could see nothing beyond blurred tree-shapes and thicket. The horse ducked and wove amidst them, taking us deeper and deeper into the forest.

I don't know how long we ran. I remember only speed, and chill, and bone-bruising jolting. We met a fallen bough, and the horse twisted beneath me. I lost my grip on the mane. The horse gathered itself to leap on further into the shadow. I made a grab for the pommel and missed. As the horse jumped, I slid forward, helplessly. I was falling… My head struck something hard.

Darkness and silence.

I awoke to a dull headache, and the smell of wood-smoke. Someone had spread a wool blanket over me, and under my head was a makeshift pillow. I opened my eyes to the grey light of evening, filtered through tree limbs. When I turned my head, I could see a small fire, and, beyond it, a tethered horse, and more trees.

No point, then, in asking where I was. This could only be the forest of Surluse. I started to sit, and a hand was placed gently on my shoulder. Turning the other way, I found myself looking directly at Gaheris.

He said, "How do you feel?"

"I'm not sure. I want to sit up."

He slid an arm under me, and helped. Then he said, "Can you see clearly? No blurring, or spots before your eyes?"

"No, they're all right."

"And you don't feel sick?"

"No. My head hurts, though."

"Aye." He was still supporting me with his arm. He shifted a little so that my head rested against his shoulder. "You've no bones broken, that I can tell. But I'm afraid I couldn't find your horse."

"I'm just glad you found me." He looked away, discomfited. "What do we do now?"

"We're stuck here for tonight, at least. I want to be sure you're all right." He glanced down at me again. "Evan has a good head on him: he'll have folk searching by now. Either they'll come, or we'll bring ourselves out tomorrow." His voice was briskly certain. "Are you comfortable? I'm sorry I could do no better by you."

"It's not your fault, Heris."

But he didn't answer that.

It was another damp, chill morning. I was stiff from lying on the ground, but my head felt clear. I sat up, and stretched. The fire had gone out. A few feet away, Gaheris was asleep with his head on his saddle. He had neither cloak nor blanket: both had been wrapped around me. As I rose, he yawned and turned. We talked little as we struck our makeshift camp. I drank a few mouthfuls of water from his canteen, and used about an eggshell-full to wipe my face. Breakfast was half a slice of bread. Gaheris apologised twice for that, but I noticed that he ate nothing himself. He lifted me onto the back of his horse, and led us into the trees.

We pushed through thorn and bush, followed narrow deer tracks past immense oaks, ducked between scrub ash and birch.

Birds called alarum at our passage, and rustled half-seen through the boughs. We couldn't see the sun, nor much of the sky. There was no sign anywhere of people. After a couple of hours, we came to a small stream. The water was brown and cold. The horse drank it thirstily. Gaheris, more cautious, would not let me drink until he had tasted it. "Muddy."

"But safe?"

"Who knows?"

Lunch was another half-slice of bread, a lump of cheese. Gaheris excused himself while I ate, and started us moving again on his return. By sunset, we had found nothing but thickets and more trees. As he lifted me down from the saddle, I said "Are we lost?"

"No," he said, shortly, and began to unsaddle the horse.

"Is there anything I can do?"

"You might find some fallen wood: we'll need a fire. Don't go too far away."

He'd insisted on that all day. Stay within earshot, better still within sight, even when in need of privacy. Turn your back, but stay close, within easy distance. Yes, and though he'd left his shield strapped to the saddle, he'd kept his sword to hand, and worn his mail. He watched the forest with wary eyes.

None but dark tales emerged from Surluse forest. Fell creatures, madmen, and treacherous faerie. My horse could hardly have taken me more than a few miles into it, yet here we still were. Something was wrong...

I gathered a double armful of twigs and small branches. They were damp: our fire would be a dismal affair. Gaheris finished untacking the horse, and spread the saddle blanket on the ground. He made me sit while he started the fire. It smoked and gave off little heat. He opened the saddle bags, and drank a mouthful of water before passing the canteen to me. He looked tired: his hair needed combing and mud streaked his face. Somehow, I doubted I looked much better.

He passed me an apple, then hesitated and did up the saddle bags. I said "Aren't you eating?"

"I ate before."

Over the years, I'd heard his fellows use a large number of epithets for his honesty. Every single one had been a variation on the extreme. The favourite tended to be one coined by Kay: crashingly. Gaheris's honesty even lay at the heart of this trouble over Lamorak and Margawse, for he had remained desperately, painfully silent, in the face of almost all questions. "You'd need to be stupid not to spot Heris lying," Luned had once said. "I've never known anyone so inept."

He was lying to me now. I put a hand on his arm. I said, "I don't think you did."

He flushed, looking at me sidelong. "Well, happen I forgot." I held his gaze. He shook his head, then gave me a quick, rueful, smile.

I said "How bad is it?"

"We have only what food I was carrying when your horse bolted. Not a lot." He looked down. "Still, it doesn't have to last long. We'll be out soon."

"Are you sure?"

"Well…" He laced his fingers. "We're not very lost. I know where we are to a degree. And I know any number of places where we aren't."

"Like Camelot, or Tintagel, or Carlisle?" I said, and he laughed.

"Aye. But we will be searched for. I'm certain of it."

"Will they find us?"

"Yes." He said. And then, "I think so. Gavin wouldn't give up. Nor your Gareth."

"If he is my Gareth, these days."

"He's always yours." Gaheris sounded unusually fierce. I gazed at him in some surprise. He blushed even more, but continued "It's my fault, this trouble you're in, not his."

"You said that before."

"Yes." He leant over, and prodded the fire. He said "What food we have might last through tomorrow. After that… I've no bow for hunting, but I know how to set snares, and I can live off the land, to a degree. I learnt that, campaigning. Happen we won't be comfortable, but we won't starve."

We wandered two more days, seeing nothing save trees and birds. It grew colder. I made Gaheris take back his cloak, but it was too cold to sleep. My bones ached, and my hands grew chapped and sore. I made sporadic attempts to tidy myself, but my hair snarled in Gaheris' small comb, and my over-dress was stained and torn. Gaheris looked tired under the dirt, and his beard was growing raggedly. Meals were erratic and basic. Of the three of us, the horse fared the best, for there was some greenery suitable for it to eat, and it seemed to suffer less from the cold. The third day differed somewhat from the preceding two: it began to rain. That evening, we couldn't start a fire at all, and perforce went colder still and hungry. Gaheris looked at me, shivering under the blanket, and swore. Then he apologised, and unbelted his sword: that night we shared the covers, the blade naked between us. There were more days after that, and more nights: I don't remember how many. Once, a white deer bounded across the path before us. I stared after it dully, while Gaheris crossed himself.

I said "We should follow it."

"How?" he said. "The horse would break a leg in those thickets."

Perhaps that was the first day I saw the knight in grey, I'm not sure. I recall the slow sensation of being watched growing over me with the passing hours. And then looking into the trees to see an indistinct shape hovering several yards away, beside a tall birch. I turned to tell Gaheris: when I looked back, it was gone. After that, I saw it several times a day, although never clearly, never close. Gaheris saw nothing. He thought I was hallucinating, I could tell, though he went out of his way not to comment.

He still swore that someone, sooner or later, would find us. I was less sure. If Gareth no longer loved me, if he loved my sister... He would never deliberately harm me, nor act maliciously. But perhaps he would not hunt too hard. I would have such thoughts late in the night, cold and uncomfortable on the damp ground, and be shamed by the memory come morning.

There came a time when nothing was caught in Gaheris's snares, when we could find no early berries, no roots, no stored nuts. We were deep inside the forest, surrounded by oaks so vast they might have been growing in Abraham's time. The ground was barren: mud and dead leaves. The horse plodded along with sunken head, suffering now as we did from hunger. It rained more or less continuously: I could not remember exactly what warmth had felt like. And I was so tired, I kept falling asleep on horseback, and Gaheris kept waking me up again. When I opened my eyes, black spots swam before them. The knight in grey was riding parallel to us: I waved to him, and smiled. He bowed to me from the saddle. "There," I said to Gaheris, "you were right. They've found us."

"You have to stay awake," Gaheris said.

We were following another deer path. After a while, it forked, and Gaheris made to turn right. The knight in grey stood beside the other branch. I looked at him, and he beckoned. "No," I said to Gaheris, "The other way."

He looked at me oddly. I picked up the reins to turn the horse. I said "We have to go left." Gaheris shrugged, and led us that way. The track wandered under the trees, narrow and winding, and the knight in grey paced us in silence. It began to grow dark, and Gaheris wanted to look for somewhere to camp. I shook my head at him. We skirted trees and picked our way among fallen branches. "We must stop soon," Gaheris said, "There'll be an injury, if we go on much longer. It's too dark."

"Not yet," I said. The knight in grey nodded to me, approving. We went on along the path as night came in. The rain slackened to a fine drizzle. I could barely see my hand on the pommel, but the knight in grey was clear before me, glowing with his own faint light. We plodded on in silence. The path seemed wider and smoother. The trees were spacing out.

Gaheris said "What's that?"

I peered into the gloom. He was pointing forward, past the knight in grey, at a dim pale smudge. I said, "I don't know." We moved on towards it. Gaheris drew his sword, holding it in front of him. I could hear something, water flowing ahead...

The path came to an end. The knight in grey halted and pointed. There was a small glade, edges indistinct. The sound of water perhaps attested to a small stream bisecting it. In the centre of the glade stood a square white pavilion, lit from within. From its flag-pole a pennant flew, device invisible against the night sky. Gaheris called out "Hello?" There was no reply. He released the bridle. "Wait here," he said to me. Then he crossed to the pavilion, and went in.

I looked at the knight in grey. He nodded once, and faded back into the wood. Gaheris came out of the pavilion. "There's food, and a fire, and candles, but no people. It's probably a trap."

"I don't care," I said, dismounting. "I'm so hungry."

"Aye," Gaheris said, "but..."

"It could be months before we're found, or find our own way out," I said. "It could be never."

"I don't want your blood on my hands, too."

"I don't want to die of cold in the forest."

We looked at each other in silence. Then he sighed, and said, "As you wish, then."

Inside the pavilion stood a low table spread with food and drink: fresh bread, roast meats, cheese, apples, honey. The wine was warm and spiced. On a stand to one side stood a bowl of heated water, and soap, and towels. Candles burned in tall silver stands. A fire burnt in a neat stone pit. There were piles of cushions, worked in silk and brocade. Against the sides were two cots, made up with thick blankets and linen sheets. In a sack by the door were oats for the horse.

"Someone was expecting us," Gaheris said.

He insisted on seeing to the horse while I washed. The water was scented, and stayed clear, even when I washed my hair. There was a small hand mirror beside the basin, and I sighed over the state of my gown. Small chests stood at the foot of both the cots: on an impulse, I opened one of them. A shift, worked in green at neck and cuff, and a russet over-gown. I changed, rolling my soiled garments into a heap, and pushing them into a corner. When Gaheris came back in, I was brushing out my hair. He said "There's an enclosure, out there, laid out as a stall..." Then he noticed my clothes.

"I think the owner won't mind the loan."

"I've always liked that colour." He hesitated. "I'd forgotten how pretty you are." Then he blushed scarlet, and looked at his feet. "I'm sorry. I never could govern my tongue."

"Do you still think this is a trap?" I asked him.

"I don't know." Unexpectedly, he grinned. "If so, it's a rare fine one."

He wouldn't let me go outside while he washed and changed. I sat on the end of one of the cots with my back turned. I felt unreasonably calm and happy, as if I'd finally found sanctuary from all my pain. I think Gaheris may have felt much the same way: when he came to hand me to table, he was smiling.

Despite the time we'd taken, washing and tidying, the wine was still warm in the jug and the roast meats hot. The taste of it all was splendid. I think I ate my fill, yet the table seemed scarcely depleted. There was an enchantment here, for sure. Licking honey off my fingers, I noticed that Gaheris had started frowning.

"What is it?" I asked.

"Nothing... I'm wondering if there's to be a price. I mind what happened to Gavin, years back..." He stopped, suddenly, and drank another mouthful of wine. "Well, I'll be the one to pay it. I owe you that."

I was warm, and full, and perhaps a little drunk. I said, "You keep saying that. But I don't see how any of this can be your fault."

"I should have insisted we took the long way round the forest."

"You were blaming yourself before that." I drew in a deep breath. "You blamed yourself the night of the test." He looked down. "Why, Heris?"

"Because it's true."

"Is it?" I ran a finger along the rim of my wine cup. "Did you force Gareth to be unfaithful?" Gaheris made no answer. "Tell me what happened."

He rose, and went to the flap of the pavilion, lifting it to look out into the night. After a while, he said "I don't know, precisely. Gareth and I quarrelled. That's all."

"What about?" He was silent. "About Lamorak de Galis?"

Gaheris inhaled. "Yes. About Lamorak."

"Tell me," I said.

"I don't know if I can." He looked down. There was another long silence. Outside, it seemed to be raining again. Gaheris dropped the flap and came back to the table, where he poured himself more wine. Then he said, "Gareth thinks it's my fault Lamorak died."

"So I gathered. But you didn't kill him."

"I'm not sure." Gaheris stared into his cup. I looked across at him in surprise. Glancing up, he met my eyes, and shrugged. "Oh, I didn't strike the fatal blow. But I misjudged some things." I watched him without speaking. "I botched the business with mother. So Agrin and Mouse went off after him."

"And Gareth thinks you should have stopped them?"

"Gareth," said Gaheris, "thinks I shifted the blame for mother's death from myself to Lamorak." His tone was utterly flat. Something in the line of him hinted at the famous Orkney temper. He shook his head. "I expect Gavin would say that was irony."

It took me a few moments to work that one out. Then I said, carefully, "Are you saying that Lamorak killed Margawse?" He was silent: his eyes slid away from mine. "Heris?"

"It isn't important any more."

"It is to me."

He swallowed more wine. "Gari's strong on honour. Upholding it. He thinks I failed. He feels sorry for Luned, because she's tied to me." He hesitated. "And he likes to rescue people. My fault. I'm sorry. Agrin has always said I'm stupid."

I said "But it was you who offered blood reparation to Lamorak's brothers."

"Hypocrisy. Or bad conscience." Again, that flat tone, that shadowing of anger.

"According to Gareth?" I said.

"You mustn't blame him." Gaheris put his cup down, and leant towards me. "He's right. Lamorak died because of me. Because I..." And he stopped, abruptly, and looked away. "It was an accident, my mother's death. Lamorak had had an *affaire* with her, but I meddled, and he tried to break it off. She attacked him, knifed him, and he pushed her away. The fall broke her neck." He swallowed. "When I found them, all I could think of was getting him away before the others found out. I thought I could take it on myself... I told Lamorak to go away and stay away. He didn't listen." He halted, briefly, studying his hands. "Agrin found out about the *affaire,* and decided that that was grounds enough. When Lamorak came back... I'd no way of warning him. Oh, Gavin wanted to fight him fair, but the others... They had to have a scapegoat, you see. Couldn't soil their hands with a brother's blood." He looked across at me again. "You see: I messed up."

Slowly, I said "Does Gareth know what happened? Exactly, I mean."

He shook his head. "Why haven't you told him?"

"I've never told anyone, till now. The way Gari feels about me, he wouldn't believe me anyway. And there's no point to it. Lamorak's name has suffered enough. He was my friend."

"What about your name?"

"Doesn't matter."

"Heris," I said, "this is a mess."

"Aye." Unexpectedly, he smiled. "I've a rare talent for them. And for growing maudlin in my cups."

"Do you think we'll ever find a way out of this forest?"

"Yes." He rose. "It's late. We should sleep."

I rose in turn and smiled at him. There was wine warm within me, and light and shelter where there had formerly been only cold and confusion. I was safe, safe... It was the wine, perhaps, that gave me courage, but it was the sense of security which led me to stand on tiptoe and kiss him, once, very lightly, on the lips. "Good night, Heris."

"Good night."

I awoke clear-headed and warm. Sunlight filtered in through the sides of the pavilion. The blankets were thick and real over me. But for the rest... I rubbed my eyes, sitting up, uncertain if I was yet fully awake. The canvas was old and stained: lichens grew on it in patches. The cushions were rotted through, discoloured and damp. There were no candles, no dishes, no bowls. The table had lost a leg, and lay mildewed at a rakish angle. My original clothing lay folded over one of the chests, clean and neatly mended. Across the pavilion, Gaheris's mail coat had been buffed and cleaned. Our one set of saddle bags appeared now to be full to bursting. I crossed myself. Then I pulled my kirtle over my shift and set about rising. There was still water in the ewer, and it was clean, although cold. On one of the stools rested a loaf of new bread, a flagon of ale, and a large wedge of cheese. I finished dressing, then prodded Gaheris with a finger.

He sat up, and looked. I said, "What happened?"

"I don't know. Some kind of magic." He frowned. "We'd best move on. Could be dangerous to overstay our welcome."

Over his protests, I went out to tack up the horse, while he washed and dressed. The pavilion was as worn from the outside as it seemed from within. It stood in a small glade, with moss underfoot, tall old trees round about, and a small stream crossing one corner. There was no sign of my guiding knight in grey. The sun was up: today we would go dry.

The horse seemed as rested as I was, although the stall had overnight transformed into a tethering post and a rusted bucket.

There were still oats at the bottom, and they were fresh and good. The tack had been cleaned and mended, like everything else. I saddled and bridled the horse quickly, then led it round to the front.

Gaheris came out of the pavilion with the saddle bags. "Enough food for a week," he said, "For the horse, too. Plus what we've been left for this morning, and the blankets, and a second cloak."

"We've been well looked after, here."

"Aye. God be thanked." He crossed himself.

We ate and made ready to leave. Gaheris, superstitious like all his kin, paused to pour a few drops of ale on the threshold. Then he looked up, and his face went utterly still.

"What is it?" I followed his gaze upward, to the tattered pennant which still fluttered over the pavilion. It had once been white, perhaps, and the device worked on it in red and green and brown. A snake, coiled up the stem of a single flower.

I knew it, of course. The serpent rose. Lamorak de Galis' personal badge.

We didn't talk much, that day. Gaheris was preoccupied, struggling, perhaps, with his old demons. The open glade and clear weather had given us a chance to guess approximate directions, and around noon I climbed a tree to confirm them. Gaheris was surprised at that. I smiled. Luned isn't the only tomboy in my family. I tried, a time or two, to tell him of the knight in grey, but it soon became clear that the subject distressed him. It seemed our lives would never be disentangled from the matter of Lamorak. Lamorak had died somewhere in this forest, at Orkney hands. Perhaps our pavilion had been his last living home: both of us, I think, thought so. Neither said it. And then there were the ghost tales. Yet, if ghost indeed it was, it seemed kindly disposed to us. Something of the safety I had felt in the pavilion travelled with me still. It seemed I had been running away from my bereavement and confusion, deep into this forest. But now I was ready to move on. Neither my lost daughter nor my cracked marriage were forgotten, but I had remembered something else. Once, I had possessed the strength to rule my own lands and hold out against all comers; the strength to be myself, independent, intact. I had found that again.

We slept dry, that night, if outdoors, and I awoke to find Gaheris's arm about my shoulders, despite the sword between us. I was still safe. It was another warm day, and we made good progress in a direction which we both considered to be south west. The forest around us had started to change. Dark, close-packed, heavy oak gave way to wider-spaced beech and sycamore and chestnut. Underfoot was low bracken, and sometimes grass. We passed through glades of bluebells, startling birds and small beasts. Amidst the trees, deer cropped shoots, and watched us with wary, liquid eyes. In a small clearing we came to a spring, surrounded by worked stone, and with a cross carved above it. The water was clear and cool in my cupped palms. It tasted sweet. Gaheris, as ever, hesitated to drink, yet followed me. This was more like the forest I remembered of old, filled less with shadow than with mystery. I rode without a veil, and with my cloak rolled behind me. I would be as brown as any farm girl. I felt young, and very free.

Something had changed. When Gaheris helped me dismount that evening, I lingered with his big hands still on my waist, and said "You always do this. I could get down alone."

"Aye," he said. And then "It is a habit I have from Gavin. He calls it courtesy." He smiled as he spoke, and there was a glimmer of laughter in his voice.

We were very close. His hands still steadying me, one of mine on his shoulder. I could feel his breath on my hair. He added "Do you mind?"

"No," I said, looking up at him. "I like it."

We were merry over our small fire, and from time to time our hands touched, passing the flask, the bread, the knife. I liked that, too. I remembered Essyllt, creamy in the tower room, so long ago. I was seeing Gaheris through her eyes. I did not think about

Gareth at all. And when Gaheris made to lay the sword between us, I put my hand over his, and shook my head.

"I wonder," he said, as his arms came around me, "if we should not have drunk from that spring?"

My hands tangled in his hair, found the shape of jaw and throat. I said, indistinctly, "I have no idea." I kissed him. "Are you saying we should stop?"

He kissed my neck, and his hands made a start on my lacings. "Very probably", he said, good-naturedly. "What do you think?"

"Umm." Another kiss. "Don't know. Maybe later…"

Later, there was laughter. I propped myself on my elbows, and looked down at Gaheris as he laughed and laughed, spluttering somewhat as my hair got into his mouth.

"What is it?" I demanded.

"Nothing." He was breathless. "I was just thinking… Gavin sets such a bad example."

For some reason, that struck me as funny, too.

Five

That was our last night in the forest, and we lingered over it, unknowing. We rose leisurely, and late, and lost more time playing over breakfast. The horse was patient with us, cropping grass, and refraining from looking resigned. It took me three attempts to mount. I kept being distracted, Gaheris's hands on my waist, his strength, his warmth... The sun shone bright around us and birds sang, it seemed, in every tree. We idled our way along the deer paths. Perhaps that was itself some part of the enchantment of this place, that it drew us out of all sense of responsibility.

Around mid-afternoon, we came to another glade, and a stream. The latter ran wide and fast-flowing, with a stone causeway laid athwart the narrowest part. On the nearer side stood a pavilion of weathered green; above this flew a pennant of plain white cloth. Gaheris and I looked at each other, and he put a hand to the hilt of his sword.

The tent flap lifted, and a man stepped out. He wore blackened mail, without surcoat or sash. His bucket helm had no crest, and hid his face entirely. There was no device upon his shield. His voice, when he spoke, sounded muffled and strange, even though his words held no surprise at all. He seemed to look us up and down. Then he said, "I am the guardian of this ford. None shall pass, save they win the right by force of arms."

"Fair enough," said Gaheris. "The terms?" And then, straightening a little, "I mean, I accept your challenge, sir knight," He was not quite taking the situation seriously: nor was I, come to that, light-headed on sunshine.

"I have not," said the stranger, "made you a challenge." There was a small pause. "I do not fight with churls."

Gaheris is as much an Orkney as any of his brothers. His chin came up, at that. But he said only "No more do I. Your terms?"

The dark figure regarded us in silence for a long moment. "A serjeant run away with his master's horse and arms? And mayhap his master's lady, too. I will take all three from you, and leave you grateful for your life."

"Oh, will you?" Gaheris said, sounding very like Gawain. "I'll take your terms, Sir Arrogance, and we'll see who's the churl."

"Then arm yourself," the stranger said. I kept my eyes on him as Gaheris unslung his shield and adjusted his mail: he had no helm, lost somewhere in our descent into the forest. As he turned to tie back his hair with a thong, he touched my arm. "I'm sorry about this."

"Not your fault, surely?"

"If I looked less disreputable... If he shows any sign of beating me, you're to put my horse to the gallop, and get away across the ford before he can lay hands on you."

"And leave you to face his annoyance?"

"Yes." Gaheris turned back to face the stranger, and drew his blade. They advanced to meet each other in the centre of the glade. Both moved warily, circling, trying to gauge the other's worth. Gaheris was the taller and heavier, but the stranger seemed quicker on his feet. The first two or three blows were almost perfunctory, aimed to test rather than damage. Then the stranger let out a yell, feinted low, and aimed a cut up under Gaheris's shield. Gaheris twisted left, catching the edge of the blow on the rim of his shield. The stranger pulled back and cut high, in time to deflect a blow himself. A flank cut, and Gaheris chopped down with his shield, slashing at the stranger's arm. Around us, birds cried alarum and fled away into the wood. Blow followed blow, loud and incongruous in the sleepy sunlight. Inch by inch, Gaheris, fighting defensively, gave ground. His face was set, eyes intent on the stranger, oblivious to all around. A twisting cross-body cut caught under his guard: blood dripped from his forearm. The stranger used his own shield almost like a second weapon, charging

Gaheris's sword, seeking to shunt it aside. It was a style of fighting I remembered from somewhere before.

The stranger aimed another blow high, then pulled back before it could connect. Wrong-footed, Gaheris made an awkward parry, leaving his left side open. I watched the sword striking down, glittering wickedly in the sun. Gaheris lunged across himself in desperate motion, and drove the rim of his shield into the stranger's mid-section. The sword-cut connected with his shoulder, and skidded off his mail. The stranger pulled back again, gasping, and Gaheris brought the edge of the shield up in a sweeping body-blow, with all his considerable weight behind it. He followed it with a solid strike to the stranger's knee with the flat of his blade. The stranger dropped.

Gaheris put a foot on his sword-wrist, and levelled his blade at the eye-slit of the helm. There was a short silence. The stranger let his sword drop. Then he said, in a different tone, "All right, I yield. Can I get up now?"

"You're still a bloody maniac." Gaheris sounded furious: I looked at him in surprise. He was flushed; his eyes were narrow and intent.

"Indubitably." One-handed, the stranger was struggling to release his shield. He wasn't making a very good job of it. "But I should like to get up."

Gaheris muttered something inaudible, and stepped back. The stranger sat up, removed his shield, and rubbed the wrist which had been stepped on. "You weigh too much," he said, conversationally. Gaheris made no reply. The stranger climbed to his feet, and pulled off his helm.

Safere the Moor, Palomides' brother, and one of the companions of the Round Table. I must have looked surprised, for he caught my eye, and made me a small bow.

"Churl, am I?" said Gaheris. And then, "You're supposed to be in Gaul."

"I became bored. Gaul isn't very interesting unless one has Claudas' favour." Safere went back to rubbing his wrist. "I see, king's son of Orkney, that you still desire to break my bones."

"You were supposed to keep Lamorak in Gaul."

"You were supposed to protect him from your charming brothers, beautiful Gaheris." There was a long silence. Gaheris looked down. Then Safere said, silkily, "But Little Snake was wilful. He never would do what I told him."

Gaheris said "You can hate me all you want. But there was a lady's honour threatened here." Safere spread his hands, and smiled. Gaheris looked across at him, and added, "And for no reason I can think of. You'd hardly have a use for her."

The Orkney brothers have enemies in the most unexpected places. I inhaled, wondering if Safere would renew the fight. But he only shook his head, and started laughing. "Granted. But I could always have escorted her back to her husband. You're headed in quite the wrong direction for Arthur's lands, you know."

I said "We're on our way to my estate at Kinkenadron."

Safere looked across at me, speculatively. "All unchaperoned? Irregular, surely, even for the Orkney clan."

"Shut up," Gaheris said, through clenched teeth.

"Or you'll make me?" Safere smiled. "I'm certain we've had this conversation before."

"We lost our companions in the forest," I said. "If you know a way out, I'd be grateful if you'd direct us."

Safere glanced at Gaheris, who looked away. "As it happens, it's for that reason that I put myself in your way. *Your* safety," and he made me another bow, "has never been in doubt."

Gaheris said "What exactly are you up to?" But Safere only smiled again, and shook his head.

Within two hours, we were at the edge of the forest. Flower-spattered meadow ran away before us down to an earthen road. A party of riders made their leisurely way along it, accompanied by fluttering bright pennants and a distant sound of music and laughter. Safere nodded once to me, and faded back into the trees. I looked at Gaheris. "What was all that about?"

"Lamorak." Gaheris looked away. Then he looked back, and smiled. "Let's go."

Half-way down the meadow, the riders caught sight of us, and halted. Several waved: as we drew nearer, a couple of them rode forward to meet us.

It was my cousin by marriage, Essyllt, the queen of Cornwall. She embraced me, warm and perfumed, and smiled at Gaheris. "My goodness," she said, laughing as ever, "just look at you! Whatever happened?"

"We got lost," I said.

"Oh, that horrid forest!" She hugged me again. "Well, you're safe now, lovey. You shall come and stay with me."

Later, bathed and changed and well fed, I curled up in the window seat of her luxurious solar, and told her the whole long tale. Her lovely eyes filled with tears when I related the part about Gareth and Luned. She said "Oh, but it's all my fault. That ridiculous horn."

"No. I'm glad I know, It's better. And other people knew before. They tried to warn me. Medraut, for one."

She let it pass, shivering in delicious, vicarious horror at our experiences in the forest. When I came to the part about the night after we found the spring, I blushed, and fell silent.

Essyllt clapped her hands. "There!" she said, "Revenge is sweet, isn't it?"

I had been gazing into my lap: I looked up. "It wasn't revenge. I didn't even think about Gareth. It was just… Gaheris thought it might be some spell in the springwater."

"And," she prompted, "was it?"

"No, I don't think so. I just wanted to, just for myself."

She crossed the solar, and sat down beside me. "And now?"

"It won't happen again," I said, confidently.

I suppose I could easily have travelled on to Kinkenadron from Essyllt's summer palace, but she urged me to stay. She kept a warm, welcoming, informal court; it was simple to sink into it. Gaheris, I think, would have left had Tristan been there, but the Cornish champion was away in the north. Dinadan was there, and Gauter; and Essyllt's complacent husband, my cousin Marcus, stopped by from time to time, when his duties brought him to the neighbourhood. I'm fond of Marcus. He'd been kind to me and mine, even though he'd been unable to prevent Ironside's siege of my lands. I felt comfortable and at home, surrounded by friends who offered no pity and expected nothing. I felt young again.

Gaheris and I did not speak of what had transpired in the forest, although we spent a great deal of time in each other's company. He seemed happy, too, and I wondered if he had also escaped the clutches of old grief and trouble. No one spoke of Lamorak, any more than of my lost child, or of faithless Gareth. "How indolent we are," I said to Gaheris one afternoon, as we wandered in Essyllt's rose garden.

He shrugged. "It suits you. You're prettier than ever." Then he blushed and hastily began to talk about horses.

I think I might have slid gradually into staying there forever. I had neither need nor reason to leave. From time to time Gaheris expressed concern over the whereabouts of Alison and Evan, or wondered if he should let his brothers know of our location, but as far as I know he took no steps concerning either. The rest of June passed us by, and July began: it would soon be time for the harvest. I laughed, and danced, and played with Essyllt's courtiers by day, and at night slept without dreams.

Around the beginning of August, I realised that Essyllt was once again up to something. She'd been conducting a superficial flirtation with a young knight from West Cornwall, but the indications were that it was starting to pall. Marcus, indulgent, proposed summoning a tourney to amuse her, but she pouted, and complained she would have no champion. The next day, she started making up to Gaheris.

We were on the south terrace. Essyllt had had her chair carried inside, and reclined instead on a pile of cushions. I was perched on a low wall, engaged on a piece of embroidery. Dinadan for some reason was lying at my feet and getting in the way. Amant, the current favourite, had begun picking at a lute, but Essyllt abruptly frowned, and waved him away. "I'm tired of music. I want someone to read to me." She looked around at the assembled company. "Prince Gaheris?"

Gaheris had been conducting a low-voiced unromantic conversation with Brangwen about bee-keeping. He looked up, startled, as Essyllt beckoned him over. He didn't read aloud at all well: his voice was a steady monotone, and he stumbled over the longer words. Gawain would have made a pretty game of it, smiling at the queen as if the words were written for her alone. Gaheris appeared to be feeling picked on. "Oh, dear," murmured Dinadan to me, "another lamb to the slaughter."

"Gaheris has more sense," I said, and surprised myself with my own vehemence.

Essyllt insisted on keeping Gaheris by her for the rest of the day, and all of the next. By supper-time on the second evening, I was fuming.

It was, of course, thoroughly irrational. I didn't wholly understand it myself. My sister had taken Gareth from me, and I had been powerless. Some reprehensible part of me was determined to win this lesser match, perhaps from sheer spite. After the meal, Essyllt called for dancing. When the figure brought us together, I caught Gaheris' arm, and said "Take me outside."

He looked perplexed, but obeyed. Out in the courtyard, he said anxiously "Are you ill? Shall I call one of the maids?"

"No… It was a little hot in there." Essyllt might soon start wondering where we were. I drew him across the courtyard, and into one of the tack-rooms. "I wanted to talk to you."

"Of course." He handed me to the single stool, then leant against the wall. "What is it? Is it Gareth?"

"No," I said, before I could think too hard about that. And then, "Do you like the queen of Cornwall?" He shrugged. "She's making it plain she likes you."

His face cleared. "It's all right, Llinos. Agrin has it I'm stupid, but I'm not that stupid. She's my host's wife. And then, I'm not over-fond of Tristan's temper. I was Gawain's squire long enough to know how to duck if I have to." He smiled. "You mustn't worry."

"I wasn't." I looked at him, big and pragmatic and straightforward. "Heris, were you ever in love?"

"I don't think so." He considered the question for a moment. "Not really. "

"You're too sensible."

"Perhaps." He studied the back of his hands. "Or perhaps I'm just too dull."

"You always do that," I said. "You're your own worst critic."

"Aye, so Gavin tells me."

He wasn't looking at me. I rose, and went to stand before him. "Heris?" When he didn't reply, I put my hand against his cheek. "I wish you wouldn't be so hard on yourself. I don't find you dull or stupid. I think you're lovely."

He inhaled sharply, then he caught at my hand. "Llinos, don't."

"Why not?"

He shook his head. "A lot of reasons."

"So?"

"It is adultery. And incest. A sin." He swallowed, and looked down. "Because revenge is a poor reason, that hurts the avenger as much as the target."

I said, "I don't want you to make love to Essyllt." I'd started to cry, silently. He looked up, at that moment, and saw the tears.

He said "I'm not intending to."

"She gets what she wants. Like Luned."

Gaheris cursed. For an instant, I thought he would turn away. I said, quickly, "Don't leave me," and his brows drew in, worried.

He said "What can I do?"

"Hold me."

He hesitated. I swallowed, and added, "Please." He shook his head again, but his arms came around me. I leant my forehead against his shoulder, and put my own arms about his waist. Warm, and solid, and strong.

After a moment, he began to stroke my hair. Very softly, he said "This is no good."

"I know." But neither of us let go. I said "That spring, in the forest..."

"That was an excuse," Gaheris said. I looked up at him, and he smiled.

I said "The sin is already committed, then."

"We do not have to make it worse."

"Heris, I'm tired of being good."

"Aye."

We looked at each other in silence for a while. Then he said, carefully, "Once could be excused, I think. Especially in those circumstances. But twice..." He paused, and drew in a long breath. "It isn't that I don't want to. You're beautiful. I've always thought so. But Gareth loves you more than his life."

"That didn't stop him sleeping with my sister." And Luned would have had none of Gaheris's scruples. My throat was tight. I was shaking. "I can't do it any more. I can't just be Gareth's wife. I lost his child, and I lost him: all I have left is myself." My voice rose. He put a finger to my lips.

He said "Gareth is in hell without you."

"Then he should never have done as he did."

"Oh, sweet Jesu." Gaheris closed his eyes. "I'm no good for you. I'm no good at complicated things."

"This isn't complicated."

"It will be." He opened his eyes again. "I told you: I have a talent for getting into messes." He looked away from me, and his face was troubled. He had his own demons, as I had mine.

Some burdens are lighter when shared. I reached up and turned his face back towards me. "Heris, I don't care."

He gazed at me for the longest while. Then his arms tightened about me, and his mouth found mine.

143

He was right about the complications. Even in Essyllt's relaxed court it was not easy to carry on an illicit liaison. And then, I had no experience in subterfuge. Within two days, I think, most of the company was aware that something was going on. Essyllt herself took it well, kissing me, and whispering, "Never again?" with a wicked light in her eyes. But once commenced, I had no desire to stop. Gaheris came to my chamber late at night, or in the early afternoon, when most of the court rested. We met in the rose garden, in the hay- loft, behind the dovecots. I suppose we were not in love, but there was a great deal of affection between us, and a great deal of passion. I was beginning, at last, to understand Essyllt.

I was also beginning to understand Gareth. My loneliness craved the comfort and consolation of Gaheris, and I had chosen seclusion in the first place. How much more necessary such reassurance must have seemed to Gareth, abandoned at court, and vulnerable to love-hungry Luned. I said as much to Gaheris, He looked at me thoughtfully, and said, "Luned has made him very unhappy."

"And you?"

"I don't love my wife. It wouldn't be fair of me to be jealous." He kissed my fingers. "I'm angry at the hurt to you and Gari."

"Did you know?" I asked him, remembering our conversation on Mayday.

He shook his head. "I knew she had a lover, but I was not certain who… Gareth wasn't the first, you see: there have been several. Lamorak, for one."

"And you don't mind?"

"About Lamorak, or about Luned?" His tone was curiously wary. I looked at him. He said "It has been said that I killed my mother for jealousy over Lamorak."

"But you didn't kill her at all."

"No."

This was dangerous ground. Very carefully, I said, "Who said that?"

He turned his face away. "People. Agrin."

Here was another of those dark currents which ran through the Orkney clan. I stroked his hair. There was something vulnerable about Gaheris, for all his size. He did not know how to defend himself. I said, "You let your brothers bully you."

"Aye." He turned again, and his lips twisted a little, self-mocking. "Gavin tells me so at regular intervals. Loudly, usually."

I laughed at that, and kissed him. "Your family is so involved with itself. That isn't all bad. You and Gawain have been very kind to me. And Medraut tried to warn me about Gareth and Luned, months back."

"Oh, Mouse has trouble with his conscience." Gaheris' voice was abruptly absolutely flat. I'd learnt to recognise that tone. It signalled pain. He added "Mouse would feel badly about hurting *you*. You're guiltless, by his lights. Whereas I… He didn't give a tuppenny damn about Gareth's anger. But Gareth and Luned…"

"Heris," I said, "what are you talking about?"

"Lamorak. As usual."

"But why should Medraut feel badly…" I stopped. Gaheris was watching me. His eyes were afraid. I said "It was Medraut who killed Lamorak?"

He swallowed. "It was an attack from behind. If he'd only used a sword, I might have done something, had time to make Lamorak move… But it happened so fast… Poor Gavin didn't even see it." He stopped, passed a hand across his eyes. "I'm gabbling. Sorry. Yes, it was Mouse. He shot Lamorak in the back with a crossbow. Neither Gavin nor I could do a damn thing about it." His voice cracked. "And I can't make myself forgive him." His eyes were dry, but the look in them was terrible. I put my arms around him, and held on, finding nothing to say. He rested his cheek on my hair. Medraut had led him into betrayal. And Gareth had helped him blame himself… Finally, I said "Does Gareth know?"

"I don't know," Gaheris said. "And it makes no difference now, anyway."

145

Six

Despite Essyllt's apparent lack of interest, Marcus went ahead with his planned tourney. The entire household was thrown into amused disarray. Dinadan and several others were dispatched to spread the word. Brangwen embarked on an energetic reorganisation of the accommodations, driving Essyllt to a succession of day-long rides and picnics. It was very easy to become mysteriously detached from the main party on such excursions, I soon discovered, and remembered with distant pain how Gareth had vanished from Guenever's Maying. "Sweetheart," said Gaheris, "ride back to Camelot, and see him fly to be with you."

"Would you come with me?"

"I have bloody hands."

It was to be a small tourney, with jousts for love, and no prize greater than applause, and a seat at dinner beside Marcus. The older squires and knights elect were also to be permitted to enter the lists, and as a result it was agreed that all should bear blank arms. Tristan still absented himself, but Palomides made the trip, and was rewarded with one of Essyllt's sleeves to wear as a token. Dinadan, after much cajoling, appeared with an apron tied about him. He'd begged it off the chief cook, to whose venison pasties he had vowed eternal devotion. Marcus elected him 'most shameless' on the spot. A few days before the tourney, Essyllt had mock-solemnly presented me with a scarf embroidered with my own green Kinkenadron lion. Gaheris bore it for me, pinned to his shoulder. A handful of the local lords came over, and the meadows were gay with pavilions. "Who do you like as the victor?" I asked Gaheris.

"I don't know some of the neighbours. But most likely Palomides. Or Andred, if he's lucky. "

"Not you?"

"Me?" He laughed. "Kay says I have all the combat style of a duck."

For all that, he fought well, the first day, and I sat that night at dinner with the victor's wreath of roses in my hair. The second day, the wreath adorned, amidst much laughter, the greying head of the chief cook, while Essyllt tried (quite successfully) to console Palomides, who'd cracked a rib when his horse trod on him. Gaheris himself had taken a nasty blow on his left forearm, and kept dropping things.

The third day was the last, and the largest: it was for this that any long-distance visitor would aim to arrive. We were all up bright and early. Essyllt was in a state of high excitement: she'd convinced herself that Tristan would turn up. She had a new gown of deep rose silk, and kept fidgeting as we tried to lace her into it. She caught my hand as we went down to the stand, and pulled me to her. "I'm so glad you came to me," she whispered. "Are you happier, lovey?"

"Yes," I said.

"I knew it." She kissed my cheek. "Your Gareth will perhaps I earn to be more attentive in future."

I hadn't the time to go to the combatants' enclosure to wish Gaheris luck again. (I'd already done so once today, a little before dawn, as we rose.) I caught his eye as he waited by the rails, and smiled. He smiled back and saluted me, as I took my place amongst Essyllt's ladies. The heralds blew the first call, and the third day's contest began. There were a number of new arrivals. The blank shields made it difficult to identify them, but Palomides beside the queen recognised several, and kept us informed. One of them was Safere. I held my tongue, though my heart sank within me.

Palomides also provided a commentary on style. After an hour, I began to see why Essyllt always claimed he bored her. Dinadan, I learned, was erratic, Andred too nervous, Gauter prone to over-correction… It would probably have been fascinating to another

147

knight, but I had trouble keeping my face straight. Essyllt yawned behind her veil. "And what about our first-day champion?" she asked, perhaps with a touch of malice. Gaheris had wrong-footed Palomides twice in the single combat.

"Heris?" Palomides missed her tone. "Too defensive. And he spends too long analysing his opponent's style. Used to teaching, rather than exploiting weaknesses"

Midday came and went. We munched on pastries and fruit in the stand, while the combatants battled on in the heat. Essyllt was sulking: there was no sign of Tristan. It was airless; dust rose from the field, coating skin and clothes. Gaheris was having another good day, although his wrist seemed to be giving him some trouble. He'd had a series of straightforward victories over local knights, and a longish successful combat on foot against Andred. Now he watched from the enclosure while one of the grooms watered his horse. He'd removed his helm; he looked hot. A further handful of newcomers had arrived and were arming up: there were perhaps ten or twelve rounds to go before the melee. Gaheris had taken Dinadan down just before lunch. In the mid-afternoon heat, he must now face the open challenges to hold or lose his position. I was worried, a little, about Safere. With Orkney rivalries, there was always an element of danger. In the enclosure, Gaheris re-fastened his helm, and mounted. Here we went again...

Mid-afternoon. Gaheris held on to his place. Essyllt had decided that Tristan wasn't going to put in an appearance after all, and was taking her mind off it by flirting with her husband. Palomides was sulking, in turn. Gaheris' encounter with Safere had come and gone: Safere now watched from the paddock fence. From time to time, our eyes met, and he smiled, cold and composed. The pages brought round fruit and cider. Only an hour or two now, before the king declared a halt. The day began, blessedly, to cool down. A final small party of latecomers appeared, and began to haggle with the marshals. In the break this caused, Gaheris rode over to the stand, visor opened. He was flushed and sweating: he hooked his shield over his saddle, and shook out his wrist.

"Does it hurt?" I asked.

"Only when I think about it. Mostly it's numb." He smiled. "That's the worst of bone bruises."

"I'll take a look at it, later," Brangwen put in. "I've a salve."

He bowed to her. "Thank you." A pause. "Man, you've hot summers in Cornwall."

"And very soggy winters," said Brangwen, as I handed him up my cider cup. He took it in his bad hand, used the other to lift my fingers to his lips. The herald sounded the recall. Gaheris quickly drained the cup, and returned it to me, before riding back into the field. I blew a kiss after him.

"Your majesties," announced the senior marshal, "Three new challengers." Essyllt looked up, and peered at the newcomers with sudden enthusiasm, hoping for Tristan. One of them was very tall: otherwise I could discern nothing to distinguish any of them. Marcus signalled assent to their participation, and there was a brief discussion amongst the newcomers as to ordering. Gaheris waited at his end, rubbing his arm.

The newcomers reached a decision, with some jostling and noise. A knight in plain blond armour rode into the lists. Gaheris caught my eye, and smiled, then lowered his visor.

Dust rose up around them as the horses thundered down the field. One pass, with no hit. On the second, Gaheris broke a lance on the challenger's shield. A third pass, and the challenger struck a glancing blow on Gaheris's shoulder. Gaheris pushed the tip aside with his shield, and the challenger, forgetting to let go, lost his seat. Gaheris reined in, and looked at Marcus.

The challenger climbed to his feet, and drew his sword. Marcus nodded for continuance. A squire came into the compound to take Gaheris' horse: another had already caught that belonging to the challenger. There was a pause. Then the combatants closed. Some instinct made me look across at Safere. This time, he didn't smile. There was something wrong with this fight... The challenger moved fast and angry. Gaheris was tired. He used his shield poorly: that arm was giving him trouble. I turned to Marcus. "Cousin, stop this fight."

"What?" He looked at me, perplexed.

"I've a bad feeling... Heris is hurt."

Marcus reached across Essyllt, and patted my hand. "He'll be all right, love. And no one's broken the rules." I looked at Essyllt, who shrugged. Then I turned back to the field.

To this day, I do not know exactly what happened, or how. My angle of vision was wrong. Gaheris remembers being wrong-footed, and clipping the central railing. And the challenger... He can recall only instinct-level sequencing of attacks. But what I saw was simple, Gaheris over-reaching, and stumbling into the barrier, the challenger closing in to follow up, perhaps a little too fast, and both men going down in a tangle of metal and shields and splintering wood.

There was a long stillness. No one moved. Then the challenger slowly rose to his knees. There seemed to be a great deal of blood. Safere had jumped down from the fence and was arguing with one of the stewards. The marshals came hurrying down the line. In the enclosure, there was an outburst of shouting, then a slight figure came jogging into the field, head uncovered. He was dark, and on his surcoat was worked the device of the pentangle. Gawain. Something wrong... I came to realise that Brangwen had her hands on my shoulders, and that I was struggling with her. "Llinos, wait!"

"Let go." It was simple, if undignified, to slip under the rail. I heard Essyllt call after me as I gathered up my skirt and ran. None of the stewards tried to stop me.

Gaheris had still to move. Blood spread beneath him, and I couldn't tell its source. "An artery severed," said Safere's cool voice in my ear. "Your veil, Lady Llinos, and that small knife." I handed him the items, numbly, and dropped to my knees. The challenger was beside me, struggling with his helm. A moment, and a hand touched my shoulder. Gawain.

I said "Is he dead?"

Gawain looked at me oddly. Then he turned to the challenger. "Will you let me do that, man? You've your wrist-strap caught in the lacing of your aventail." His fingers moved deftly over the offending area.

I caught his arm. "Gavin, is Heris dead?"

He turned and stared. I said "There's so much blood... he hurt that arm yesterday in the melee." Gawain had gone white. "Gavin, what's wrong?"

"I should have known him." He sat back on his heels. "But Gari would have it was Ironside." He swallowed, and glared at the challenger. "Now will you see where your jealousies have brought us!"

Gareth finally dragged his helm off. He was as pale as his eldest brother. Weakly, he said "I didn' t know... I thought..."

"Oh, you're a mighty man for thinking," Gawain said. "And for assuming. And here's Heris paying for your assumptions again." I remembered Agravaine all those weeks ago, accusing Gawain of favouring Gaheris, and I put my face into my hands.

Without looking up, Safere said, "Will one of you cease quarrelling, and summon Dame Brangwen?" One of the stewards ran back to the main stand.

Gareth said "Is he...?"

"He lives," Safere said. "No more can I tell you: I regret I am better acquainted with necromancy than any healing art." I think we all stared at him. "Prince Gawain, you have steady hands. You might assist me by removing his helm." Gawain moved to do so. Gareth reached a hand out to me, hesitated, withdrew it.

"Llinos." He stopped, swallowed. "Sweetling, I swear I didn't know."

All those nights without him, and now I could not look at him for crying. He said "Gavin's right. I was jealous. I didn't think. I saw him kiss your hand, and he was wearing your token..."

"It was combat for love," I said, and he fell silent. Gawain and Safere had removed Gaheris's helm. He was unconscious, and a bad colour. I touched his hair with my fingers, and sobbed.

Perfume surrounded me, and a swirl of soft fabric. Essyllt's warm arms closed about my shoulders. "Come away, lovey," she said, gently. "There's nothing we can do here."

Later on, Safere came to the queen's solar to report. He'd washed his face and hands beforehand, but here and there on his clothing were bloodstains, and he looked tired. I was afraid to ask. Essyllt held my hands and said, "Well?"

"He lives." Safere hesitated. "The sword-cut severed the tendons as well as the artery, and the wristbones are crushed. The arm is broken, and also the shoulder. Prince Gawain says he's had a fracture there before." I remembered that: Christmas five years ago, when Lamorak had fallen on him in practice. Safere continued "Also several ribs. Those and the shoulder will heal. The arm as well, probably. The rest…" He hesitated, and looked at me. "He's going to lose that hand. With the tendons cut, he'd never use it again anyway."

We had found Lamorak's white pavilion, and won relief from cold and hunger. And Gaheris had looked down at me, and vowed that should there be a price, he would take it upon himself. I swallowed, and stared back at Safere, who had known that we were lost in the forest. I said "Did you know that this would happen?"

"No."

"But…" I stopped. "Why are you doing all this?"

He ran a hand through his hair. Then he said, "Lamorak. Is there another reason? I loved him, but he thought himself in love with your Gaheris."

I think Gareth tried to see me later that night, but Essyllt turned him away. She treated Gawain the same, but a little before midnight another visitor was permitted entry. Very tall, taller even than Gaheris…

Kay the seneschal kissed both our hands, while I said, "But why are you here?"

"Common sense," he said, accepting a chair. "We had a message from the queen of Cornwall that you and Heris had turned up here, and I wasn't about to let Gawain and Gareth go charging about by themselves. The Orkneys," and here he favoured Essyllt with a satirical glance, "have no sense of proportion."

I looked at Essyllt in turn. "*You* sent a message?"

"I wrote to the King of Logres," she said, defensively. "I thought someone might be worried. And," and she looked down, "I thought that husband of yours could use a lesson."

"Good intentions," said Kay, crossly, "are more likely than the Saxons to send the lot of us to early graves. Not," and here he turned his dark look on me, "that I'm overly impressed by all this rushing about in fits of panic, either. It wastes a lot of time, and it never seems to turn out well. Just look at Lancelot."

I looked at Essyllt, who gazed back at me blankly. Kay added "Not that Gareth was much better, moping around at court. He used to burn everything when he was a scullion, too." He caught sight of our faces, and sighed. "My wife says I'm about as sympathetic as a lump of granite. But someone had to come along and mediate between Gareth's idealism and Gawain's brotherly love. Just sorry not to have done a better job."

"Kay," I said, "tell me about Lamorak and Gaheris."

He looked at the floor. "Nothing to tell, really. It was no one's fault, what happened." He looked at me. "But I don't think anyone could have prevented it, either."

"I have no right to ask," said Gareth, "but I beg that you will hear me out just this once." He spoke to the floor, on his knees before me in my small room. I'd found him there when I returned from a fruitless visit to the infirmary. He had kissed my hem. He looked pale, and tired, and unhappy. It seemed likely Gawain had been on at him all night. I longed to comfort him. I was afraid to try. He said "I've wronged you so much. I don't know where to start."

"Sit down somewhere," I said. I sat on the bed, pleating the coverlet with my fingers. Gareth rose, and found a stool. We looked at each other in silence.

He said, softly, "I love you so much." I looked down. He went on, "I am so ashamed."

"For loving me?"

"For mistreating that love." He swallowed. "You were so unhappy, when the baby died, and I felt so useless. You didn't seem to need or want me any more. I didn't know what to do." I twisted my hands in the coverlet, and tried not to cry. Gareth said, "I wanted so much to help you."

I looked up. I said "I was afraid. It hurt so much... I needed to hide."

"Yes." He sighed. "But I didn't understand, then. I am so sorry."

He, too, was close to tears. I wanted to go to him, to hold him and take the pain away.

I stayed where I was. I said "I shut you out. I realise that."

"I love you," Gareth repeated. He rose, and went to the window, "Everything was such a mess, I don't know. Agrin at Heris's throat over mother's death, and then Lamorak..." He paused, drew in a long breath. "I don't know how to explain. I was angry with the whole family for Lamorak's death, but Heris... Perhaps I needed someone to blame for my own misery, and he was there. Lamorak loved him, you know."

"Safere told me."

"I don't understand Heris. I never have. I was six years old when he was sent off with Gavin as a hostage to Arthur. I remember he hated thunderstorms and winter greens. He was always the quiet one. He never seemed to want anything, or at least he never mentioned it if he did. He still doesn't, come to that." Gareth turned, and leant on the wall. "He's so meek. It's easy to blame him for things."

"For Lamorak," I said.

"For Lamorak." Gareth looked at the floor, shaking his head. "I couldn't understand how he could stand by and let Lamorak die... Gavin told me, over and over, that Agrin threatened to drag him bound if he didn't go willingly. I still don't understand it. I'd have fought Agrin to a standstill."

"Gaheris," I said, "has no faith in himself."

"Oh, God. And we all bully him, I know. You should have heard the fights Gavin had with Kay on that subject on the way down here." He looked up again. "Anyhow. The Lamorak business. I could give you any number of rationalisations. Heris didn't do as I would have done. He knew who was responsible, yet he brought no complaint. They're all excuses. The truth is much simpler. I was confused, and lonely, and I wanted to hit out."

"What happened?"

Gareth swallowed again. "He was blaming himself, of course. If Heris had been around at the time of the Flood, he'd have found a way to feel responsible for that, too. So he offered his life to Aglovale de Galis right in front of everyone, and Aglovale refused him and made peace, of course... It all looked so empty, so false... I lit into him for it." He stopped, rubbed his hands together. "I've never fought like that with any of my brothers before. I called him every name under the sun, I threatened to disown him, I raked up every grievance, large and small, I could think of. Jesu, I even accused him of collusion in Pellinor's death. And he took it. He made no attempt to defend himself. When I finished, he just looked at me, and said 'Agrin won't kill me on account of common blood, and Loval de Galis is too damn forgiving. Perhaps you'd care to do the job, and put me where I can do no more harm'." Gareth stopped again, and passed a hand across his eyes. It was all I could do not to go to him, "I should have realised then that he was as miserable as I was. But I only saw what I wanted to."

I said "I'm so sorry. If I'd had the courage to come back to court..."

"What?" Gareth came to the bed, and sat down beside me, taking my hand in his. "Sweetling, this is no more your fault than it is Heris's. I was unhappy and I made a terrible mistake." He looked down. "The first in a whole series. A few days after that, I found Luned crying on the terrace. She told me it was over Heris, someone had taunted her... To this day, I don't know if that's true. But I felt sorry for her. I was lonely myself, and here was someone who needed me, someone I could help. My brothers were either avoiding me, or acting like I was crazy, and you didn't seem to want me around." I gave a small gasp, and he put his arms around me. "I'm sorry," he repeated. "I never meant for anything to happen with Luned. I suppose I thought I was being brotherly, to begin with. But over the next few weeks..." He stopped, pulled a face. "She needed me, it seemed. More fool me for being so selfish. I've hurt her, too. I didn't love her. I don't even like her, much. But I enjoyed the comfort."

I straightened in his arms. "I understand that."

"You do?" He looked surprised. I don't expect you to forgive me, but..."

"The business between you and Heris isn't for me to forgive, but as to the rest..." I inhaled. "Let me go, Gareth. There's something I have to tell you, too."

He released me, slowly. He looked vulnerable, a little afraid. I said "What did you think, yesterday, when you saw me at the tourney? You said you were jealous."

"Yes." He looked rueful. "I'd given you every reason to give up on me. And when I saw someone else with your token... Gavin's right. I just jumped to conclusions. That old fool Ironside lives locally, and he was so keen on the idea of you that he besieged you for two years..." He blushed, and looked at his hands. "What you must think of me."

"Well, I don't much care for your opinion of my taste." He glanced up, and smiled quickly. I went on, "But you weren't entirely wrong. You mistook the man, but not the situation."

There was a short silence. Gareth stopped smiling. He said, softly, "Paid in my own coin... No, I deserve it." He wrapped his arms around himself. "You and Heris?" I nodded. "Are you in love with him? I can bear anything but that. I think I can bear it."

"No."

"I wonder what Gavin would call this?" Gareth's tone was light, but his voice shook. "Ironic symmetry? I don't even have the right to ask you why."

"It wasn't revenge," I said, "whatever it looks like. Heris, at least, wouldn't do that." Gareth looked at me sidelong. I continued. "The first time was almost an accident. We'd been lost for days in Surluse forest. Everything was very strange; it just happened, somehow. And later... He made me feel safe. Reassured." I put a hand on Gareth's arm. "It wasn't his doing."

Gareth's expression was strange. Raggedly, he began to laugh. "Well, I can't say a word about it; it would be sheer hypocrisy... I'll lay you straight odds Heris tries to shoulder all the blame for this, too, once he's conscious. Let me see: he'll say something like he wronged me with my wife, and the loss of his hand is only fair punishment?" He stopped, abruptly, and drummed his fingers on his knee. His hand shook.

I said "You're angry."

"Bloody furious." He turned. "I know I don't have the right to be. It's all right. I'll be better in a moment."

We sat in silence for a few minutes, while he drew in several long breaths. Then he said "Are we all right, do you think? Or are we over?"

"I love you," I said. "I don't know about the rest."

He took my hand, and kissed the fingers.

A long time later, he kissed the corner of my mouth, and said "What about Heris?"

I stiffened in his arms, looked at him warily. He sighed, and continued, "I meant simply that he's in a hell of a mess, and a lot of it's my fault. What can I do?"

"I don't know." I stroked his face. "He thinks you're right to condemn him: if you apologise too much, he'll probably feel worse."

"He's lost a hand," Gareth said, and shivered. "I shall live with that forever."

I thought about Gaheris, kind and straightforward and alone. I said, "I think the trouble is inside him. You can't rescue people from themselves."

"I love my brother," Gareth said, and started to cry.

157

It was almost a fortnight before I was allowed to see Gaheris. Brangwen had barred the whole family from the infirmary on the (perfectly reasonable) grounds that we were not conducive to peace and quiet. Gawain took it surprisingly well; it was Gareth who fretted and fumed, and tried to bribe Kay, fruitlessly, to take messages. Before being let in myself, I practically had to swear on the Bible to be calm and sensible.

"Is he still in danger?" I asked.

"No more than usual, with a family like his," said Kay.

He looked awful, frankly: his colour was poor, and he'd lost a lot of weight. His left arm and shoulder were heavily bandaged; the arm ended in a neatly wrapped stump. The sight of it made me want to weep. Seeing me looking, Gaheris smiled and said "It's all right. I just have one arm a little longer than the other."

"Oh, Heris." I sat on the bed and kissed him, carefully, on the cheek.

He said, "I feel better than I look. I nearly had a relapse yesterday, when Kay brought in a mirror." That made me laugh. He took one of my hands in his single one, and said "You are all right, aren't you?"

"Yes. Yes, I'm fine."

"I'm glad. You deserve to be happy." He hesitated. "Did Gareth…?"

I said, hastily, "Gareth sends his love. He's probably going to drive you berserk, trying to wait on you once Brangwen lets him in here."

"There's something to look forward to."

There was a silence. I held onto his hand, and looked into the dark- circled grey eyes. "You know, Heris, just for the record, I love Gareth…"

"Aye."

"No, let me finish. I love Gareth, so I can't really blame Luned for loving him too. But all the same," I reached out, and touched his face with my other hand, "I think she's blind, not seeing what she has in you."

It was another two days before Brangwen let Gareth visit, and then only for five minutes, and under her supervision. I hovered outside.

Gareth emerged red-eyed and distressed. "He apologised, Llinos. *He* begged *my* forgiveness." He stopped, and swallowed. "I'm beginning to see why Gavin gets so angry with him. Of course, I stopped him, and tried to explain, but Brangwen threw me out."

"Good for Brangwen," I said.

Seven

I don't know if, in the end, Gareth ever did get the chance to have the conversation he wanted with his brother. I rather think he didn't. It was painfully apparent that Gaheris was distressed by the whole business, and in the end I suspect they simply agreed to both stop apologising. Neither knew quite what to say to the other, and Safere, who might have been able to throw some light on Lamorak's motives in the matter, had simply disappeared again. Tension reigned for some time between Gareth and Gawain, but the latter could never stay really angry with a brother for very long, and they eventually patched things up.

It was well into October before Brangwen pronounced Gaheris healed, and even then he was pale and easily tired. Kay, by that time, had returned to Camelot, but Gareth and Gawain and I stayed on in Cornwall. Essyllt was happy enough for the company. Tristan remained obstinately absent, and I think Gawain made a consoling substitute. She had hopes of pairing Brangwen with Gaheris, I think, but nothing came of it. Given the way her last scheme had turned out, I couldn't help feeling relieved. In mid-August, Alison finally made her way to me. She and Evan had not, after all, been able to raise the alarm. Around that last corner on the road, there had been another landslide. Alison had been found two days later, wandering dazed and feverish, by a shepherd. Poor Evan had been killed outright. I lit a whole branch of candles for him in Essyllt's small chapel.

We made our way back to Camelot, finally, in time for Christmas, riding in easy stages along the safe, interminable, coastal route. Gawain and Gaheris bickered amicably about sheep-rearing and politics, sword-play and root-crops. Sometimes, Gareth joined in too, and the king's highway rang with the sound of the king's nephews insulting each other. And two days before Christmas Eve, we came back to the court.

I found my sister Luned in her own room. She was packing. She halted when I came in, and stood there with a gown in her arms. She said "What do you want me to say?"

"I don't know," I said. "What do you want to say?"

She turned away, and laid the gown carefully in a chest. I said, "Where are you going?"

"The convent at Shaftesbury." She looked across at me. "I can't watch you with Gareth any more. And what I have with Gaheris isn't a marriage. It doesn't matter whether he's kind or unkind. I can't live like this."

"Are you so sure?" I said. "Gaheris…"

She held up a hand. "You know, sometimes I think the king got us the wrong way around, when he made our marriages. Oh, not you and Gareth, but… Laurel and Heris would go well together, I think: they could be nice, and sensible, and kind. Whereas I… Agravaine might beat me, but at least I'd have something to react to."

I found I had nothing to say to that.

Down in the hall, the family had gathered, checking and rediscovering each other. From the gallery, I could hear Agravaine winding up to lecture Gareth about injuring brothers. Gawain the mediator stood in between, putting in occasional critical words to either side. Medraut was at his shoulder, looking as ever as if awaiting his turn. Gaheris, quiet as usual, sat on the foot of the stair, listening. I sat down beside him, and rested my elbows on my knees. He looked down at me, and smiled.

"Well," he said, "I've two days, I reckon, before Agrin starts in on me. Do you think I'll survive the anticipation?"

PART THREE:
KNOTTED THORN

Now

In the grey hour before dawn, the pilgrim came walking across the bleached grit where the river once flowed. His head was uncovered; a ragged cloak flapped from his shoulders, sending flickers through his shadow as it fell before him. In one hand, he held a staff; the other hung loose at his side. He moved with neither haste nor hurry, as if he walked simply for its own sake. His face, his shape, the colours of his garments, all blurred into grey against the morning haze and the dead white of the sand. I could not tell if he looked to right or left, not at the distance. He did not stop, as most do, to gape at my brother's bones, strewn all along the rim of the bay.

He did not know, then, what place this was. He would not know what awaited him, if he did not turn back.

Few travellers do, if they find their way to my door. Few know I remain here at all. Stories lose their meaning once the heroes move on.

I watched the pilgrim from the curve of the stair that winds up the outside of the remaining tower. Even at this hour, the steps were warm underfoot. By mid-morning they would be baking and I would once more be restricted to the undercroft and the remains of the kitchen. Above me, Palug stretched out along the parapet, pupils widening, flexing large paws. His tail draped down the wall beside me, stirring up dust from the stone. The heat does not disturb him, any more than it does the gravel and the dusty soil and the bones. His like was here before my family. He will be here long after I am ash. I looked up at him, and he twitched an ear in my direction.

"I don't know," I said, and he yawned, showing yellow teeth. "There's nothing here for him. He's not my concern." Palug flicked his tail, beating time against my arm. "You go and inspect him, then. I have work to do."

Palug heaved a sigh and settled back down, resting his chin on his forelegs. We each have our duties, he and I. I reached up to scratch behind his ear before turning and climbing back down the stairs. The jug was too light in my hand: every month, it seems, there is less and less dew to collect from the dish on the roof. I would need to make the long trek inland on foot soon, though I had hoped to wait until the season turned and the nights grew longer. The pilgrim would have to fend for himself: there was nothing here that could be spared. The sand crunched under my feet as I crossed the courtyard: no matter how much I swept, it blew back in to mound up against the walls and work its way into the remaining rooms. Not that it mattered any more; aside from Palug and myself, the land was empty and forgotten. We are no more than shadows who were left behind.

You don't know my name. The names of those like me are seldom recorded. Our very presence is barely noted. We are like the stone flags and the wooden benches, background that is assumed. And that... that has served me well, as the years go by and men forget.

I let myself in through the kitchen door and set the jug down in the niche beside the fireplace. It's the coolest place left in the fragments of Caer Arian, apart from the undercroft, and the safest. There's no place for fresh water in the dark spaces underneath the tower, not since my sister took flight and my last brother was slain.

We were six, once, kin to the Lady, the first four born two and two, as is proper. "Two for the air and two for the water," she would say, as she braided our hair. And then, to the youngest of us, "And a gift of men." Four born directly of her womb, two fathered by the lord of the sky and two by the lord of the sea, and two brought by the land and its peoples. My first sister was as beautiful as the full moon, with her great dark eyes and her hair the shade of raven feathers. My second sister was as bright and bold as the flowering broom, with wheat-coloured hair. Every lord and warrior and poet for miles came courting them, hoping to win a glance, a smile, a word. And then, my brothers, light and dark. They were the pride of the warband, strong and straight in the embroidered tunics we women made, each of them skilled with blade and spear and bow, feared on the battlefield and revered at the hunt. Poets vied to hymn their deeds, and the sisters and daughters and wives of all our neighbours sighed after them as they rode by. And me, the small brown rockling, sheltered under our mother's gaze. The children of Penarddun, from the silver castle, the brightest jewels in our mother's crown.

You know my mother. On clear nights, she still shines down over you. But you can no longer seek her blessings, not since the iron warriors came and severed her stair from earth to sky, cut the bright from the dark, and left me and Palug here to keep vigil over memories and bones.

I took the rush basket from its hook on the wall, and left the kitchen through the ragged gap in the south wall. My eldest sister's lover made that, crying betrayal against my brothers, long ago in in the earliest days of the iron warriors. Once, the walls of the castle had risen high above the sand and water, white as seafoam and hung with the banners of my kin, visible for miles around. I remember their fall, the heavy slow thunder of stone breaking on stone, the scent of salt, the scouring of wind-blown sand on my skin. The broken stones were long worn smooth by water and time, the walls lost, the deep ditches silted shut with mud and grit and shell. My feet took me across them, towards the spindle of rock beyond. Here had stood our water gate, in those before times, where our mother had shown us how to read the stars on the surface of the sea and our seafather had taught us to swim. Under my shift, my wings stirred against my shoulder-blades at the memory and I arched my back to silence them. The rock here was still cool and the sea for once had been kind, leaving small pools amidst the drying weed. A handful of molluscs joined the skeins of wrack and sea kale in my basket. I dipped my head to the west in thanks, one hand going to the space over my heart where I wore my father's mark.

It was brightening now. The sun had climbed up over the distant hills, staining the places of men in red and amber. There was no sign of the pilgrim. Perhaps he had come to his senses and turned back towards the land. I let myself dawdle on my way back, enjoying the cool underfoot while I could. All too soon the day would turn to pounding heat and light. As I came back into the kitchen I could hear the click of Palug's claws on the flagstones and went out in the courtyard to see what he was doing.

The pilgrim sat on the rim of the dry well, his staff and pack propped beside him. Palug sat on his haunches a few feet away, crunching something between his jaws. As I approached, the pilgrim rose to his feet and made me a surprisingly elegant bow. "Good day to you, lady, and my apologies for arriving unannounced."

I'm not my mother. I have no use for court fanciness. I said, "I saw you walking clear enough."

"Aye."

"We have no food or water to spare, and you'll sleep on the ground outside if it's shelter you're after."

"I've done that often enough." There was an accent, a burr, to his voice that tugged at memory. I'd heard voices like his before, somewhen, back in the days when my second sister held her court, and mortal men came courting her and danger. For he was mortal, this pilgrim. I could smell it on him. He was tall, as tall as I remembered my eldest brother, and broad, and past first youth. Grey threaded through his sandy hair and beard; he had the wide shoulders of a fighting man, but his tunic hung loose. He was missing his left hand. My sisters might have thought him handsome. I didn't know: I've never been much of a judge of men. He continued, "And if you're short of food, I've bread and meat I can share."

That explained what Palug was eating. I shot him a dusty look and he ignored me. He'd do as he pleased, as always. As to me, the sun was well over the horizon: I couldn't linger outside much longer. I said, "Stay or go as you please: it's nothing to me, unless you try to come inside. Then my companion here will have a thing or two to say." I nodded at Palug, who yawned.

"You have my word I'll not intrude." The pilgrim said.

"Then do as you please." I started to turn away.

"Lady…" Hesitation in that burred voice. I looked back, ready to be irritated. "I've a question, of your kindness."

I'm not kind. I've no time for it. I said, "What, then?" and let my sharpness show.

He bowed his head again, all court grace. "I'm looking for somewhere, for Caer Arian. I'd be grateful for any direction you might give me."

"You don't need them," I said. "You've found it."

Then

The castle lay off the coast of Nordgwalia, marking the bounds of the lands of men. By night the walls shone silver-white, shimmering with the roll of the waves. Bright pennants flew from the tops of the towers, blue and green and gold. By night, the moon painted a shifting path across the surface of the water, white and silver and grey. From time to time men set out at low tide or sailed small boats, trying to reach it, yet mostly it eluded them, hovering just a little further ahead, until they grew weary of their quest and turned back, or else vanished forever to join the drowned companions of the deep. The castle had no need of their company then; my siblings had each other for that; nor did they need the wheat and meat and milk that men produced. Our fathers, lords of sea and mountain, kept us well supplied with sweet water and grain and vegetables, and my mother's gardens overflowed with fruits of all kinds. Sometimes my siblings rode wave or wind to hunt and brought back fish or boar or stag, and men cowered and called them storm and tempest and nightmare. In garden and solar, chamber and hall, they danced and made music, composed poetry and practiced sword and spear and bow, wove and spun and embroidered, crafted in wood and bronze and gold, studied law and numbers and the ways of the world from our mother. The eldest swam with their sea kin, teasing the younger two siblings who must contend with mere human limbs, and were teased in turn when they took flight. Life was all youth and plenty and we siblings paid no heed to anything outside ourselves. Each solstice, our mother descended from the sky to hold her court and her vassal lords came to seek her judgement or advice, bringing gifts of gold and silver and carved bone. Once each year, she rode forth, all of her children in her train, to visit each vassal in turn and inspect the domains they held for her. Sometimes mortal men glimpsed her as she rode and came rushing in our wake seeking wisdom or treasure or love, and made songs of her beauty and her strength.

Lady of the Wheel, they called my mother; Queen of the changing moon; and her rule was akin. Now fickle, now clear. The lords of Arfion worshipped her and obeyed. Until the iron warriors came seeking riches and power from the labour of others, driving out or killing or enslaving the Arfionedd, who inhabited the land at that time. At first, they were careful, hiding their desires behind gifts and fine words, thinking in their pride that they would fool my mother. But from her silver throne she saw into their hearts as if their flesh was water and sent them away unsatisfied. Secondly, they rode against our castle with their iron swords and spears, thinking a woman would have no defences. But she summoned our fathers and my siblings took up their own arms and again the iron men were turned back.

But the third time... The third time, their leader, whose name was Pellam, built a great pyre of thorn-wood, on which he sacrificed his best horse and bull and even his favourite hound, and through it summoned the lord of fire, who has long hated and feared my mother and her kindness. And he took counsel with the lord of fire, and between them they conceived a plan. Then Pellam sent for the remaining elders of the Arfionydd, who now toiled in their fields or served in their halls. "I have erred," he told them. "I have erred and I seek pardon. I came to these lands like a raging lion, slaughtering those who would have welcomed me and sowing these fields with blood. Like the lion, I believed myself king of all around me, and I treated your queen with arrogance and disdain. I was ignorant in my pride and I have committed great harm. Tell me, you who are wise and good, how can I undo what I have done? I cannot restore the lives of your kin, but I will return to you the lands and rank you once held and labour beside you as your neighbour and friend."

The elders were old and wise as humankind count such things, and to begin with they did not trust him. But he bowed low to the elders and raised them up in his place, making himself their servant and swore on his life and those of his unborn children that he would do everything they bade him, pretending to them that he was stricken with awe and reverence for my mother and now wished only to serve her. And the elders, who loved my mother, believed him and gave him their support. And the seasons turned and the leader kept his word to them, and at the end of five years he came again to my mother's court, and kneeled before her unarmed and alone and swore to be hers for the rest of his life. And my mother looked again into his heart and this time it appeared pure, and brimming with love and reverence for her. For she did not know that the lord of fire had given Pellam an amulet that would hide his true nature from her. At first, Pellam offered her marriage, after the fashion of his kind, and the elders trembled at his daring. But she only smiled, and turned away his offer in gentle wise. "For a day or so, your kind can live in my light. But linger too long and it would consume you. Marry a daughter of men, and all will go well with you."

Pellam was displeased with this answer and anger welled within him. Yet the amulet hid this from our mother as he bowed and praised her wisdom. But he frowned as he rode back to the lands of men, and in the shadow of his wooden hall he took counsel again with the lord of fire. "Women are fickle," said the lord of fire, "and all women are weak. Seek out her weakness and you will gain mastery over her."

So Pellam waited and watched and studied as the seasons turned, until it seemed to him he knew all there was to know of my mother. "She has sons," he said to the lord of fire. "Children make women weak. I shall gain power over her through her sons."

"Perhaps," said the lord of fire.

At first, Pellam thought to win over my brothers, for in his arrogance he assumed that men came first with my kin as they did with his. But though they hunted his woods and drank in his hall, and gave him counsel when he asked them, he could gain no more influence over them than any other man, nor did they agree to be his messenger to our mother. So he watched some more and waited some more, and this time he noted that it was my sisters who sat at my mother's side when she held her court and made her judgement. He studied them, the dark and the fair, and saw that both were beautiful and skilled, but that the elder was the quieter and more thoughtful. He saw that it was my first sister who spoke for our mother when the latter returned to the heavens, and not, as he had assumed, my two bold brothers. And so he made a new plan.

The lives of men are short and age comes to them quickly: Pellam was no longer young and bright-headed and limber, but my siblings, born of earth and sea and air, were still in the flower of their beauty. So he summoned to him his younger son, newly returned from fostering and just entering manhood, and said to him, "Tell me, what must a man possess to gain respect and honour?"

The younger son, whose name was Garlon, thought a while. Then he said, "A sword and a shield and a horse, so he may shine as a warrior."

"What else?" asked Pellam,

"A spear and a hound, that he may hunt."

"What else?"

"Golden rings and fine garments, so that he may be admired"

"Indeed. And what else?"

"High birth and renown," said the son, and frowned.

Pellam, seeing that he could think of nothing more, said, "All that is true and yet there is one thing more. A man must have dominion over land and people. Listen: you are my son and I love you well, but my lands must go to your brother, for he is the eldest. But to our west lies another land, which has only a woman to rule it. I grant that land to you, if you can find a way to take it."

Now

"Ah," the pilgrim said, and looked about him. "Then I thank you for telling me, and I crave your pardon for not recognising the place."

"It isn't what it was," I said, tone curt, and again turned to go.

Again, his voice called me back. "I was here before… it was a while back, I grant you."

I considered him anew. We received few visitors from human lands even when my mother still lived amongst us, and almost none in recent years. I did not think I recalled this man. Human men change so fast and look so similar. I shrugged, "If you say so. I do not remember."

"No. I'd not expect you to; you'd another guest at the time."

"That might have been." In the days when my brothers held the castle, men came from time to time to pay renders or attend courts. Perhaps this man had been one of those minor vassals, or one of their servants. I thought the latter more likely. His clothing, his voice: neither suggested even human gentry. "It does not matter. As you can see, we no longer offer hospitality."

He nodded. "All I ask is time to rest, and an audience with whoever now holds this place, when it is convenient to him. As I said, I have food and water of my own."

"You have your audience already."

"Then you are chatelaine here?" He bowed again. "Forgive me, lady, when last I came, this castle was held by the Lord Brandelys."

"No more," I said and he looked worried. "If you come with me, you can see what became of him." I walked the short distance across the courtyard to the remains of the east tower, and pointed back out across the sand, to the headline where the ravens wheeled. "There he is. Speak with him if you wish, he will not hear you."

Then

Men speak of spring as the season for love, but it was winter when Garlon son of Pellam came to the Silver Castle. Nor did he come on horseback, dressed in court finery and bearing gifts. Rather, he walked to our gates, dressed in homespun, with his feet bare and head uncovered, and asked only for shelter and a corner to get warm. He spoke softly, and kept his head bowed, so that my brothers, who had seen him as a child in his father's court, might not know him. And under his garment he wore the amulet that the Lord of Fire had given to his father.

My mother was away from home: the nights were long and at their most dark. Frost formed on the walls and roofs and walkways. My sister saw him enter, shivering in his thin garment, with his feet unshod, and her soft heart opened to him. Without asking what kind of man he was or whence she came, she rose from her seat on the dais and offered him the warmest place by the hearth. One maidservant was dispatched for blankets; another for hot ale and bread and meat. And she took the fur from around her own shoulders and draped it over his, and bade him welcome. "This is a bitter night to be traveling," she said. "Please, rest in my hall, and stay until the weather grows warmer."

Then Garlon looked at her and saw that she was not beautiful, as human men count such things, but her face was kind, and her hands gentle, and he smiled to himself inside, thinking that the love of such a woman would be easy to win. And thus he set himself to woo her, but slowly, softly, so that she would not see the nets he wove about her, but rather believe she came to him of her own accord. He made himself useful about the castle, helping to chop wood and build fires, to sweep away used rushes and replace them with fresh, to carry water from the well and flour from the mill. When my sister's gaze fell upon him, he bowed and looked away, playing humility. "That is a good man," she said to my eldest brother, "and a kind natured one. He was not born to serve, yet he finds no shame in it."

"Perhaps," said my brother, but he too watched Garlon, and his gaze was measuring, and he made note to speak to our mother when she returned, for he was not wont to trust so easily. But already winter turned towards spring and the leaves unfurled in our orchards, and our mother did not come, for the longer days deterred her. For Garlon had called again on the lord of fire, to raise barriers and hamper her progress. And then, as the children of mortal men grew ever more powerful in our islands, so the paths between sky and land weakened. Thus our mother could only watch from above as Garlon wove his nets ever tighter. And as spring in turn gave way to summer, my sister summoned our siblings to the orchard, and in their sight placed consort bands on Garlon's wrists and throat.

At first, it seemed that my brother's fears were misplaced, for Garlon made great show of his love for our sister, placing her comfort and happiness over his own, deferring to her as his lord in all things, and seeking neither wealth nor status for himself. But when the nights grew long and at last our mother returned to the Silver Castle, he found reason to be elsewhere, for he feared her gaze might penetrate the magics that sheltered him. And that year ended, and another and another, and with each passing season Garlon worked himself closer to power. He sought, he said, to shelter our sister from the harsher duties of governance, which pained her tender heart. He wrapped his own notions in tempting skins of comfort and support, offering to lift from her shoulders any necessity to be harsh in judgement. At first she demurred, but pebble on pebble his influence grew, until she depended on him for every deed and word and thought.

"You were wont to be kinder," my eldest brother said.

"I was weak," my sister returned, "and all around me took advantage. You, for one."

My brother made no answer, but from that day she was ever colder with him, and he spent more and more time away from the castle, taking my younger brother with him. Garlon rejoiced, for in their absence he might more easily extend his own power, bringing in human men loyal to him and to the lord of fire. And at the end of summer, my sister conceived a child, which up to that time had not been possible between my people and humankind.

Up to that time, she had been strong and active, riding all day to the hunt and then dancing half the night. But now she grew pale and listless. My younger sister gathered herbs and wove spells, but nothing seemed to help. As the babe grew, so my elder sister waned. "We must summon our mother, and soon," my younger sister said. But it was summer, and the power of the lord of fire at its height, and her entreaties went unheard.

"I will send for the best healer of my own people," said Garlon, and in this guise he summoned the lord of fire into the very heart of the Silver Castle. My younger sister sent messengers, then, searching for my brothers all across the lands of gods and men. At midday on the longest day, my elder sister was brought to bed, with only Garlon and his healer to attend her. Her pains were great: it is said that her screams could be heard from Aberffraw in the north to Arberth in the south, and the hearts of all who heard her were chilled. A day and a night she laboured, and a day more, until at sunset a child was born, dyed red with her blood and the rays of the sun. "A son," said the healer, and Garlon smiled, seeing in the child all his plans come to fruition.

"We shall have a feast," he said, and summoned his servants. He gave the babe to the wife of his chief man, who had lately lost her own child. "My son shall be as human as his father: no taint of his mother must be allowed to remain." And he and the feigned healer departed the chamber, leaving my elder sister all alone, for they had no further use for her and hoped she would die.

She was indeed weak, and her heart ached within her to see how the man she had loved betrayed her. But she was not defeated. Summoning what strength she still possessed, she rose and dragged herself to the narrow window. From below rose the scents of roasting meats and the cries of men celebrating the birth of her son. But she paid them no heed. Instead, she fixed her eyes on the sky and called with her force on her siblings and our mother. For in those days, we had the power to speak to one another from afar, though only at times of great need and danger. Our brothers, far away across the strait, heard her summoning and set spurs to their mounts. Our second sister, shut away in her chamber where Garlon had confined her, leapt to her feet and went to her own window. But our mother, in her palace beyond the horizon, did not yet hear, for the lord of fire had had great pyres built around the castle walls to hamper her vision.

Seeing the fires, my second sister added her skills to the summoning. From her tiring chest, she took a silver mirror, and set it on the windowsill. Then she took a candle, made of the purest, palest wax and placed it before the mirror, so that its light was reflected ten-fold. She tilted the mirror so that the pure light might shine outwards and upwards towards the darkening sky.

Across the strait, my eldest brother saw the light and bade his horse carry him even faster. "For we must reach the sea's edge as soon as we may." My second brother did likewise and their noble steeds gave their all to aid them, though their sweat mingled with blood and their hearts were like to burst within them. And within no more than minutes they arrived at the strand, and my brothers dismounted and ran to the water, where the light cast by the mirror formed a fine thread over the surface. "Now," said my elder brother, and both brothers took off their silvered steel helms, holding them to catch the light. To this, they added their shields and even their fine swords, until the thread became a ribbon and the ribbon a pathway, reflected up and up, over the horizon and the acrid smoke of the lord of fire, and at last reaching my mother in her realm. And she looked out along the path and saw her eldest daughter betrayed and bleeding, and fury grew within her.

The lord of fire likewise saw the path, and a shiver grew within him. The sun was set, sunk below the sea, and his power lay at its nadir. "Build the fires higher," he commanded. "And cover all the tower windows, so that the women may not work their witchery." But the people of the castle heeded him not, for Garlon's festivities were well underway. The silver path grew ever brighter until, in a great rush of wings, my mother returned at last to our castle. Tall she was, and beautiful in her anger and she struck at the lord of fire with her great steel talons and the razor edges of her feathered cloak. And the fire lord summoned his own weapons and they fell to battle, there in the castle yard, each causing the other great wounds. At that moment, too, my brothers burst through the gates, each wielding sword and spear, so that Garlon's men fell like dry corn before them. Hearing the clash of arms, Garlon himself entered the fray, and the castle rang with the sounds of war. In her chamber, my eldest sister sank to the floor, feeling her pains come once again upon her. And there, all alone, she gave birth for a second time, this time to a daughter. Knowing that death would soon take her, she took her daughter in her arms and blessed her and commended her to our mother's care, and then, with her last strength she pronounced a curse on Garlon and all his kin. "As you hid your nature from me, so shall you forevermore be hidden from human eyes and hated and shunned. And may your kin ever lose what they love and find instead only misfortune, until a human man, born in blood, shall come here seeking nothing and trust my kin without question." And with that she drew her final breath and fell dead, her daughter at her breast.

My second sister, in her tower, felt the death and cried out in her grief. And the castle walls heard her cry and echoed it, so that every stone sounded the knell and the whole building shook. In the courtyard, Garlon too cried out, as his body faded before his eyes. My mother, wild with grief, took the lord of fire in both clawed hands and cast him out through the curtain wall and into the deep sea beyond, so that the water boiled and hissed and steamed. Garlon's surviving men dropped their weapons, dismayed, and my brothers drove them out through the gates, Garlon among them, for he was yet visible to their eyes. But Garlon was treacherous to the last, and as the gate swung closed, he let fly his last dagger, given him by the lord of fire, and fuelled by his own bitterness, and it struck my second brother through the eye and slew him.

Three days our mother remained in the silver castle, and throughout those days the sun did not rise, nor did any warmth come forth across the land, and the skies were dark and heavy. The walls of the castle were stained from the pyres and broken in many places: beyond them the sea raged, flooding more than half of our orchards and taking great bites out of the lands of men. Our mother, my second sister and my eldest brother washed and prepared the bodies of their dead, and laid them in caskets of glass and silver, that their fathers, the lords of water and of air, should know what had happened. And my mother took the newborn children, the boy and the girl, and fed them herself, and declared them her own. But Garlon's mark was already upon the boy, so that his shape was strange and hair grew over all of his body. "Even so," our mother said, "he is my daughter's child and mine." And she made my older siblings swear to treat him well. Through all this, her wounds pained her greatly, for they would neither close nor heal here on land. And at the end of the three days she knew she must return to the heavens or die herself, and so she summoned my surviving siblings, and blessed them and gave them the castle to rule. For in her battle with the lord of fire, one of her wings had been near severed, and she knew that even in her own sanctuary it would take her many many lifetimes of men to heal and she might never be able to return to the castle and her children.

And that was the first of our sorrows.

Now

The pilgrim said nothing at all for a long time, staring at the bones. I wondered if he might choose, then, to pick up his staff and pack and be on his way. But he only stood, while the sun crept higher and my skin began to prickle, gazing at my brother's remains. After a while, Palug stirred himself to pad across to us. I shot him another disapproving look, but he ignored me, settling down where the flags were warmest and dropping his head to his paws with a sigh. I was beginning to think I would have to leave them there, trusting to Palug to keep watch, when at last the pilgrim sighed and shook his head. "I'm sorry for it, though he was a hard man."

In some ways. But my opinion of my brother was no one's business save mine. "He was himself."

"Aye. I've a brother like that myself.

I had no interest in his family. I had enough trouble with my own and the sun was hurting my eyes. I made no reply, hoping he'd take the hint.

He did, which was a small mercy. "But I'm keeping your from your own duties. Forgive me, lady. I'll find myself a corner to rest out of your way. Though…" and he hesitated.

"The north tower is sound enough: you may rest in the lower chamber, if you wish, though there's nothing in there but dust."

"Dust and I are old friends." This time he did smile, and something sparked in my memory. I had seen that smile before, somewhere, somehow, for all the man himself was unfamiliar.

Perhaps that was why I said what I did. "I've matters to attend to today, but if you can wait, I'll have time to listen to whatever it was you've come to say once evening falls."

"I've no hurry. It's you that's doing me a courtesy, anyway." Another bow. "This evening, then, and may your day be blessed, lady."

I've no use for the blessings of men, nor of their gods, who stole my mother and severed the silver castle from our kin of sea and mountain. And I needed to be out of the sun. I gave him no answer, then, as I turned and walked away.

This time, he did not call me back.

Then

"Before everything," my mother would say, "there was the water and the wind. Each courted the other, dancing and whispering, showing their finest skills. The wind granted water speed and change; water gave wind colour and depth. And in time out of their dance they spun the mountains and the plains and the islands. And where wind and air touched were born the spirits of air and water, while land and air birthed the spirits of mountain, and water and land brought forth humankind. And each had their own domain and ability, as it should be.

"And that is the world that was and is and will be." Here she would gesture, first raising her left arm towards the sky, then extending her right arm towards the sea, before finally turning her head to face the landward side.

"And human men worshipped us as gods," my second sister would say at this point, lifting her chin and drawing her spine straight.

"Some did," my mother said, "and some did not. But we are not gods, my love. We are ourselves. Each of the peoples make their own choices when it comes to gods." And my eldest sister and brother would nod, and my middle sister would frown, while my middle brother gazed out of a window and dreamed of hunting.

Or so my middle sister told me. My memory does not reach back so far. To me, my mother was a god, serene and knowledgeable. Now... all I know is that the gods cannot be trusted, for some are fickle and some fey, and they do not care about anything outside themselves.

If my mother's time was the morning of our lives, and my eldest sister's the full day, the time of my second sister and of the knights was our dusk. The castle and its lands – what remained of them – belonged now to my second sister and she was filled with bitterness and rage. She made no attempt to rebuild our broken walls, nor to remedy the damage done to our orchards, but let the elements and growing things do as they willed. Leaving our eldest brother to watch over what remained, for nine times nine full cycles of our mother's orb she rode through the lands of men, observing their needs and desires and weaknesses. At the end of that time, she returned to Caer Arian and took counsel with our brother. And she rode out again, to spend nine times nine cycles studying with our mother's cousins, the great ladies of Caer Gloyw, who knew magics beyond the imaginings of human men. And all the while, my twin and I grew as wild as the lands about our home, for our brother paid us little heed, and our tutors were the spirits of water and air and wood.

When our sister returned at last, she seemed changed. She no longer spoke harsh words nor frowned nor stormed. Rather, she was become as a great lady among human men, soft-spoken and gracious and gentle. For long hours she closed herself away with our brother, and when they emerged he too was changed. In all things, he now ruled over our lands. Like our sister, he did not try to rebuild what had been broken: rather, he made treaties with the men of the land, and they came with cartloads of timber to build a feast hall and guest chambers of ash and oak and beech. Lord Brandelys, they called my brother, for his dark hair and eyes, and took him as one of themselves. My sister they named Alaw, for her golden hair and lily-pale skin. Neither my brother nor my sister did anything to disabuse them of the notion. Our new halls were filled with light and colour and scent, for we wove hangings to brighten their walls, and strewed their floors with sweet rushes and thyme and meadowsweet. Where the outer bailey had stood, my brother planted a fine garden, where our sister sat at her embroidery or her harp, or sought at last to teach my twin and me the skills of a court. Once the buildings were done, my brother sent messengers far and wide, inviting the mortal lords, not as vassals but as friends, and the new halls filled once again with feasting and laughter and music and dancing. And our sister smiled, dancing now with one lord, now with another, until they were all mad with love for her. But she showed no more favour to one that another, with the result that they often came to blows. They wooed her with songs and poetry and gifts of gold and silk and fine horses. Some sought her hand from my brother, who told them that she was free to make her own choice. Some thought to steal her away, and yet somehow she always eluded their snares. Some departed on quests, vowing to impress her with their skill and courage. One or two lay down fasting at her door. My twin and I watched and wondered. Some of the suitors paid court to me also, not in truth but as a means to gain access to my sister. But most of them ignored me, plain and small as I was. Still, she made no choice, showed neither favour nor preference, though the men took up arms in tourneys to impress her. They won battles and slew great beasts, brought her treasures that they swore came from the end of the world, or swore vows to quest or wander or fight until they won her love. And slowly, in ones and twos, her suitors began to die.

And that was the second of our sorrows.

Now

"I think," the man said, "that I've been here before. A long time ago. I was with my brother. One of my brothers."

He spoke to himself, or perhaps to Palug. Stretched out along the floor of the undercroft, I could hear his voice filtering down through the cracked walls, dry with dust and outside heat. Somewhere up there, above the castle, the sun trod his path to zenith, but down here it was cool and I was safe. Rocked by the salt waves, I let tail and wings unfold, and closed my eyes. The man's voice was a warm rumble through the stone.

"It was different, then," the man went on. "This place, me. Everything, maybe. There were orchards, half wild, with fruit of all kinds. Perhaps it was autumn, though the sun shone and the weather was fine. And perhaps I'm wrong. Agr… One of my brothers always says I have a rotten memory. But I remember plums and pears and the scent of ripe apples. My oldest brother loves apples and there so many different varieties…

"There were vines, too, growing up the castle walls. Gavin – my brother – said it was a sign the Romans must have been here, once, long ago. He thought the lord should mend it, said it would make a fine dwelling. We could see the tower for miles, as we rode, and he pretended he knew all the pennants. He was so young back then, eighteen at most. We both were so young. There was a fine hall, too, with carvings of ravens and hawks on the beams, and pavilions, though we didn't see those until we were closer. It was so beautiful." He hesitated, and I found myself catching my breath, as if I feared to distract him. I heard Palug yawn, and the man laughed.

It had been a long time since I had heard mortal laughter; any laughter at all, save my own. His laugh was nothing special. I wished he would speak again. His voice reminded me of autumn, and the year turning back into my mother's hands. I drifted in my saltwater, waiting.

"I'm boring you," the man said, speaking to Palug. "I don't suppose you care about the memories of men. But I've no other coin in which to pay you for your hospitality, other than stories. You've had the last of the dried meat and I doubt you care for stale bread. And this place... it's like the walls want to hear." I started at that, eyes opening. Did he sense my attention, here below? Or was it some remnant of my sister's magic still haunting the castle walls?

"It was beautiful," the man said, "Beautiful and strange, and it made me uneasy and I told my brother so."

Then

"I don't like it," I say to Gawain as we make our way through the tangled trees. "There's something uncanny here. It's too early for so many apples."

"We're a long way south and west from home," he says. "It gets warmer here sooner, that's all. You worry too much, Heris, and that's a fact."

"Someone has to."

"What for?" Making a long arm, he reaches out and plucks an apple from a nearby branch. ""Nothing uncanny can smell this good." He tosses the apple to me and picks another for himself. "You're a worrywart, and you never do recognise simple good fortune even when it bites you on the backside."

"Better that than be forever riding into traps. There's something strange here. An enchantment, maybe."

"Enchantment, or blessing? This is the High King's kingdom now, not the old world of wars and treachery. I should have got you away from mother much earlier. You see enchantment and trouble everywhere." He pauses for a moment to take a bite of his apple, then grins at me, showing his fine teeth. "Tastes like a perfectly normal apple. You've got to get over jumping at shadows. You'll be a knight yourself one day, and the king can't have men who turn their backs on adventure."

I wonder about that myself, but there's no sense arguing the point with Gawain in this mood. He's just nineteen, the hero of the king's wars and the darling of the court. Even the new queen, the beautiful Guinever, smiles on him. She named him her personal champion at the last May Day revel.

He's a knight such of those from story and song, and I already know I'll never be his equal. I'm sixteen, too tall for comfort, awkward and clumsy, forever knocking cups off tables or tripping over my feet and my tongue. "You'll grow into your height," my uncle the king tells me. "Just look at Kay."

He's kind, my uncle, and means to reassure me, but Kay is a great oak of a man who scares the daylights out of all the squires and pages. I can't imagine ever being like that. The only person I can reliably scare is myself. Not that I'll tell the king that. He has matters far more important to manage.

Gawain finishes the apple and tosses the core away into the undergrowth. "Come on, then. Don't you want to find out what's happening here?"

Not particularly. But I don't say so. It's our duty, as servants of the king, to discover what occurs throughout Logres and its dependent realms. It's why he sends his knights out questing. Well, that and keeping them from being forever underfoot eating the storerooms empty. So I urge my mare up to join Gawain. "Do I have any choice? You're the knight, after all."

"Not really." He leans over to slap my shoulder.

"I still think there's something strange here. Maybe you shouldn't have eaten that apple."

"You definitely spent too much time with mother," he says. "Not everything away from her grasp is a trap." And he sets his horse to a trot down the path through the trees and I have no choice but to follow. There's a familiar taste to the air, fresh and sharp. For a moment, I'm back home in Orkney. "The sea," Gawain says.

"Salt marsh, more like." But I say the words to myself. There's no holding Gawain back in this mood and anyway the sea-longing has its clasp on me. The trees are thinner here, the ground starting to slope downhill. On the horizon I make out the shape of a castle, banner flying from its towers, and behind it the grey shimmer of the sea.

"The lord is at home," Gawain says. "Come on, I'll race you!" And before I can respond he's off, galloping over the grass towards the castle and the shore and the sea. My mare tosses her head, eager to follow, and I let her go. Perhaps Gawain is right. Perhaps I do worry too much. The war is over and Arthur is safe on the throne, and we are young and free to explore this land and win glory. The smell of the sea fills my lungs, salt tingles on my lips and I let out a whoop as we thunder onto the white sand. Ahead of me, the tail of Gawain's bay gelding streams out: I can almost touch it. He glances back at me and I flash him a grin. Then we're neck and neck, racing along the strand towards the castle on the headland. A handful of wooden buildings cluster outside, some with banners of their own. Flower-strewn grass surrounds them, interrupted here and there by an arbour or an outdoor bower. Whoever this lord is, he lives well. I slow a little, scanning the scene, and with a yell of triumph Gawain pulls ahead, reaching the end of the beach about a length and a half before me. He halts and looks up, trying to identify the various emblems displayed on the banners.

I'm supposed to be learning those, too. A knight is expected to recognise his fellows and I already know the devices of Arthur's allies and regular warriors. I'm still hazy about a lot of the knights and lords who joined us after the war: a lot of people have changed their arms since, as well, distancing themselves from the taint of opposition. Including Gawain, I suppose. He chose Arthur over our father, and has never borne the Orkney shield. Bishop Baldwin granted his device when he was knighted: a red pentangle (symbolising the unity of Logres and the virtues of knighthood, apparently) on a white field. I don't have my own badge yet: I wear Gawain's on my surcoat. He might, I suppose, have taken back the Orkney shield after our father surrendered and swore fealty. But he would not. "Let Agrin have it, if he wants. And the lands too, for all I care. I don't want any of it."

Our mother was angry at that, for all she'd urged him to take Arthur's side. She's possessive of everything she touches, be it land or kin. I'm glad to be far from her. I miss my other brothers, though. But I'm happy to be with Gawain.

There are those at court who say he's set his sights higher than Orkney, that he sees himself as Arthur's heir and successor. Some hint he wants that role sooner rather than later, as if he was as scheming and heartless as our mother. They don't say it where he might overhear. His temper is already legendary. But they forget about squires and pages: we might as well be invisible. They forget I'm Gawain's brother, as well as his squire. The first time I overheard that slur, I was ready to fight. I have the Orkney temper, too. I recall my fists clenching. I took a step forward, and a hand came down on my shoulder. Startled, I looked up and there was Kay, shaking his head at me. "Leave it, lad. If you make something of it, they'll just think you and your brother have something to hide. Go take a walk outside to cool off, and leave the gossips to the king and me."

I did as he suggested. You don't cross Kay if you're a squire. Or if you're a knight, most of the time.

I don't recognise any of the banners displayed ahead. Not that it signifies: whoever they are, they won't recognise me, either. But they'll know Gawain. He's the King's nephew, the Queen's champion, the Flower of Knighthood and the handsomest, most gifted knight at court. Still, he's frowning when I halt beside him. He twists in the saddle, and says, "What do you hear?"

It's an odd question. I consider. The slow rhythm of the waves against the sand. My mare and Gawain's gelding, still breathing hard. The wind in the grass. I tell Gawain as much.

"Is that all?"

"Well, you talking." At that moment, my stomach rumbles and I blush. "Us, I guess!"

"Us," he repeats. "But no one else." He gestures at the wooden buildings. "There's no one about outside, cooking or fetching wood and water. No smell of food or horses. There's no one here."

"Maybe they've gone hunting?"

"The servants would still be here. And there would be guards."

"Well then, perhaps…" but I can't think of anything else and my voice drifts into silence.

Gawain puts a hand to his sword. "Maybe you were right after all, Heris. Maybe there's some enchantment here."

Now

I remember this voice. The thought bubbles up within me as I float. I remember... what? Something in the rhythm of his speech, the way he turns a phrase. Something familiar. Kings and knights and wars: all the trappings of mortal men. Not that, no. But something... An overgrown orchard, a beach, a castle by the sea. That could be many places. The bright pennants and empty halls. A shield. A pentangle shield.

My eyes snap open. I know this man. I know.

I remember.

Then

The pentangle knight arrived like any other man, all pride and self-satisfaction on a high-stepping horse. Like the others, he was clad in mail, with an embroidered surcoat. His head was uncovered, the sunlight striking red lights in his dark hair. He was followed by a lanky squire on a nondescript mare, who nevertheless had something of the same air as his master. The knight's shield was covered, but the device on the surcoat was a pentangle in red. We watched them ride along the beach, my siblings and I, up on top of the tower. "He rides well," my brother Brandelys said. "And that's a good horse. This one is a man of rank, I think."

My sister Alaw shrugged. "A man is a man, all the same." She leaned forward, resting her white arms on the wall. "Which game shall we play with him, do you think?"

"Let it be as you please."

She paused, brows drawing in delicately. Then she smiled and whispered something to Brandelys. Her fingertips danced over the stone, speaking to the magics she had woven within them. "We shall have good sport, I think." Then she turned to me. "And you, little sister, have a part to play also. Are you ready?"

Her will was mine in those days. I nodded and bowed.

"Then it is agreed." She clapped her hands, beautiful in her delight. "To arms, my loves. Tonight we go to war."

Now

My sister never taught me any of her magic, nor did I ever ask to learn. And later, after the pentangle knight, when such skills might have served me, I could not do as she had done and ride out to seek tutors. Her magics had trapped me as certainly as those she had used against her suitors. I was bound to Caer Arian and its lands. Palug might have left, had he wished. But, aside from hunting, he had no interest in travel nor in studying – if he had been capable of the latter. He was as indolent now as he had been while our sibling lived and I... I was as powerless and little and plain. Had I possessed some beauty, I might perhaps have found a way to draw humans to me, if only through rumour and lust. But there was nothing about me or the ruins of our home to excite travellers and, in truth, it suited me thus. Oh, a handful came anyway, and Palug frightened them away or else I drove them forth with harsh words and treats and pebbles. One or two were not alarmed, and lingered a day or two, as if seeking knowledge from the stones. These I watched from my undercroft, gleaning what knowledge I could.

They were not important, they had no bond to me or my kin. But now... The rumble of the man's voice pulls me from my waters, slithering up the steps to the courtyard. Outside, the sun is hot and sharp on my scales: I draw my wings in close, to protect their tender membranes from its teeth. I move silently. The man will never hear me. He continues speaking, in that low brown voice. "The buildings were empty. They looked like they hadn't been used in years. We checked them all and found nothing. Yet the banners looked new. Gawain wasn't laughing any more. We searched until there was nothing left to search except the sea and the distant castle. We were the only ones there. Until we weren't.

"We should leave," I said.

"Without finding the adventure? We haven't tried the castle yet."

"There's something wrong here. I bet the castle's part of it."

"All the more reason to investigate. If there's evil at work, it's our job to put a stop to it."

"I suppose. But, Gavin…"

"If you please, Sir Knight…"

A small voice spoke from behind us. We both turned. Gawain put a hand to his sword again. There before us was a girl, a little scrap of a thing, like a wren. She wore a gown of faded green homespun and her head was bare, hair darker even than Gawain's. She kept her eyes downcast, hands twisting in her dress. She didn't look like an enchantress, she looked like a lost child. She drew in a breath and looked up. She had pretty eyes, amber, like a hawk. She said, "My mistress sent me to bid you welcome, and to ask a boon."

Then

My sister sent me with a message and a token. We had played this game before and I had no need of any magic. Human men seldom see beyond themselves, anyway. I kept my voice soft and my gaze averted, as if afraid, and the knight relaxed, releasing his sword. I relayed the message, focusing my attention on the knight. He was handsome, in his way, with a look to him that reminded me just a little of my own kind, of the lords of air and water who once frequented Caer Arian. But for all that, he was just a man, eager to help the lady I told him of, oppressed by her cruel brother. "My Lady Alaw offers food and shelter, if you will protect her against Sir Brandelys."

"My sword is at her service," and the knight bowed to me. "Take us to her. We will do all we can to aid her."

Human men seldom stop to ask what strengths, what powers women may hold in their own right. I led this knight – 'Sir Gawain', he styled himself – along the causeway to the castle, which my sister had spelled to look whole. Wrapped in her magic, I brought them to the lower postern gate on the seaward side, accessible now while the tide was out. The knight set me on his own mount, behind him:

when we reached the gate I bade him let me down, then opened it with a key. It led to a shallow passage. I urged them inside, locking the gate behind us. "Your squire and horses must wait here until it gets dark, lest Sir Brandelys see them. Good Sir Gawain, I will escort you to my lady."

The knight dismounted, throwing the reins to his squire, and followed me through the mural passages to the south tower, while I made great play of the need for silence and care. My sister awaited us in the solar, seated in the window with an embroidery frame, her golden hair unbound. I watched his eyes widen at her beauty, as I served them wine and sweet cakes, and she, all trembling voice and wet lashes, begged for his aid. Her long fingers brushed his arm and he shivered. She wiped away a tear with her veil and he fell to his knees before her, swearing to obey and protect her to the best of his abilities.

"See to the squire," she whispered to me, as she led the knight to her inner chamber. "Reassure him and feed him. I intend to take my time with this one. He's pretty. And get your twin to see to the horses. There's no need for them to suffer for the sins of their masters."

The squire was where I'd left him, leaning on the passage wall while the horses drowsed. He straightened at my approach. He said, "Where's my brother?"

"He dines with my lady," I told him. "He's safe and well. I'm to take you and your mounts inside, and find you lodgings. Sir Brandelys is in his cups and will notice nothing." He looked uncertain, but his brother was within, and so he let me lead him into the inner courtyard. Palug loitered there, yawning. The squire eyed him dubiously and insisted on seeing to the horses personally, while I tapped my foot and Palug gave half-hearted aid with untacking and grooming. He never cared much for work of any kind, even then. The squire was patient with both horses and my brother, and thanked them for their service. "And thank you, too, damsel," he said, and made me a bow.

"I'm a maidservant, not a damsel," I said, and took him across the courtyard to the kitchen. Palug tried to follow and I waved him away, not trusting his tongue if he got at the ale.

"How should I address you, then?" the squire asked. "I'm Heris – Gaheris. Gawain is my older brother."

Mortal men seldom troubled themselves over me, save as a means to get access to my sister. Most of them referred to me as 'girl', if they noticed me at all. One or two attempted to kiss me and were met by my teeth or my knee. None had ever thought to ask my name. "Thorn. You may call me Thorn."

I waited for a comment, a sign he intended a flirtation. But he merely nodded and said, "Thank you, then, Mistress Thorn, for good bread and meat and decent ale." And then he turned his attention back to the food.

I watched him in silence for a while. He ate like one starved. I said, "Your knight doesn't feed you, then?"

"What?" He wiped his mouth with the back of his hand. "No, he does. It's just that I always seem to be hungry. I can't seem to stop growing." He gestured at his long legs. "I don't do it on purpose, but Kay says I'm a blight on the king's storehouses, and Agrin…" He met my eyes and stumbled to a halt, blushing. "Sorry. I do that, too, talk too much. Gavin says I have rotten manners."

No human man had manners worth a broken pot. But I just shook my head. "Is he a good man, your Sir Gawain?"

"He's the finest knight in Logres." His pride in his brother shone bright and for a moment I found myself smiling back.

But "Finest isn't good," I said "Many knights who thought themselves fine have found themselves wanting against Sir Brandelys. You saw the pennants."

He raised his chin. "Gavin said he's help your lady and he will. He's decent and he keeps his word. You'll see."

"Perhaps," I said.

Now

"I didn't get to see the lady until later," the man says. "Thorn showed me to a kitchen alcove to sleep, but something kept me restless."

It's baking in the courtyard. My hair is already starting to dry. I glide forward slowly, dust getting into my face and between my scales. My sisters brought me to this, each without intending to, one in her death, one when her magic broke. But it was men – men like this one – who led them to such straits and it is men who will pay. Garlon I cannot find, but the pentangle knight... I come to the opening into the bottom of the tower and pause a moment. Caer Arian is mine, now, broken as it is. It will sustain me.

I raise myself up, spread my wings. And then I slither through the arch.

Then

I sleep fitfully, for all that the alcove is warm and comfortable and my dreams are full of my mother, which always unnerves me. There's a sour smell to the castle walls, despite the fresh rushes and the fresh bread. I've seen no one save the maid and the groom. Our horses are the only beasts in the stable. This place feels uncanny, and I cannot settle. The banners, the dangerous unseen Sir Brandelys. Gawain is somewhere here on his own. I should have insisted on accompanying him. I should have listened to my own concern.

Not that I'd be much use to him. Not that he'd have let me go. He's the great Sir Gawain, hero of Logres and he doesn't need a clumsy younger brother to save him. But all the same, he's my *brother* and he's an idiot where women are concerned.

I rise and peer cautiously round the hanging that closes off the alcove. The kitchen is empty, no sign of Thorn or the groom. A great weight of silence blankets the whole building: all I can hear is my own breath. But something feels wrong. I cross the kitchen barefoot and open the door to the courtyard. It's a cold night: overhead a thin chill sliver of moon shines amidst clouds. Against the sky, the line of the curtain wall is briefly ragged. Then it shimmers and becomes whole. I draw my knife. I was right. There is enchantment here.

I'm halfway across the courtyard when I hear the clash of metal from somewhere above me. A single light shows at the top of one tower, the only one that, by moonlight, is still whole. I take the stairs two at a time and go sprawling at the top, as someone sticks out a foot to trip me. I drop my knife and hear it clatter back down the steps. The maid blocks the doorway ahead. She glares at me as I struggle to my feet. I can't fight a woman. I hesitate, looking for a way to get past her, and she shoves me backwards. I grab her arms to stop myself from falling and we both stagger against the door. It swings open. I can smell woodsmoke and blood. Over Thorn's shoulder, I see Gawain, clad only in his undergarments, fighting a great mountain of a man. Gawain has his sword, but the other man – Sir Brandelys – has mail and a hauberk and a hefty two-handed blade. Lady Alaw is behind them, sitting on the bed in her shift and smiling.

I know that type of smile. I've seen it all too often on my mother, excitement and malice all mingled together. I struggle to free myself from Thorn's grip and she sinks her teeth into my shoulder. I can't hit her… I grit my own teeth and use my weight to try and get her pinned to the floor with a knee. She twists, which at least frees my shoulder. Something – no, someone --- pounds at my back and I turn as best I can just in time to get the groom's fist in my face.

Him, I can hit. I scrabble to my knees, letting go of Thorn, and make a grab for him. We lurch sideways into a wall, and I get another glimpse of Gawain. He's faster than Brandelys, and lighter on his feet. But Brandelys has the advantage of armour and reach… Thorn hits me again, this time in the back, and I twist to hold her off. The groom stamps hard on my foot and gets my other elbow in the gut as a reward.

Light flashes on the edge of my vision. Not the swords… Gawain has Brandelys backed against the fireplace. Behind him, Lady Alaw rises to her feet, a wicked long knife in her hand.

I yell, "Gavin, ware behind!" and my brother spins, just as Alaw lunges at him. He can't stop the blow: I see the horror on his face as momentum brings his blade down, slicing into Alaw's slender white neck. She drops to the floor, blood spraying in all directions, and everything turns to chaos. Brandelys lets out a mighty roar, swinging at Gawain with all his might. Gawain side steps and slips in the blood. The blow hits the bedframe instead, bringing the hangings down in a tumble of splinters and dust.

The tower shakes. Brandelys, overreaching, tumbles forward and Gawain takes a step back, waiting for him to get back on his feet. A good knight never strikes a fallen opponent... Brandelys' sword is tangled in the bedclothes. He grabs his sister's knife and slashes at Gawain's left leg. I push both groom and maid aside and make a leap for his back.

The tower shakes again. Chunks of wood break from the beams above us, crashing to the floor. Great chips of rock tumble from the chimneypiece. Brandelys, off-balance, misses, and I find myself next to Gawain. He stares at me, wide-eyed with shock.

"We have to get out!" The groom drags at my arm. I don't understand why he's suddenly helpful. He tugs at me again. "Come on. Move. The tower is going to break." As if to underline his words, the tower shakes a third time, with a mighty groan, and a massive block of rock breaks away from the ceiling and crashes through the broken bed. The groom is pushing Thorn out the door and down the stairs. I get hold of Gawain by one hand and pull him after them. We scramble down the stairs, thumping and bumping into each other, and then we're in the courtyard, and the horses are there, somehow free from the stable. I can't see Thorn or the groom. "The lord... Sir Brandelys..." Gawain says, and tries to move back into the tower. I dig in my heels and hold him back.

"The ceiling is down. He's dead by now. Come on." I get him onto his horse. All around us, the castle walls are grinding and swaying. I mount myself, and, grabbing Gawain's reins, get us both out through the gate and onto the causeway. The horses' hooves kick up spray: a bitter wind whistles past us. After a moment or two, Gawain straightens in the saddle and pulls his reins from me. Ahead, the shoreline is silver-white in the moonlight. From behind, the crack and thunder of falling stonework drowns out the sea. The horses are running flat out. Something whistles past me, leaving a long burning along my right arm. In front of me, Gawain twists and snatches something from the air. He braces himself in his stirrups and throws whatever-it-is back towards the madness behind us. There's a long moment of stillness and then a great cry erupts, like the cawing of a thousand ravens.

And then we're on land, on a muddy track through a saltmarsh. The wind drops. The horses slow to a trot.

"Gavin," I say, "what just happened?"

Gawain's face is pale and blood-splattered. He still looks stunned. Tears roll down his face. He says, "I don't know, little brother. Nothing good."

Now

The man stops speaking in mid-sentence, staring at me, not moving. Lolling on the ground, Palug looks up at me and blinks. My breath is a hiss in my throat. My wings rattle against the stone. My stone. My walls. My castle. I have waited long years for this moment, ever since the pentangle knight slew my second sister. I know this man, now.

When my second sister died, all the magic she had woven through our walls, our lands, snapped back upon us like the warp on a broken loom. The wooden halls and chambers crumbled to ash, the land withered, the stone walls broke and tumbled to fragments and ruin. The sea overran our orchards, our meadows, polluted what remained of the castle well. Trapped in the remains of the upper tower, my eldest brother shaped a spear out of his fury and our sister's blood and cast it after the pentangle knight as he fled. But our mother's face was veiled, our luck as spoiled as Caer Arian, and the spear turned back upon my brother instead. I saw it strike him. I saw him shatter into rags and ravens. And Palug and I... There, in the lee of the fallen tower, my scales formed and his fur.

And such was the third of our sorrows.

Now, I glide closer to the man, and Palug clambers to his feet. The man still makes no attempt to move. His staff rests a few feet away, leaning on a wall. His knife remains tucked through his belt. I lift myself up to his height and stare back at him, swaying.

He says, "So that's it. I should have recognised you sooner." Slowly, carefully, he reaches for his pouch. I tense, but all he draws out is a black feather.

"They were all around us when we woke the next morning," he says. "We were miles inland, by then, but there they were. And then, a night or two back, when I first came back to this coastline, this was beside me when I woke up. It's a long time ago, what happened. But I remember, now." He turns the feather in his hand. "We rode back to court, Gavin and me. Gavin thought himself dishonoured. To kill a woman… He was ready to throw himself into the sea. He told the king and Bishop Baldwin, and they gave him penance. We never spoke of it, after that. I told myself… I told myself that some of it was a dream. The castle collapsing. The spear." He shakes his head. "We should both have known better. You see, our mother was a witch."

He ought to be afraid. Human men cannot bear the sight of me in this daylight form. He does not look afraid: he looks sad. He continues, "My brother… Gavin still bears that shame. He swore a holy oath to serve women for the rest of his life. He can't bear to see a woman suffer. He tried to find this place again, to make amends, but we never could reach here again, however we searched." He shakes his head. "I can't bring you Gavin. I won't do that to him. But there's blood enough to my account, too, these days." And he takes a step towards me, leaving his staff against the wall.

Palug pads his way to stand between us. He has grown to suit this life, such as it is. Nothing much is expected of him, aside from the occasional hunt. He sleeps and dreams as he wishes. He was not born to rule Caer Arian. Like his father, like my father, Garlon, he is just a man. I have worked to banish the taint of human blood from my own veins with hardship and bitterness. I have waited and watched and planned. I have gleaned what little knowledge I can from the rags of my sister's magic that still lingers in the walls. I have done all I can to further her will.

And it has brought me to this. The ravens, my ravens, the echoes of my eldest brother, have brought me the wrong man. Not Garlon, whose trail is lost. Not the pentangle knight. Just the gangling boy, the squire, this maimed and exhausted man in front of me. I tried once before to harm him, the night my sister died, and I failed. I have better weapons now. Let the pentangle knight lose a sibling, as I have lost mine. I dart towards him, and my long body wraps itself about him, tight, tighter. I raise my head, the one part of me that still holds trace of my original form, and I bare my fangs.

"Thorn," he says. "You told me your name was Thorn. I remember your eyes." He does not flinch. He simply stands there and waits.

From behind me there's a crack and a rushing bubbling. A burst of sweetness fills the air. I taste green, growing things. I hesitate, and from somewhere a drop of moisture lands on my skin, then another, and another. I look up. Clouds, great beautiful grey clouds, cover the sun. Rain patters down onto the stone and dust. Over the man's shoulder, I see tender green shots begin to climb their way up the walls. The rain washes the heat from my skin and I raise my hands to catch it.

My hands… I stagger, then, and the man steadies me with his one hand. I have no wings. I have no scales. Only the shape I was born to, two legs, two arms, a woman's form. The man turns his face away and a blush stains his cheeks. I am naked. My gown is in the cellar where I left it. He takes his hand from me and shrugs out of his cloak, offers it to me. Behind me, Palug makes a snuffling sound that is almost laughter.

I do not want the cloak. I am caught up in the feel of the rain on my skin. But human men are fools about such things, so I accept it and wrap it around me. Then I turn and look at Palug. He retains his great cat form. He sits atop the well, peering down inside. I join him and see that it is once again full. I dip a hand into the water, and it tastes fresh and clean in my mouth.

I look back at the man. "What did you do?"

He shrugs. "Nothing. At least, so I believe."

"You did something." I gesture around me. "This wasn't supposed to happen."

"No." He considers. "You wanted my brother, I think. But he's not here. He sailed with the king into France. So you got me instead. I'm sorry about that. At least, sort of."

"He killed my sister."

"Aye."

"He cast my brother's spear back and slew him too,"

"I'm sorry for it. He didn't know."

"Men drove my mother away. A man trapped and tricked my eldest sister."

"There are too many bad men." Again, he looks sad. "The king does his best. He'll help you send help to your eldest sister, if you wish."

"It's too late for that. Garlon took her and forced her to bear us, to force his blood into our line. He weakens us. His blood is still betraying me. It brought me the wrong man." My words trail off and I knot my hands in the cloak.

Abruptly, the man is there beside me. He takes one of my hands in his. "Lady… Thorn… I am so sorry for your pain." His voice is gentle and I remember the squire who was grateful for bread and ale. "Tell me, if you can, what it is you need now."

My eldest sister wanted love. My second sister wanted power. Men twisted both away from them. I… On the other side, Palug nudges me, rubbing his head against my arm.

No one ever asked me what I want, what I need. I have never even thought to ask myself.

Palug wants to be a cat, not a man.

And I… I want a home.

Afterwards

It rains for three days and three nights without cease. All the while, the green growing things burst from the ground, climbing the castle walls. We take refuge in my kitchen, which at least has its roof and a working hearth. I make pottage from the last of our grain and the man contributes herbs and a few scraps of apple. I don't know why I do this. I just know I can't think what else to do. By the end of the first day, there are tender new beans to add to our food; the second brings spring greens and the third berries and nuts and apples. When I climb the damp stairs to peer over the remaining walls, I think I see grain growing from the cracked white sand. Ravens wheel and call over the headland, new grass covers my eldest brother's bones.

"Your name is Gaheris," I say to the man on the first evening. "You told me it without my asking. Then you asked my name and thanked me for bread.

"Aye, well." He won't meet my eyes. He's shy, I realise.

I study him. He's a human man, like Garlon, like the pentangle knight. Like and not like. He does not seem to have the same need for mastery and conflict.

"You didn't try to defend yourself," I say on the second evening. "I meant to kill you. Yet you did nothing."

"Happen you had cause. And I... well, I have sins enough on my conscience."

The third day, while the rain still pours, I find myself telling him the tale of the castle, about my mother and my sisters and all that befell us. He listens intently, asking no questions. Afterwards, we sit in silence for a while.

Then he says, "He's dead, you know, Garlon. A knight called Balin killed him a long time ago. He was dead before Gawain and I ever came here."

"Good," I say.

"I never met him. I never met Pellam, either. I don't suppose the family was proud of either of them. I knew Garlon's brother, Pellinor. He wasn't a bad man." He stops and a cloud passes over his face. "He's dead now, too. He would have been your uncle. And Lamorak..." He stops again and looks down.

"Who is Lamorak," I ask him.

"A friend. He was my friend." He still won't look at me. "I should have realised before. Your eyes. Your eyes are just like his. He'd have been your first cousin." He laughs, shakily. "I really should have known."

That evening, the third evening, it's him who asks the first question. "Is your name really Thorn?"

"Yes," I say. "And no. My name is Draenwen, Whitethorn. But Palug always called me Thorn because he says I'm prickly."

"Ah," he says, and smiles at me.

The fourth morning the rain finally lets up. We go out of the castle and onto the old causeway. The land – my white parched land – stretches before me, green and renewed. Palug stretches, then pads away to nose about in the new fields. "You broke the curse," I say to Gaheris.

"I didn't mean to. That is, I didn't know!

"No."

"Are you angry?"

I consider the question, gazing out over my beautiful lands. "No. I don't think so. Not any more."

"Your world… the world of your kind…" He hesitates, hunting for words. It's a habit he has that I am beginning to find appealing. "It's not gone, I think. You hear stories. Sometimes, you find yourself somewhere completely unexpected. My aunts… Well, they have a way with that kind of thing. And Gawain… There was a lady he loved with all that's in him. She was like you,"

"What happened to her?" I ask.

"She went away. She could only stay seven years. He's mourned her ever since." He hesitates again, then goes on, "You could come to Arthur's court, if you wanted. With me."

"Not now," I say. There's much to be done here, and only me to do it. Palug's no more use than the waves on the shore. "But later. I'd like to, later." And I reach out and take his hand in both of mine. His skin is weather dark and work-worn.

He says, "I could stay longer and help, if you wished. I don't have to be at court until All Souls." He sees my puzzlement, and adds, "The mid-autumn."

I hold on to his hand. I say, "And if you go then, will you return?"

He raises my hands to his and kisses them, one kiss for each. "Aye," he says, "if you wish."

PART FOUR:
THORNED
SERPENT

Gavin, I'm cold.

"Race you to you the beach," Gaheris says, and sets off without waiting, down the sloping track towards the cliff and the way to the sea. The grass is springy under our feet; overhead, gulls wheel and cry. On the horizon, the sea sparkles blue-grey in the summer light. I'm laughing as I chase after him, leaping over low rocks, zagging round the larger boulders, plotting a course to cut a long looping corner off the track. Ahead, Heris glances back and speeds up as he sees me closing. He's getting tall but I'm still three years older and longer in the legs, and I stick my tongue out at his back. I reach the bend and cut left, pushing through the gorse. Twigs catch at my shirt sleeves, leave thin lines on my bare forearms. I tug them free. Somewhere nearby a raven calls. I run harder and the branches snatch at me. On the track below, Heris rounds a corner and vanishes beneath the spur. The gorse shifts, thick knotted roots grabbing at my feet, thin wiry strands twisting about my legs. I thrash and it tightens its grip. Thorns climb my body, heaving me down to the cold hard earth below. Spines bite into my flesh and close around my throat, slithering and rattling. I taste soil and rot, and the branch turns, rearing over me with great serpent fangs…

I woke with a start, heart pounding, skin stinging and prickling with sweat, the sheet part twisted around me. Danger, danger, danger…

A dream. Just a dream. I rubbed my face, staring up at the roof beams in the dim light. Beside me, my companion rolled over and opened her eyes. "Gawain?"

"It's nothing, sweetheart. Just a dream."

She moved closer, winding her arms about my neck. "A bad one? I can help with that." And she pulled my mouth down to hers. "Let me show you."

"Agrin's lost his mind."

Gaheris shrugged. "You're assuming he had one to begin with?"

"Not now, Heris."

He looked at me in surprise. I picked up a pebble and threw it into the stream before answering. "He wants to talk to the king about naming an heir."

"Ah." He'd been reclining on the bank, legs outstretched, leaning on his elbows. But now he sat up and turned to face me. "That's not good."

I threw another pebble. "I told him no. But I'm not sure he listened."

"Maybe we should send for Aunt Morgan?"

"And that would help how?" I raised a brow and he shook his head. "I threatened him with the bishop and the Holy Brothers, but I think he's serious."

"Can't you send him somewhere? One of the family manors? Orkney?"

"If I thought he'd go, I would."

It was autumn: the grass was damp beneath us; the trees were arrayed in gold and amber and ruby. Some six weeks until Advent, when Arthur's allies and vassals would begin to arrive at Camelot for the great Christmas court, and the nights growing longer and colder. Of all the times that Agravaine might have chosen, this was possibly the worst. Half the court were away at their own holdings. And of those who remained a good proportion were with the king at Gloucester. That at least provided some breathing space.

I said, "When's Arthur due back?"

"The end of the week. If things go well." Gaheris picked up a pebble of his own and turned it over in his hand, looking worried. He had reason: the king's health had been failing since the turn of summer and it grew ever more difficult to conceal it from most of the court.

Agravaine was not supposed to know. But he had always had a gift for discovering the things he should not. We sat in gloomy silence for a few moments. Then Heris flicked the pebble and I watched it bounce across the stream, one, two, five, seven... I said, "You always were good at that."

"My one talent."

"One of many." I said, and nudged his shoulder.

He sighed and settled back again. "Well, there's no use me talking to Agrin. He'd laugh. And Gareth won't be back from his lands for at least a sennight." He pondered. "Mouse, then? He's closest to Agrin."

"Maybe."

"Do you think he knows what Agrin's planning?"

"I have no idea. Want to ask him?"

"Holy saints, no!"

I could understand that. Gaheris and Medraut: that was always tricky. It wasn't a conversation I particularly wanted to have either. If Medraut was part of Agravaine's plan it wouldn't help, and if he wasn't... Well, Mouse wasn't the most reliable.

Gaheris pulled at the grass. "Maybe we should talk to the king first." Reluctance wrote itself all across his tone, but I treasured that 'we'.

"That's the best course I can think of, too. Though heaven knows I'd rather not."

"Would anyone?"

"No one I can think of, outside maybe Bishop Baldwin."

"This is a mess," Gaheris said.

"Aye. And why Agrin's so all-fired up about it now defeats me. He's supposed to be the clever one."

"Maybe it is clever." Gaheris stared at the tree overhead, gloomily. "Mother would have thought so."

"Mother wanted one of us on the throne from the day Arthur was proclaimed king. Probably before that."

"She wanted you."

I crossed myself. "I don't know." But Gaheris was right. Our mother, beautiful, cruel Margawse, had a hunger for power her whole life, and a hunger for revenge. I think she'd have married Arthur herself if she could, for all the closeness of their blood. She'd smiled when I'd been sent as hostage. I know she worked on Arthur to name me his heir, in those few feverish months she spent at court when he was crowned, while all the while scheming his overthrow, positioning her kin in both camps. Me and Gaheris for the king. Our father and Agravaine for the old nobility – Gareth, too, maybe in her mind. And Medraut... Medraut just in case both plans failed.

It is a sin, to dishonour your father and mother. I don't know if it's a sin to distrust your siblings, but I knew for certain I could not trust Agravaine.

Gaheris said, "What do we say to the king, though? I mean..." and he spread out his single hand. "It's not the kind of thing there's rules for. And then there's the queen. Should we talk to them together, or see she's warned, and if so how? It will be a cruel thing for her to hear. Do we need to ensure her ladies are ready? Or Lancelot? Agravaine's never liked her: he'd be sure to twist the knife."

If there were ever to be a tourney prize awarded for fretting, Gaheris would win it. I knew what he meant, every word, and I too worried for Guenever. If Arthur was to name an heir, it would inevitably expose her to shame.

As briskly as I might, I said, "One thing at a time, Heris. Maybe we'll get lucky and Agrin will get cold feet, or be called away, or fall in the castle moat."

"He'd float," Gaheris said. "The water wouldn't want him."

"Then maybe someone will give him a clout on the head and knock him silly for a while – not you, mind. It wouldn't be proper."

"I wouldn't mind." He grinned at me. "I could ask Kay, though. He'd enjoy it."

"So would I. But there's no tournament due, and I can't think of another excuse. And anyway, the king wouldn't like it."

"I wish something would happen to him," Gaheris said, then looked guilty. "I know, I know, he's my brother."

"Aye." I climbed to my feet, and held out a hand to him. "We should get back. I'll try and arrange to see Arthur as soon as he returns."

He ignored my hand, rising in one smooth movement. "Do you want me with you?"

He'd hate it, every minute. Like Gareth, he was never good at seeing anyone in distress, let alone causing it. He'd hate it, yet he would accompany anyway, because that was Gaheris. I pulled him into a hug. "No, it's all right. It's probably better with just me." And then, because I didn't want him to think I'd gone soft, "Besides, you'd only get nervous and say something daft."

He thumped me in the arm and laughed.

Gaheris was always there. It sounds foolish, stated so baldly. But it's the truth. Almost my entire life he was there, the diffident younger brother who other people dismissed as my shadow. I was rising four when he was born, one gloomy winter morning, the third of the sons of Lot. My mother took little interest: she had wanted a girl, and anyway Agravaine, my second brother, was her pet. Our father was even less troubled: he had no time for children. Agravaine pinched and poked the new arrival, jealous of his position. But I... I remember creeping into the nurse's room to see the baby, and Gaheris gazing back at me with wide eyes. He was far too small to play with and clearly years from walking or talking or doing anything much at all, and yet somehow in that moment, I knew that this brother was particularly mine.

He was there all through my knightly training, first observing from the side, later alongside me working with the master at arms. He tagged after me around the castle and its grounds, begged to join in games and on rides, and crawled into my bed every time there was a night storm. He was there when father first made terms with Arthur, in the wake of defeat, and Arthur specified me as his first hostage. I do not know on which of the others my father's choice would have fallen as the second: perhaps Medraut, who was a babe in arms and thus the least useful to him. But before he might speak, Gaheris, who feared his temper even more than storms, stepped forward and said, "I'll go."

Even mother was silenced. None of us dared interrupt father, and Gaheris was grey as a ghost and shaking. But he kept his head high, looking direct at the new high king.

"You have brave and loyal sons," Arthur said, smiling at Gaheris and me. "They do you credit." And so it was settled.

Gaheris was there at the dawn of my first battle, helping me into my armour, and handing me sword and spear and shield, and all the while trying his best to hide his fear, though never in his life could he tell a convincing lie. "You'll be a hero, Gavin," he said. "You'll be the finest warrior Logres has ever seen." And I smiled for him and punched his shoulder, and kept my own dread where he could not see it.

He knew it was there, all the same.

He was there at sunset, when I returned for the field coated in mud and blood and worse, unsure whether I was proud or ashamed of what I had done that day. He hugged me, careless of the gore, and said nothing as he disarmed me. There was hot water and clean clothes and food I could not eat. He was there when I woke, shaking, and this time it was him who comforted me.

The following morning we rode with the king to the crown of Badon Hill. Below us, the whole battlefield spread out in the morning mist. Crows and ravens squabbled, chasing each other from the dead. Here and there, people wandered, hunting for kinsmen and friends. The sky hung low, iron grey and heavy. I shivered and Arthur put an arm about me. "War is terrible, Gawain," he said. "You fought bravely and well yesterday. But war… War should always be the last resort."

"You lost many good men, sire," I said.

"Yes," he said. "We all did."

I was whole: I'd escaped with scrapes and bruises. Kay, the king's foster-brother and closest friend, had taken a spear to his shoulder, and Arthur himself had a long cut down one arm. Hoel and Esclabor and Ulbawes were dead: I'd seen them die. I shivered again, and Gaheris beside me stirred. He said, "Sire?"

"Yes, Gaheris?"

"I was thinking… The Saxons have parents and wives and children, too."

Arthur looked at him, a long thoughtful look. "They do. And that's why war is so awful. Never be afraid to feel compassion, either of you. If we stop caring, we stop being human."

Gaheris was there two years later, when the five kings rebelled, our father among them. There was no question for either of us by then. Arthur was a better lord – a better father, for all he was no more than seven years my elder – than Lot ever had been. In press of battle, Gaheris held my back, though he was not yet knighted, and did the work of war, although it sickened him. He was there, or

I was there, all through those early days. Gawain and Gaheris. Gaheris and Gawain. Knight and squire, brothers, the king's two nephews whom he loved full well.

I was there the first time Gaheris killed a man. Not in battle, but when some petty lord thought to ambush the king as he travelled. They came on us through trees, with swords and spears and axes and it was up to each man to save himself. When those few bloody minutes were done, Gaheris was nowhere to be seen, and my blood became ice inside me. He was fourteen, now taller than me, but lanky and wanting muscle. I hunted from body to body, fighting panic, a prayer to the Christian god, to our mother's gods, to any god, running endless through my mind, until at last I found him. He curled at the foot of a yew, beside the body of the man he had killed, drenched in blood, both his and the other man's. He met my eyes, and said, "Oh, Gavin, I didn't mean to."

I wrapped my arms about him. "I know, little brother. But you see, if you hadn't killed him, he would surely have killed you."

He never did grow comfortable with killing, though in time he accepted that sometimes it was unavoidable. Perhaps that was why he always remained diffident about his skill at arms.

Of all my brothers, he was the only one who could ever make me afraid. Not of him, but for him, because of that vein of uncertainty that ran beneath his skin. "It's a hard thing," Arthur said to me, once, "to be a man made for peace in a time of war." He spoke, I thought then, of himself, but now I wonder. Arthur was as stalwart in war as in peacetime, but there were others of our company – not only Gaheris, but Dinadan and Aglovale and quiet sensible Bedwyr – who ever preferred the quieter side of knighthood.

Agravaine was right, of course, when in a rage he accused me of favouring Gaheris. Of all my brothers, I loved Heris most, and the others felt it. Open-hearted Gareth never resented that: he had love enough in his life and never begrudged another. But Agravaine and Medraut… Perhaps, if I had loved Heris less, and them more, or at least taken the time to see how my actions harmed and shaped them; if I had examined why Agrin jabbed and picked so at Heris, why Mouse tried so hard to win attention and affection from anyone and everyone, if I had been a better brother to them both, then my tale might have a different end.

But I didn't. I failed them all. Gaheris was my favourite brother, my shadow, my second self, and I got him killed.

Lady Andrivete was waiting for us in the stable yard when we returned, and she was not smiling. Gaheris and I exchanged glances, then I slid off my horse and threw him the reins. I bowed to Andrivete, who looked upset. The day was getting better by the minute. She's the queen's chief lady and closest confidante. Whatever this was, it wasn't going to be good. I began to greet her, but she cut me off. "Sir Gawain. The queen wants you."

I bowed. "Give me a moment to tidy myself after my ride, and I am at her disposal."

"No, she says directly."

Really not good. Gaheris had dismounted and was leading our horses back towards their boxes. I said, "It's bad?"

"Yes." Andrivete is married to Kay, and probably the sanest person at court. Now, tears formed in her eyes, and I took her hand.

"It's not the king?"

She shook her head. "She's in her private office." I kissed her hand, waved to Heris, and left.

The queen's personal rooms are in the south tower. Usually, the place is alive with voices and laughter and music, as the queen and her ladies read or stitch or sing. But today it was unnaturally still. I passed the public rooms – Guenever's dining hall and audience chambers – running up the stairs, past the rooms for her ladies and her personal chapel, and up again to the top of the tower where she has her bedchamber and personal office and the great solar. From the chapel came the murmur of prayer; though other doors stood open, no one was about. I reached the final landing and tapped lightly on the closed door.

There was no answer. I waited a moment, then opened the door quietly. Guenever sat in the window, gazing out over the grey morning. She turned at my step and her eyes were red. I shut the door behind me and went to her.

I was sixteen the year she wed the king. The court was new and raw, the various wars still raging. She brought him twenty knights, a company of foot soldiers and the huge round table that sits now in the centre of the Great Hall. She was beautiful and kind and we all fell a little in love with her back then. She's the closest thing I have to a sister. I took her hands. "Tell me."

She swallowed before replying. "Oh, Gavin... she's dead." I waited as she fought tears. "Laurel. She didn't come to me this morning, and I sent a maid and she was just lying there..." She bit her lip and I folded my arms about her.

Laurel is my brother Agravaine's wife. Kind-hearted, plain, sweet-natured. I hadn't heard she'd been ill, though I hadn't seen her for several days. The truth was, few people paid her much attention, outside the queen. Agravaine did not love her, but he was a hard jealous man, all the same. Most people waited until he was absent before showing her any kindness.

I said, "Was she ill?"

"There was something, but she said it wasn't serious." Guenever pulled away from me and wiped her eyes.

"She wasn't..." I hunted for a word, "injured." Agravaine is cruel, and it would not be the first time he laid violent hands on his wife. Though to kill her...

Guenever blew her nose hard, which would have shocked most of the poets and junior knights who sighed after her. Then she shook her head. "No." And then, "I've got your shoulder all wet."

"I'll dry. And I'm too young for rheumatism."

She pulled a face at me. "Come and sit out of the draught. I swear autumn is colder every year." She took one of the high-backed chairs by the hearth and waved me to the other. "But I'm worried, Gavin."

"Aye."

"I went to her chamber, when the maid came back. She looked like she was asleep. But something..." She shook her head. "I've seen death before, you know that. From illness and injury and age.

The priest came, and the court physician and neither of them seemed concerned. But something was wrong. I could feel it."

"Where is she now? Still in her chamber."

"No. The maids washed and prepared her, and took her to my chapel. Some of my ladies are sitting vigil. And," and she frowned, "And Agravaine, of course."

"Of course." I could not, quite, keep an edge from my voice.

Guenever said, "She didn't bleed when he touched her, if that's what you're thinking."

"No." He'd be too clever for that, if this was his work.

She was silent a moment, pleating her fingers in the sleeve of her robe. "She'd been low, these last weeks, with her ailment. But I swear there was something more troubling her. Oh, we all know how Agravaine treats her, but this was different. She kept looking at me when she thought I didn't see. But she never said anything."

"She was always one to fret: you know how she took others' troubles to heart."

"That's true." Guenever considered, "Who, though? I can't think of anyone."

I couldn't either. "Maybe it was one of her relatives away from court. Or maybe she felt it wasn't her place to mention whatever it was." I sent a prayer for forgiveness to Laurel's spirit as I spoke. It might well be she was aware of what Agravaine intended, and it would have pained her tender heart to think of the queen.

It was a great pity that a horse hadn't rolled on Agravaine in battle. Or that he'd never crossed Tristan in one of the latter's red rages. Some men are safer dead, even if they are your brother. And may God forgive me for the wish.

Guenever reached out and squeezed my hand. "I'm sorry to burden you with all this. But I couldn't... I can't tell Arthur. He has enough to worry him. And he always wants to see the best in everyone.

"That's one reason he's such a fine king."

"The best." She smiled, then, and was suddenly that summer girl again. I leant forward and kissed her hand.

"I'll talk to the physician," I said. "It may be he's right, and we're hunting imaginary beasts. People do die suddenly, betimes."

"Yes." The smile fled. "Poor Laurel. She was always so gentle." She rose and shook out her skirts. "I should go and pray with my ladies. You'll tell me what you learn, yes?"

"Of course."

"I can always depend on you. Thank you, Gavin."

"I'm always your knight," I said, and bowed.

Andrivete looked out from one of the lower chambers as I descended the stairs and we exchanged a few low-voiced words. Then, as I had promised, I sought out the royal physician and he told me about humours out of balance, much as I expected. "Let your grief be tempered, Sir Gawain," he said, "She was a good lady who made her confession regularly. Her soul will surely achieve paradise."

Agravaine, I told him, would be most comforted to hear that. I thanked the physician and left. The truth was Agravaine cared for nothing and no one but himself. I needed to send a message to Laurel's kinswoman, Llinos, who was wed to my brother Gareth, and, ideally, I needed Gareth back at court sooner rather than later. That thought led to a detour to my room and then to find a confidential courier. As a result, it was past noon when I finally found the man I was actually looking for.

He was in the fourth place I looked. If I'd been less harried, doubtless I would have approached the search more logically. But as it was I checked the main hall and the tiltyard and the stable before thinking to try the library. The librarian gave me a stern look as I entered. Aside perhaps from Gareth, none of the Orkney brothers have much of a name for scholarship. I bowed to him, hoping he'd take it as a promise to behave, and entered. The man I sought sat partway down the long room, at one end of a table piled with books and rolls. He was bent over a smallish volume written in a dense miniscule that would take me most of an afternoon to decipher, and making notes on a tablet. Hearing my steps, he looked up and closed the book.

"Prince Gawain." I'd surprised him: his tone betrayed him although he kept his face neutral. He'd expected the librarian, doubtless, or another of the scholars who frequented the place.

"Safere." I nodded to him and waited. Silence makes a useful tool, if you seek to learn something from someone you don't wholly trust.

Safere was used to distrust. He narrowed his eyes, and said, "You want something."

"Possibly."

He sighed and rose to his feet. "Your family never ceases to be a thorn in my flesh. But I can assure you I haven't exchanged a single word outside the commonest courtesy with the beautiful Gaheris since midsummer. Possibly longer."

"This isn't about Gaheris." (Though one day I was going to get to the bottom of that 'beautiful.')

"Ah. Then shall we leave the library before we distress the good brother in charge too much, and you can tell me about whatever it is that is exercising you?" He led me out through the far end of the chamber and up the short stair that led to the roof and the wall walk. He continued, "As you can see, I'm disposed to be trusting today. I hope my faith is not misplaced and you don't intend violence."

"I didn't when I started looking for you." Safere seems to make a habit of getting under people's skin. The king says he's insecure. Lancelot thinks he's self-conscious. Kay says he's a professional pain in the rear.

I tend to agree with Kay. But today I needed Safere. So I sat on my irritation and said, "I promise I intend you no harm. There's something I wanted to ask you."

He studied me in silence for a few moments, and I realised he was using my own strategy against me. Lancelot also says he's one of the cleverest men at court. Cleverer, one might hope, than Agravaine. I said, "I wanted to talk to you about Laurel."

"Laurel?" I'd surprised him again. This time he made no attempt to hide it. "You do not, I imagine, mean the botanical variety, so I suppose you refer to your sister-in-law." I nodded. He said, "She has the reputation of being a kind lady. But I'm not

214

certain I have ever exchanged more than the barest pleasantries with her."

His confusion seemed genuine. I said, "How long have you been in the library."

"Since dawn, I think. Maybe a little before. Something occurred to me when I first woke and I came to look it up."

"So you haven't spoken to anyone else?"

"The librarian, and one of his assistants." He peered at me suspiciously. "Are you perhaps feeling unwell?"

"I'm fine." A coolish breeze blew from the east: I wished I had thought to bring a cloak. Then again, I hadn't expected to find myself out on the walls. I stopped in the lee of a tower and leant on the parapet. "So you haven't heard about Laurel?"

"Clearly." He stopped a few feet away, folding his arms about himself. "Not that I understand why this concerns me."

"It doesn't. At least…" I hesitated, seeking the right words. "You said something, once."

"About Dame Laurel? You have me confused with someone else."

"Not about Laurel. About yourself." I was getting myself in knots, and I rather suspected he was complicit in that. "She's dead."

"I see." He thought for a moment. "My condolences."

Gaheris once said that trying to hold a conversation with Safere was like trying to catch an eel with your elbows. He slid out sideways from everything and half the time you weren't even sure what he meant.

I'd come looking for him because I was pretty sure he was the only man at court who could help. I straightened and said, "I don't think she died a natural death."

"I did not," he said, "kill your brother's wife." He put a hand to his belt. "Nor do I choose to become an Orkney scapegoat."

That was one reaction I had not expected. I said, carefully, "I explained myself poorly. I'm not accusing you, not in the slightest." I bowed to him. "My apologies, Sir Safere."

He relaxed fractionally. I went on, "She shows no sign of injury and the physician has pronounced her death natural. But… I believe you know more of the medical arts, and, well, other related things, and I wanted to ask you if you might be willing to examine her body also."

"You believe she was poisoned." All the archness fell from his voice: he was abruptly focused. I'd seen that side of him only once before, in Cornwall, the day Heris lost his left hand.

"I think it's possible."

"You understand that such things are not exact? I may be able to tell you nothing. There may be nothing to find."

"Yes."

"It might, additionally, draw unwanted attention. To us both, I suppose, though I confess I'm more concerned about myself."

"I promise to protect you from Agravaine."

"As Beautiful Gaheris once undertook to protect Lamorak from all of you?" Something showed on his face that I recognised. A bleakness, a depth of grief.

I said, "Heris has never forgiven himself over that. Nor have I."

There was a long silence. He looked away from me, staring out towards the horizon. Then he shook his head, and said, "I just cannot avoid your family. Very well. I will do as you ask."

I found Gaheris in the chancery office, looking harassed. Kay had gone to Gloucester with the king and in his absence Gaheris was acting seneschal, a job I knew he detested. It wasn't the petitioners, nor the household details, nor even the accounts: it was the writing. He sat at Kay's desk, surrounded by account rolls and scowling at a scrap of parchment. He looked up as I entered and put the quill down with an audible sigh of relief.

I said, "You've heard?"

"About Laurel? Yes. The senior page came to tell me. So did the queen's chaplain and two of the chambermaids and for some reason one of the laundrywomen. Poor Laurel."

"Ah." He never could see it, but the fact was that half the servants were a little in love with him. He treated all of them well, knew their names, and, unlike Kay, never shouted at them, even with cause. His wife Luned thought it showed low tastes. I rather applauded it.

He pushed his chair back from the desk and stood, stretching. "Does the queen have orders for me respecting the death?"

"Probably, but I didn't ask her. I need you to do something for me."

"Oh?" There was the faintest hint of caution in his voice. He had reason: I've led both of us into trouble more times than I can recall. "What?"

"Agravaine's in the chapel."

"Aye. That's to be expected."

"I need him not to be, for an hour or so this evening."

Gaheris took a step back. "Oh, Gavin, no... Surely there's someone else. Mouse? Or Mador de la Porte? He likes Agrin."

"Mouse went to Gloucester with the king. And Mador gossips."

Gaheris sat down again. "Hell. Bloody hellfire and damnation. Agrin doesn't listen to me. You know that." He considered. "Unless you've changed your mind and you *would* like me to knock him out for an hour or two."

"Tempting, but no. I thought maybe you could tell him the queen is planning a dinner in Laurel's memory, and wants his advice on who to invite."

"I'd rather knock him out."

I ignored that. "It's a perfectly sensible request from the seneschal. Acting seneschal."

"Is the queen planning a dinner, though? He'll know if I'm lying."

That was true. Heris was the worst liar at court. "She will be. I'll get her to send you an order."

He looked at me, that measuring, faintly sceptical look that I remembered right back to when he was my squire. Then he said, "Today just keeps getting better. All right. I'll do what I can, and he'll probably be suspicious. But I need to finish this first." And he gestured at the parchment.

I peered over his shoulder. As ever, with Heris, it was mostly crossings-out and blots. It looked to be a letter, but it was hard to tell. I said, "Can't you get a clerk to write it?"

He shook his head. "No. Well, I could, but… I'm writing to Luned. Laurel was her cousin, after all. If I ask a clerk, she'll feel slighted. Though if I write it, she'll complain it's illegible."

"How about I write it, as head of the family? She couldn't see that as a slight, surely?"

"She could take a slight from the king himself," Gaheris said. But he let me take the quill anyway.

The chapel was dim. Usually, there would be great candles in all the sconces and on the stands along the chancel, and crystal lamps on the altar, so that any soul in search of comfort might find welcome. But not now, not tonight. Vespers were over, and most people were abed. I'd sent a note to the queen, asking that she draw her ladies away from their vigil, and Gaheris had played his part with Agravaine. The chapel was cold and dark and empty, the only sources of light the small red lamp on the altar, and a single lantern, which I held.

The queen had insisted on attending: neither Safere nor I had the authority to deny her. She stood beside me. One of her ladies – the damsel of the White Lands, who Heris calls Thorn – waited by the door, to deter any interruptions. Laurel's body lay on a bier in front of the alter, arrayed in her finest gown. Guenever's ladies had strewn sweet herbs around her, placed a bouquet of late roses and a rosary in her folded hands. For a silly chilly moment I wondered if Safere might balk at that latter, and I felt his dark eyes on me as he lifted it to his lips, murmuring a prayer.

"As you see, Prince Gawain, I am as orthodox as the next man," he said, and, for once, smiled.

His hands on Laurel were gentle, more respectful by far than the court physician. He examined her hands, turning them over to inspect the palms, then the nails. He frowned, said, "Bring the lamp a little closer, if you please." I obeyed. He leant over her, studying her face. From a pouch, he drew a kerchief, which he laid carefully over her lips, then breathed on it. Lifting it, he smelt it, and the frown deepened. He drew his dagger from his belt and cut a long lock of her hair. "A flame, please."

I opened the cover of the lamp and offered it to him. He shook his head. "No. Hold it steady." He held the end of the lock into the flame, which flickered, shades of green mingling with the familiar yellow. The queen gave a small gasp and moved closer to me. "Have no fear, my lady," Safere said, "No harm will come to you, and Dame Laurel is safe now from all human meddling." He reached out and snuffed the hair between two fingers.

Guenever said, "But what does it mean?"

"I'm not entirely certain; I need to look up a few things. Tell me, were any lotions or tinctures found in the lady's room?"

Guenever looked at Thorn, who said, "I believe so."

"It would be helpful if I could have them."

"I'll arrange them to be brought to you." The queen said.

"Thank you." Safere bowed to her. And then, "You understand I am not yet sure, but I believe it entirely possible that Dame Laurel was poisoned."

If I sinned by loving Gaheris too much, then I sinned more in caring so little for Agravaine. Scarcely a year separated us in age and I had grown up with him always dragging at my heels, trying to do whatever I did and hating it – hating me – if he failed. I was never as patient with him as I should have been: the gap was too little and I too young to understand. Of all of us, he was the most like our father in temperament: thin-skinned and jealous of his status. And if he resented me, in truth, as a child, I resented him also, and with less reason.

Of us all, he spent the longest with our mother, and he adored her without question. Insofar as she troubled with any of us, he was her favourite. He was left to deal with our father's rages and our mother's spite and scheming, while Gaheris and I won glory at Arthur's side. After our father's death, he came at last to court, to be knighted into a fellowship already tempered and bonded in battle. Oh, Arthur welcomed him, and offered him the same warm affection he bestowed on Heris and me, but it was never the same. Agravaine was the new man, the rebel's son, the outsider, and he felt it. He was always proud. He hated for any other to see his weaknesses. And I... I laughed at him while he blustered, and told him to get over himself.

I should have been kinder. I should have paid more attention to him, worked harder to help him belong. Gaheris, of course, was kind, but Agrin resented it: he was never a man to be led by his younger brothers.

He was always a hard man to love, but I failed him.

It was full dark by the time I got back to the chancery. The castle halls were empty: all good Christian men were asleep, as Bishop Baldwin would say. But I had one last duty, one I should have attended to far earlier in the day. But I was never as good a Christian as the minstrels would have it. And some things are hard to face.

Light still burned in the passage to the chancery office, and here and there through open doors I glimpsed clerks still at work. A low rumble of speech came from the office itself: I knocked on the door and entered. The rolls and ledgers had been cleared from the desk, which was now strewn with the remains of a meal and a number of empty bottles. Agravaine sat with his back to the door, a cup clutched in his hand. Gaheris was across from him, chin propped on his hand. He looked up as I came in, and the set of his shoulders told me he had only the thinnest of reins on his discomfort.

Two strides took me to the table and Agravaine's side. I said, "Agrin. Brother," and drew him into an embrace. Over his shoulder, Gaheris gave me a dusty look. I ignored him. "This is a sad day. A terrible one. My heart aches for you."

"She was a good wife," Agravaine said, slurring his words a little. He was more than half drunk. Gaheris rolled his eyes.

Agravaine always did get sentimental in his cups. I sat down beside him, keeping one arm about him. "She was. And a good friend."

"Yes."

I nodded at Heris. "You leave any of that wine for me?" It was the good stuff: he must have raided the king's private cellar. He rose, fetching a cup from the side table, and poured for me. I kept my attention on Agravaine. "I should have come to you sooner. I'm sorry. Duties."

"Agrin spent the day in the chapel anyway" Gaheris said, "Praying." I frowned at him.

"She was a good woman," Agravaine said. "She will go to paradise, won't she?"

"I'm sure she will." I squeezed his shoulders. "And I'm sure your prayers are helping."

"The queen kept her from me!" He said, a bitterness to his voice. "She gave Laurel inappropriate ideas. Always meddling!"

The expression on Gaheris' face told me he'd heard this before. Agravaine said, "I'd have had a better marriage without her. Yes, and our uncle would have a son."

"Agrin," Gaheris began, and in his voice I heard the edge of his temper.

Agravaine ignored him. "Arthur's sick, we all know it. He needs an heir now, and not a babe in arms, either. He needs an heir old enough to hold the kingdom."

"He has an heir," Gaheris said. "Gavin."

"I don't want to be king." I said

"So?" Agravaine said. "You understand your duty, at least. And if you really don't want to be king, then..."

"You think you'd do a better job?" Gaheris said.

"Enough," I said. "Heris, be quiet. Agrin's grieving. Let him be."

There was a moment's silence, then Gaheris rose and walked to the door. Just before leaving, he caught my eye and gave me the Look again.

Agravaine blinked at me. "You never do that. You never take my side against Heris."

"Happen Heris was out of line. He'll apologise tomorrow."

He considered that for a second or so, then took another gulp of wine. Conscience gnawed me: I took a sip of my own drink. I said, "I'm sorry, Agrin. I've been a poor brother to you sometimes."

He set the cup down. "Did you ever wonder why none of us have heirs?"

It was my turn to blink. "Gareth has his daughters."

"Daughters!" He was scathing. "We've all been married, apart from Mouse. And you've had plenty of lovelights besides. But no sons, not any of us, not the king."

"I don't know. I suppose sometimes it just happens."

"It's her. She can't bear it, you see, for one of us to have a son who could inherit from the king."

"Who?" Either he was drunker than I thought, or if I'd missed something. "Do you mean Aunt Morgan?"

He snorted. "She's only interested in daughters. She already has her eye on Gareth's youngest." I made a note to warn Gari about that. Agravaine continued, "No, the queen. She's barren and she can't stand for any of her rivals to bear a son. And that's why we need to get the king to name an heir. That, or..." And he fell abruptly silent.

"Agrin," I said, "are you suggesting the queen had something to do with Laurel's death?"

"I..." For once Agravaine the silver-tongued was at a loss for words. He swallowed more wine, then said, "I didn't kill her, Gavin."

For once, I believed him.

The following morning, Heris and I rode out again. I'd sat with Agravaine till gone midnight, when his squire and I poured him into bed: for myself, I'd slept badly, dreams full of spikes and clutching branches. We rode out through the village and up along the northeast road, before turning uphill to climb the ridge, where all was empty save for the wind and the grass and the tor stones. We dismounted, letting the horses graze, and Gaheris wandered a little further along the trail, to where a fold in the land opened out all around us, all the way back to Camelot. He said, "Five counties. You know, I don't think I've ever seen them all at once."

"That's because it's usually either raining or hazy."

"I suppose." He found a weather-worn rock and sat on it. "So: Agrin?"

"He says he didn't kill her." I took off my cloak and spread it out on the damp grass to sit on.

He pulled a face. "He's a grand liar."

"I know. But this time I don't think he's lying."

He thought about that for a while, while I watched his thoughts chase across his face. Finally, "I don't know. He's clever. And who else would want to hurt Laurel?"

"That I don't know. He's hinting at the queen."

Gaheris snorted. "That's absurd."

"Yes, and I doubt anyone will listen. If you ask me, it's part of this obsession he has with Arthur's heir."

"Maybe." His brows drew in. "Maybe you need to be careful what you eat and drink, too, Gavin."

I said, "Even Agrin would draw the line at fratricide," but he just looked at me.

We buried Laurel the following day, under a leaden sky, the court in full mourning. Agravaine stood flint-faced through the Mass and the interment, Gaheris and I flanking him on either side. Once or twice, he reached for my hand, but his expression never changed. The queen wept. So did Heris.

The interment was followed by the queen's memorial meal. She placed Agravaine in the seat of honour at her right hand, serving him herself with all the choicest foods. I'd warned her beforehand not to let him drink heavily, and Gaheris had briefed the cupbearers. Agravaine ate little, spoke less, and accepted Guenever's attentions with grace. Perhaps, for once, being the cynosure of the court had eased his pride.

It's all too easy, to see the better route once you are already sunk in the marsh.

Safere met me in the hallway afterwards. He had not been one of the select few to dine, though I had seen him at the burial, standing quietly at the back. We walked together across the inner courtyard and out into the king's garden, which was deserted at this season. He said, "I tested Dame Laurel's cosmetics. There was a tincture containing traces of dedalera. There were traces also in her hair. Some physicians prescribe it for palpitations and nerves in women."

"So she may simply have mistaken the dose?"

"Possibly." He came to a halt, gazing up at the evening sky. "You mentioned Dame Laurel had been unwell."

"Yes."

"I am no physician. But some signs of illness may also be signs of poisoning. From her hair, I think she had been exposed for some while. It would be interesting to learn where she obtained that tincture. It wasn't the court physician. I asked. You, I believe, are superstitious, Prince Gawain."

The abrupt change of subject caught me off guard. "I'm cautious. There's much to this world we don't understand."

"Indeed. Observe *Mirrïkh*, then. He is shadowed." He caught my expression, and added, "I believe you call that star Mars."

"Difficult times ahead."

"Yes. But, I wonder, for whom?"

The king returned two days later, and much of my time was once more absorbed by him. He looked tired, and Kay was visibly anxious, which is never good news for anyone else. Yet Arthur took up his heavy workload once again, without comment to anyone (save, perhaps the queen). Gaheris, when I asked, shuffled his feet, looked out of the nearest window, and started talking about horses. I left it alone: Arthur would tell me when he chose and it was not my place to pursue it.

Agravaine, too, resumed his usual duties, though the king would have granted him surcease. I began to hear murmurings, from the servants and ladies and some of the knights, about his bravery. "Poor Sir Agravaine," Dame Elyzabel observed to me one evening as we dined. "He bears his grief so nobly." Medraut, sitting opposite, made a choking noise and I kicked him under the table.

"He's holding up pretty well," I said. ("He's smug," said Gaheris, later. "He's never been so popular in his life and he loves it.")

Laurel's maid had left Camelot: when I tried, in odd moments, to gain further information about the tincture, no one seemed to know anything about it. A week passed, and another, and Kay began preparations for the Christmas court. I watched Agravaine as closely as I might, but after that one drunken evening he made no further mention of speaking with the king, nor did he seek a private audience.

"Biding his time," Gaheris said.

"Perhaps he's changed his mind."

"Perhaps yours has gone soft." And that conversation devolved into a wrestling match.

The week before Christmas, Luned returned to court. She arrived at dusk, unaccompanied, wearing a dark cloak over her novice's habit. I learnt later that she requested to be shown immediately to the king. We were once more at dinner: a steward showed her into the great hall and announced her. "Dame Luned, sire." Beside me, Gaheris drew in a sharp breath.

Arthur smiled at her, rising and holding out his hands. "Dearest Luned. Welcome. Come, sit and eat with us."

"Sire, I dare not." Luned dropped to her knees, eyes downcast. "I am here to throw myself on your mercy." I looked at Heris: he shook his head.

"And you have it," Arthur said. "You've travelled far and you must be cold. Please, we can speak of serious matters later."

"I cannot." She raised her head, and, to my surprise, she wept. "I have done great wrong, sire. It's my fault that my cousin Laurel is dead."

A low murmur ran up and down the room. My brother Gareth, who had returned to court the week before, slipped his arm about his wife, Llinos, whose face was white. Gaheris shifted towards me, and muttered, low-voiced, "I don't like this."

No more did I. I kept my eyes fixed on Luned as she spoke. "Sire, my cousin wrote to me some weeks ago, about problems she was experiencing with her heart. Since I took up residence at

Shaftesbury, I have made some study of herbs, and she sought my help. She didn't wish to cause concern by asking the court physician, nor to distress her good husband, Sir Agravaine." I elbowed Gaheris before he might snort. Kay, seated next to the queen, was suddenly finding his plate very interesting. Luned drew in a long breath. "I only meant to help her. But... I fear I made an error in my preparation, and instead I brought about her death." She dropped her face into her hands, and sobbed. Across the hall, Llinos half-rose from her seat, and Gareth pulled her back. I heard Gaheris beside me swallow hard, and I put a hand on his arm.

He was always soft-hearted. But Luned had brought him nothing but pain.

The king said, "Dear Luned, did you ride all this way at this season over such a concern?"

"Yes, sire."

He left his place, coming round the table to take her shoulders in his hands, and lift her gently to her feet. "Dear niece, everyone knows how much you cared for your cousin. She had been suffering ill-health for some time; my physician himself believes it was that that brought about her death. Do not reproach yourself. You did nothing wrong." Luned sobbed, and he folded her in his arms. "Come, now, sit with me, and rest. You'll feel better when you're warm and comfortable again."

I looked for Safere amongst the diners, found him partway down the hall, a few places beyond Gareth. He was watching the drama with a thoughtful expression. He would not meet my gaze. Arthur, meanwhile, led Luned to the high table, where Kay had vacated his place. He saw her settled, and Guenever leaned round him to clasp Luned's hands and whisper words of comfort.

"Sire." The voice was Agravaine's. I tensed. He had risen from his own seat and now stood at the foot of the long table. He looked sad. "May I speak?"

The king looked at Luned, then said, "Very well."

`Agravaine bowed. "I believe, sire, that you are correct. My wife tried hard to hide her suffering from me, but a husband knows. I find it all too possible, that, seeking relief from her pain, Laurel might have taken more than she should of a remedy." Luned's eyes widened. "I am certain Dame Luned intended only to heal: I know the great affection that joined her and my wife."

Luned gasped. Gaheris made a faint gagging noise and I elbowed him again. She said, "Sir Agravaine, you comfort my heart." Someone sniffled; I noticed at least two ladies wipe their eyes.

"That was well said, nephew." Arthur said. "You do us all credit. Let us drink together in Dame Laurel's memory, and be at peace with each other."

If I failed Agravaine, we all failed Luned. From the king down, none of us ever took enough time to understand her. She was a woman like a haw bush, all angles and edges, with no veiling graces to soften the edges, and guarded by the spines of her temper. Her quick mind refused to pretend or soften or dissimilate: the court and its pastimes wore her patience thin. "A shrew," said Sagremore, after her tongue cut at him once too often. "Difficult," said Guenever, and sighed. "Lonely," said the king, sadly.

Gaheris did his best, but in truth he no more wanted to wed her than she him. And for Luned, their marriage was a token of everything she did not have. She lived always in the shadow of her more beautiful, more loveable sister Llinos, who had everything Luned wanted, most of all Gareth's love. We all tried, in some fashion or another, but Luned could not be satisfied nor healed. A man like Safere, perhaps, clever and quick and self-contained, might have succeeded. But Safere had no use for women, and Dinadan avoided her, and Balin was dead ere ever she came to court.

Agravaine, as far as I could recall, had ignored her most of the time. Not even Medraut, who is the most indiscriminate flirt at court, ever paid her much attention. "She's spiteful," he said once, "and she hates fun." I think, when she chose to leave court and retire to the convent at Shaftesbury, we were all relieved.

Christmas is the busiest of the annual feasts, and the largest, and this year was no exception. Arthur had summoned all his vassals and lords from across Logres. As ever at such times, Kay and the queen reorganised the court lodgings from top to bottom, to make space for the guests. I found myself sharing with Gaheris (who had given up his room to Luned) and Medraut. Gareth and his family were in the west tower, while Agravaine, out of respect for his bereavement, had been left undisturbed in his usual quarters. While the rest of us bustled about with preparations, he had taken to spending long hours in the chapel or out riding with Mador or Malagant or others of his closer friends. I went with him a time or two, and found him sullen company. "So no change there," said Gaheris.

"Maybe he's really grieving," I said.

"He's really something," Medraut said, slightly muffled. He had taken advantage of the new arrangements to conduct an inspection of both my and Heris's wardrobes. He finished fighting his way into a sage green surcote belonging to Gaheris. "Is this too big across the shoulders?"

"Yes," Gaheris said. "And anyway, I wanted to wear it myself tonight."

"Fair enough." Medraut shrugged out of the garment and threw it to Heris. "Gavin, are you wanting your blue cotte?"

"It'll be short on you, likely," I said.

"But the colour matches the embroidery on this shirt perfectly." And Medraut waved a pale green shirt that I was pretty sure belonged to Gareth.

"Don't you ever wear your own clothes?" I took a pair of my hose from him.

"I always wear my own mail." He grinned at me. "And my own braes. Mostly."

"You can try the cotte," I said, "if you can find it."

Medraut abandoned Gaheris' clothing chest and went to rummage through mine. "Talking of Agrin, though. Do you think he's gone full Lancelot?"

It took me a moment to parse that. "Do you mean the sudden piety, or are you suggesting he's gone mad?"

"He's always been mad," Gaheris said. I ignored him.

Medraut sat back on his heels and considered. "Mostly all the chapel-going, I suppose. I saw him talking to Bors yesterday at dinner. Bors! Some people might consider that a form of madness."

Gaheris snorted and I gave him a quelling look. "Bors is all right."

Medraut shrugged. "And he's practically stopped drinking."

"There's a loss," Gaheris said. "I prefer him passed-out drunk. It's less annoying. And safer."

Medraut paused and looked over at him. "Me too, Heris?"

Gaheris flushed. "Let's not, Mouse."

There was a nasty silence. Heris stared at the floor, Medraut watching him with an oddly sad expression on his face.

I said, "Has Agrin said anything to you in particular, Mouse?"

"About God?"

"About what's going on with him?"

He bit his lip. "I... He talks a lot of nonsense lately. About Laurel and hell and... well, nonsense. I think he thinks he's going there – hell, I mean – because of how he treated her." He frowned, "He ought to think that, anyway."

I said, "So he hasn't mentioned anything else?"

"Not particularly." He went back to his inspection of my clothes. "Gavin, do you never fold *anything?*"

"No point. Not when I have brothers who jumble everything for me."

"He's complaining about the family honour again, if that helps," he said. "And our Duty. You know, usual Agrin stuff. Be close to the king. That sort of thing."

I exchanged a glance with Gaheris. "He's not talking about the queen?"

"No." Medraut was curious. "Should he be?"

"She's been good to him, since Laurel died," Heris said. "Happen he's feeling more kindly towards her."

"Well, he hasn't said anything to me." Medraut found the green cotte and brandished it with a triumphant air. "He did say I should be marrying, though. He suggested I make up to one of Claudas' daughters at the feast. Or maybe Malagant's sister. Though why I'd do that I don't know. She must be ten years older than me. And anyway, I don't want to get married. I was rather hoping..." and he stopped talking abruptly and went slightly pink.

"I don't want to know," Gaheris said, with a mild shudder. "You won't woo anyone wearing that old thing of Gavin's, anyway. It's years out of death, and the moths have been at the sleeve."

"Ah, but the colour becomes me. Dame Helawes told me so yesterday. So did Lavaine, now I come to think of it.

"They're both blind, then," Heris said, and Medraut threw one of my shirts at him.

"He – Agrin, I mean – keeps saying it's what mother would have wanted. Though I always rather thought she wanted Arthur's head on a pike and you on the throne, Gavin."

I crossed myself. "Heaven forfend."

"Or herself," Medraut went on. "Or maybe Agrin. Not me, though. I was always an afterthought."

I exchanged another look with Gaheris. Medraut added, "For what it's worth, I think he really is upset about Laurel. As he should be. She was nice and she deserved better than him."

There was no arguing with that. Medraut pulled the cote on, and belted it with, astonishingly, his own belt. "Well, I'm off. Kay has duties for me." He smiled at Gaheris, aimed a punch at my arm and left the room. We heard him start to whistle as he ran down the stairs.

"I swear," Gaheris said, "he must be the vainest man at court."

I nodded. "Almost makes me miss Tristan."

"Not me." Gaheris sat down on his bed. "You think he knows anything?"

"I'm not sure. He might not, or he might just want us to think he doesn't. With him it's never easy to tell."

"Aye. He genuinely liked Laurel, though. Mind when he first came to court?"

I remembered. Laurel had been Medraut's first love, and he'd always retained a kindness for her. Whatever he might do – and his morals were sadly flexible – he would not connive at harming her. I said, "All the same, we should probably keep an eye on him."

"It's Christmas. He'll be too busy flirting with everyone." Gaheris looked uncomfortable. "He probably wouldn't talk to me anyway, not about that. And…" He went silent and studied his feet.

"He wants to make amends," I said.

"Aye. I don't mind that. It's just the talking beforehand."

"Heris," I said, "it needs mending."

"Yes. But…" He rose. "I should be about my duties too."

I caught his shoulder as he passed me, and gave him a quick, hard hug. "I'll watch Mouse."

He clasped my arm and left.

I can't see you, Gavin. It's so cold.

The branches make a dry rattling sound as they close about me. They wrap about my limbs, my chest, drawing tight like serpent coils. My breath catches in my throat, like kitten claws. Tiny thorns, tiny sharp teeth, bite through my shirt, drawing blood. It's cold. My breath hangs white in the air before me. The slow drag-draw of the sea far below fills my ears; overhead birds circle, trading strange hissing calls. I shift and the branches tighten and I gasp. My veins burn and tingle, like frost, like poison, and the more I move the more they scald. Narrow leaves blind me: somewhere out there, ahead along the path, is Gaheris, and I cannot see him, I cannot reach him or know that he's safe. I twist and tug at the thorns, feeling the blood spill down my body, slick on my skin, and from somewhere he's calling my name…. "Gavin… Gavin… Gavin…"

"Gavin!"

I woke with a start, skin sticky with sweat, heart thumping. Gaheris stared down at me, solid and real and concerned. He said, "Gavin, wake up."

His hands were on my shoulders: I struggled free and hauled myself up to my elbows.

"You were dreaming and thrashing and yelling. Nightmare?"

"Yes." I licked dry lips and he poured me a cup of water from the pitcher on the small table. The room was lit by two candles: Medraut's bed was empty and still piled with clothes. Nothing new about that. I said, "Sorry if I woke you."

"You didn't." Gaheris suddenly found the back of his hand very interesting. A blush spread its way slowly up his neck.

I considered him. "Working late?"

"Something of that sort." He really is the worst liar. I patted his shoulder, and the last vestiges of the dream dropped away.

"How's Thorn?"

He smiled, face going gentle. "Everything. Everything good."

I sat up properly and drank more water. "I must be losing my touch. Here I am abed while my brothers play the gallant."

He gave me a shove. "Getting old, Gavin?"

"Perhaps," I said, and shoved him back.

Solstice Eve, the queen decided she wanted to make the short ride to the Holy Church at Aquae Sulis, to hear Vespers and take mass with the holy siblings there. Most of the great lords and sub-kings of Logres had arrived over the last several days and Camelot was filled with music and laughter and bustle. Kay was fit to explode at every moment, and most of the pages were already running riot, and even Bors occasionally smiled. We still expected Mark of Cornwall and Claudas of Armorica, so the king elected to remain at Camelot. But he gave leave for any of those who wished to accompany Guenever. Thus, a little after noon a small party began to make it way along the northeast road. It had snowed the last two days, and the countryside spread out around us clad in ermine and silver, gleaming in the thin winter sun. Birds wheeled above us, setting off small avalanches as they descended to perch in trees and bushes. The country people waved and smiled as we passed, and Guenever distributed sweet cakes and fruits preserved in honey and shiny copper pennies to the children. No one in Arthur's lands went cold and hungry; by law, everyone received enough food and fuel, supplied by his lords, and any lord who failed in the duty faced his full justice. We were merry, that day as we rode, singing rounds and carols, passing flasks of cider from hand to hand, laughing and at peace. We had almost a full hand of Orkneys. I rode between Gareth and Gaheris, close to the queen, while Medraut flitted between the ladies, and Agravaine, black clad and sombre, accompanied the queen's chaplain and Dame Luned. Only Liinos was wanting: she had remained at the castle with her two daughters, who were too small to make the journey there and back in one day. Llinos and Laurel.

"The queen is laughing at me," Medraut said, riding back to join us. "Nobody takes me seriously."

"That's because you're half daft," I said.

He heaved a dramatic sigh. "Nobody wants me today."

Gareth reached over and patted his arm. "Never mind, Mouse. We're happy for your company."

"You're obliged to be. We're related," Medraut said. And then, "And most of the time you don't take me seriously either."

Gaheris turned his measuring look on him. "We do when you do serious things, Mouse." There was a small, uncomfortable pause.

Then, "Gavin," Gareth said, "you're a terrible role model; you do realise that? I swear Mouse is getting to be almost as bad as you ever were." I aimed a mock punch at him, and the tension broke.

The abbey gates stood open; the holy brothers and sisters gathered in the forecourt to welcome us with smiles and blessings. Lay brothers took our mounts; the lady abbess and the priest led us to the guest hall, where we were offered spiced ale and new bread and honey. The queen had gifts for the community, from herself and from Arthur, which she presented to the abbess. The room was warm, and scented with applewood from the fire: a great air of peace lay over us all. Even Agravaine, for once, forbore to frown. The church itself shimmered in jewel colours, tall pillar candles striking sapphire and ruby and emerald from the windows; the high altar glowed in gold and silver and scarlet. Garlands of greenery, holly and ivy and fir, adorned the railings and the lintels of the doors.

The Romans built the first church here, so Arthur once told me, over the vestiges to an earlier shrine to different gods. I bowed my head to any and every god present, and said a silent prayer of my own for my winter lady, my Rhanillt, who had loved me as no other and taken away with her the better part of me. When I opened my eyes, Gaheris stood at my side once again. He knew, of course. Gaheris always knew.

Thorn had not come with us for the service. Like Rhanillt, she had different gods. We listened to the priest as he retold us the tale of the journey and the cold and the byre. Afterwards we came one by one to the altar rail to partake of the sacred mystery.

I was glad for that, later. Glad for us all, even... Even for those who are no longer my kin.

It was dark when, at last, we filed out of the church. The moon was half-full, hanging over the fields. The snow below reflected back its light, blue white against the black. It was cold; we would have ice come morning. I saw Gaheris make a slight bow to the moon overhead, then cross himself and look faintly guilty. There were no clouds, and I was glad of my heavy cloak and fur-lined gloves. Several of us carried lanterns; we rode by their light and that of the heavens above us. A deep stillness lay over us all; when anyone spoke, their voice was low. The sacred mystery, perhaps, held us yet. Even Medraut was quiet, gazing up at the stars as he rode by my side.

Palomedes told me some of their names in his tongue, once. Alnasi, Altair, Alsuhail, Denebola; lovely musical names like water flowing. "In the winter, out on the high plain, they shine in their thousands," he said. "The sky there is more vast than anything you can see in Logres."

I would like to see that sky, one day. Now, I told over the names to myself, and Gaheris, on my other side, surprised me, chiming in, "Alnilam, Eltanim, Almaysan, Thuban." I looked at him, and he said, faintly defensive, "Lamorak taught me. I suppose he learnt them from Safere." He hesitated. "I was thinking about him, back there in the church. Lamorak, I mean. He'd be close to thirty now, if he..." He looked past me at Medraut, and fell silent.

"Heris," Medraut said, "I... About Lamorak, I...." But Gaheris only shook his head and put his horse to the trot, riding up the line to join Gareth.

Medraut sighed. "He won't listen."

As gently as I might, I said, "This wasn't the time."

"It never is."

"No, I suppose not." I looked at him and there were tears in his eyes. "Heris never was good at talking about things that distress him. He doesn't like remembering; it hurts too much."

234

"No." Another sigh. "Do you think that the priest was right? Can a man really be cleansed of all his sins?"

"I'm not the man to ask about that. Try Lancelot or Percevale. Or Bishop Baldwin."

"But could it be possible?"

"I don't know, Mouse. There are things I've done, things I regret… But it's not up to me to ask if they can be forgiven. If I can be forgiven. Heris would probably say it's not up to him, either. But… I just try to do better now, better than I did back then."

He thought about that for a while. "So, if there was something…"

I never got to hear the end of the sentence. We turned a bend and ahead a horse screamed in pain. Medraut gasped, and the sky shattered into a hail of arrows.

Chaos. From the front of the line, someone yelled, "Take cover!" and someone else cried out as they were struck. Red pain stung along my right arm; an arrow skimmed past. Smoke billowed across the road, blurring sight. A gust of wind set the lanterns flickering, turning everything into grotesquerie and puppet play. Someone – it was Gareth – shouted, "To the queen!" I pressed my mount forward. Steel clashed and sang behind me, and I looked back to see Lavaine defending himself against two men on foot and armed with spears. I started to turn, to go to his aid, and another knight – Mador? – came riding from the rear, sword lifted. His horse cannoned into one of the spearmen, knocking him down, while Lavaine struck the other. Mador's sword came back round a bright arc, to sheathe itself in Lavaine's throat. From somewhere beyond me, another voice cried, "Treachery! Defend the queen!" and then Mador was on me. The night devolved into blood and steel and violence.

I couldn't see Medraut. I couldn't see any of my brothers. I remember Mador going down in a bloody spray, and turning to fight off another spearman. I remember catching glimpses of my comrades through the smoke; Dodinel grappling with a man in black mail; Erec fighting two at once; Dame Andrivete setting her horse over the wall to gallop away across the field, an armoured man in pursuit. A man came at me, screaming, armed with a great axe, and my sword took him in the chest. To my left, Astamore went down under the hooves of a mare I recognised. I pressed towards him, and someone cut me off. I heard Gaheris swear, caught a glimpse of him cutting the shaft from an arrow that had lodged in his thigh. I pressed forward again and saw Gareth, defending the queen against three men in leather and mail. No insignia anywhere, save our own. I killed another man, then another, pushed closer to Gareth and Guenever. I couldn't see Agravaine anywhere. I couldn't remember where he had been in the line. One of Gareth's opponents went down, and another came to replace him. Patrise appeared from somewhere and took up position to Gareth's right, intercepting the new man.

A woman screamed: I twisted round. Luned was backed against the other wall, one man holding a blade to her throat while another made a grab for her bridle. I turned my gelding towards her, and the animal checked, stumbled, as an arrow whistled by to lodge in his neck.

Gaheris materialised from my right, grim-faced and bloodied. He took the first spearman in the back, whirled round to slash at the second. And then… Luned behind him shifted, leaning forward, and Heris swayed and crumpled forward over his horse. Luned nodded to herself, a thin long knife in her hand. And then she looked up, straight at me, and she smiled.

I raised my sword, urged my faltering horse towards her. A man dropped before me, and another, and another, and then the horse was stumbling, falling, a spear in his neck, and I too was falling and the world went black.

Gavin, are you still there? I can't see you. Gavin, I'm so cold.

The thorns coil about my neck, bitter and sharp as hatred. My legs, my torso, my arms, all are held down, bound to the dry earth by bands of green and brown. My breath freezes in my throat. The branches writhe about me, their touch like scales, speaking in tongues of ice and pain. They slip here and there, taste my flesh, lick my blood from dripping pointed fangs. The air tastes of salt and iron and ash. I can't move. I can't breathe. I can't see anything anymore, except the twisting branches and the spines and the cold dark sky. I can't push through and Gaheris is out there ahead of me, where the sea hisses and turns…

I came to on a cold stone floor, stained with mud and blood. My hands were bound behind me: to one side I glimpsed other men, likewise bound and left to lie. Erec, his face bloodied, and garments torn. Patrise, looking scared. I twisted, and my arm stung where the arrow hit me. Gaheris lay to my other side, unconscious and pale. There was a lot of blood…

"He's awake." The voice came from behind me. Footsteps approached, and a hand caught in my hair, pulling me to my knees. "The lord will want him."

"Take the other one, too." I didn't recognise either of the voices. Nor do I recognise the courtyard in which we are confined.

"He's still out."

"Wake him up, then."

The man let go of me, and moved towards Gaheris, kicking him sharply in the side. Gaheris groaned and rolled over. I tried to struggle to my feet, and the second man grabbed hold of me from behind. "Be good, now, Sir Gawain, and maybe our lord will be nice to you."

"Your lord can burn in hell."

He backhanded me, knocking me forward again. Erec caught my eye and shook his head. The guard pulled me back up, this time hauling me to my feet. It took two of them to get Gaheris upright, and he was barely conscious. I said, "For God's sake, untie his hands. He can't hurt you in his condition."

"Not without the lord's permission."

"Let me help support him, then."

They looked at each other. I waited. Then one of them shrugged, and said, "Let him get covered in blood. It makes my life easier."

It wasn't simple, not with both of us bound, but somehow I managed to get Gaheris propped against my shoulder and the guards steered the both of us across the courtyard and in through the doors. Heris flinched with every step and I longed to be free, to take down these men who tormented us and whichever lord they served. I kept him as steady as I could. "I'm here, Heris." I said. He murmured my name, almost too low to hear, and the guards laughed.

I studied their faces. These men, I would remember. These men, I would kill. Step by step, they pushed and pulled us, across a small antechamber and into a great grey hall, lit by smoky tapers and strewn with dirty rushes. A dais stood at one end, bearing a high-backed chair covered with furs. Two men stood beside it, one to either side. One the seat itself sat a man I knew all too well. I knew all three. Malagant of the Summer Isles. Medraut. And, on the high seat, Agravaine.

The guards gave us one last push, and Gaheris lost what balance he had, toppling us both forward. The fall wrung a sharp cry from him, and Agravaine… Agravaine smiled.

"Not so high and mighty now, Gavin," he said. "How does it feel?"

"I'll get back to you on that," I said. I looked from one to the other. Malagant smirked. Medraut wouldn't meet my eyes. "How does it feel to you?"

He gestured, and one of the guards kicked me in the back. I caught my breath, and refused to let the pain show. I went on, "Brus sans Pitie, wasn't it? I mind Lance got you out of that one. And then Lucius, or was it Galapas? I lose track. You've been captive so many times."

"Hurt the other one," Agravaine said, and I twisted to shield Gaheris.

I said, "All right, Agrin. It feels bad. Is that what you want to hear?"

He smiled again, showing his teeth. "Perhaps. You have a choice, brother. Back me as king against Arthur, or I kill you both." He looked at Gaheris. "Heris first. Slowly. You get to watch."

He wanted to kill: it was writ clear on his face. He wanted to see us both suffer as much as possible. I inhaled, slowly, trying to think. I said, "I don't understand. What are you doing?"

"Really?" He knew I was prevaricating. Agravaine is many things, but he's no fool. I looked again at Medraut, trying to catch his eye. Agravaine has neither conscience nor compassion, but Mouse… Mouse is easily led. Agravaine said, "I would have thought it was obvious. Or are you asking so Heris will understand?" Gaheris stirred and muttered something that sounded distinctly uncomplimentary. It didn't reach Agravaine. The latter continued, "The finesse is wanting, I grant you – that's your fault, going around asking questions. My original plan was a lot more subtle. But…" and he shrugged, "I intend to be king. Arthur is failing; the vassals," – here he glanced at Malagant – "are asking questions, and, well… Right place, right time."

I said, "And Laurel?"

For a moment an uncertainty flickered in his eyes. "I didn't want that. But she saw something she shouldn't have and she might have said something to the queen. So I asked Luned for a way to keep her quiet for a while."

"You asked for a poison."

"No. That was Luned. She killed Laurel, not me. It's not my fault."

Gaheris had been right: he was mad. But I didn't say it. Instead, I waited. Agravaine never could resist an audience. He went on, "You've made it clear you don't want the throne. I'm the next oldest."

And utterly unfit. But I didn't say that, either. "The vassals, maybe. But what about the subkings?"

"Malagant is with me, as you see. So are Claudas and Brian. The others will come round."

I did calculations in my head. Of those three, only Malagant held lands near Camelot, and he was the least powerful of them. For Brian, or more particularly Claudas, to bring their forces would take weeks, particularly at this season. Malagant's men must be occupied guarding this fortress. If I could get word out, somehow… If some of our party had escaped…

Gaheris swayed against me, and slipped to the floor. I said, "I need time to think, Agrin. And Heris needs a physician. He's bleeding too much."

"So?"

"He's our brother."

"He's not important. You can have your time to think. That's it." And he signalled to the guards. "Take them to their quarters."

"Wait," I said, "Agrin…" He rose, and walked away from me. I tried again to make Medraut look at me. "Mouse, please, make him listen. Heris will die."

"Good," Agravaine said, without turning.

The guards grabbed me, dragging me away. I called, "Mouse. Mouse, *please*…" But Medraut still would not look at me.

It wasn't a pit.

That was the most I could say. The guards left us in a small semi-circular chamber at the base of a tower. It was bitterly cold, unfurnished save for dirty straw and a couple of old pallets, and lit only by the glow of the torches on the other side of the door, and a sliver of a window high above. A chipped bowl held dirty, frozen water. At least they untied our hands. I helped Gaheris onto one of the pallets, and used both of our cloaks to cover him. He clutched at my hand, gasping with the pain of moving. "Gavin?"

"I'm here."

He needed clean water and fresh linen and the best physician in the land. I had none of these and precious little hope of getting them. My outer garments were foul with mud and gore. I tore the sleeves from my shirt, chipped at the ice with the clasp from my cloak. "Heris. Heris, listen. This is going to hurt. But I need to stop you bleeding."

"Right."

I squeezed his hand, then began to pull the remains of his surcoat and shirt away from the wound in his side. He cried out, and I swallowed. It was a narrow puncture, deep and mean, already red and hot to the touch at the edges. Black blood oozed from it. I had seen such injuries before. Most men died within the hour. Those that did not... the majority lasted no more than a handful of days, wracked with pain and fever. A very few lived, never again whole or healthy or comfortable. My eyes burned me. "I'm going to try and clean the wound now, and pack it. Stay with me."

"Yes, Gavin." His voice was a thread. I wiped the blood and dirt away as best I might, rolled the cleanest part of one sleeve into a tight ball, and bound it over the puncture with further strips from my shirt.

"There. Done." I wanted honey, or wine, to keep the area clean. I wanted thunder-herb and marigold. I wanted, more than anything, for my brother to live. I sat beside Gaheris as the night grew darker, and, in the fortress beyond, men shouted and sang. I wiped the blood from his side, repacked the wound, whispered prayers to every god I could name. He drifted in and out of consciousness, speaking now and again, calling for this person and that. Me. Gareth. Thorn. Lamorak.

Sometimes, I think, he knew I was there.

Sometimes he did not. Over and over I did what I could to call him back to me, talking, telling over all the quests and battles and tourneys we had shared.

"Gavin... are you still there?"

"I'm here, Heris."

"I can't see you."

"It's dark, that's all."

"Gavin, I'm so cold."

I lay down beside him, then, careful not to touch his poor injured side. I wrapped my arms about him, stroked his hair away from his face. "I'm here, Heris. I'm with you."

"It hurts..."

"I know. But it will be better soon, I promise."

I held him, there in the cold and the dark, while Agravaine made merry over our blood. And there, in my arms, in that bitter chamber

– at the lowest point in the night when God has his face averted and the world is at its most unforgiving – Gaheris, my shadow, my second self, my most beloved brother, died.

I don't know how much time passed before a key turned in the lock, and the door opened, filling the chamber with torchlight. I still lay beside Heris, trying somehow to keep him warm, hoping he would stir, speak, take a single breath. I could not weep; my heart was lead in my chest, my eyes drier than Palomedes' great plain. The door closed again, and Medraut's voice said, "I came as soon as I could. I had to wait till Agrin passed out: he wouldn't let me out of his sight. I've got water and bandages and salves from the leech's store. And candles." I heard a scrape of flint, then further light blossomed against the cold stone.

"Mouse," I said, "Go away."

"What?" There was a clink of pottery as he set whatever he carried down, then he touched my shoulder. "Are you all right?"

I sat up, pushing him away, hard. "I said *go away*."

"But…" he said, looking from me to Heris and back. And then, "No. Gavin, no. Agravaine promised…"

I came to a crouch and he flinched. "Agravaine is a liar and a traitor. And you helped him."

"No," He said again.

I grabbed him by the shoulders, shaking him to and fro. "Yes, Mouse, yes." He made a small frightened noise, and I dragged him forward, forcing his head over the pallet. "Take a good long look. Gaheris is dead. Your brother is dead, and you helped kill him." My hands itched to move from his shoulders to his throat, to wring the life from him. Let Agravaine feel what I felt. Let him bear the same burden, the same loss, of the brother he loved the most.

Gavin, no.

It could not be Heris. Heris lay dead at my side, never again to temper me. And yet, there was his voice. I took a long, ragged breath, and threw Mouse away from me, back against the icy wall. "Your fault, Mouse."

He curled up into himself, shaking. Dark marks marred the shoulder of his tunic; my hands printed in Gaheris's blood. He wrapped his arms around his knees and began to cry, great retching sobs that seemed like to pull him apart. And I…

I envied him. I had no tears, nothing save the weight in my chest and the cooling embers of my rage. I waited for a few moments, then moved to sit by him. "There, Mouse. You'll make yourself sick." He tensed for a moment, then all at once turned and buried his face against my lap.

Once, long years before, when Rhanillt faded and died, Gaheris held me thus, while I wept and raged and pleaded. I had never thought to find myself again in this situation, nor in such company. And yet, somehow, my anger died away and my thoughts softened towards this brother who I knew so little.

"I'm sorry, Gavin. I'm so sorry…"

"Aye."

"Agrin promised no one would get hurt. He said he'd send the doctor in an hour or two, that he was only trying to soften you up…"

"Agravaine's word is worth less than a bent penny."

"He said they were just going to persuade the queen to take the veil…"

I raised his head, and wiped his face with the edge of his cotte. "Mouse, you know better than that."

He gulped, then said, "He said… said it was the only way I could ever do any good. That the king needs an heir… And I wanted to belong."

"You do belong."

"No… You and Gareth… You're both so far above me. And Heris… Heris hated me for Lamorak, and Agrin was the only one who ever really bothered with me… I'm an idiot, aren't I?"

"Probably," I said.

He sat back on his heels, and blew his nose on his sleeve. "I was jealous of Lamorak. He had everything I wanted, the skill at arms, and the admiration and the popularity. Even mother liked him more than she ever liked me. So I…" His voice shook. "Agrin told me I was defending the family honour and I so wanted to believe him and afterwards Heris would never let me apologise or explain… and now it's too late." The last words threatened to become a wail and I gave him a small shake.

I said, "We'll talk about this later. I promise you, on my honour. On Heris's memory. But right now… Can you get me out of here? I need to tell the king what we know."

He swallowed hard. "Yes. Yes, I think so. Most of the guards are drunk or asleep or both. I can get you a tunic and a cloak, say you're going on patrol."

"The queen?"

But he shook his head. "She's locked at the top of the main tower, with Luned and Malagant's sister to watch over her, and only Malagant has the key. And the other knights are in the undercroft. You can't get to it except through the main hall. Some of Malagant's men are sleeping in there."

"Just you and me, then," I said. "Agravaine will kill you if he suspects you let me go." He blinked at me, and I patted his arm. "And Heris. I can't leave him, not here."

He nodded. "I think I can arrange that. There are wounded men in Malagant's guard. We can say one died and we're taking him for burial. Give me ten minutes."

He hesitated at the doorway, "Gavin, are you sure? I could say you knocked me out… I don't care what Agrin does to me. Not now."

"Well, I do," I said. "I'm not losing another brother."

"Agrin…"

"Agravaine's not my brother any more."

Outside, it was damp and grey. We rode out through the postern, where drowsy-eyed guards barely looked at us as we passed. I followed Medraut down the lane that led to the nearest hamlet and its church, leading the packhorse that carried Gaheris. The snow was beginning to melt, churning the ground to slush and mud. We passed the church, and turned down a track towards woodland. I said, "What about patrols?"

"Malagant doesn't have that many men. He sent everyone he could spare after Gareth. They haven't come back."

"Gareth got away?"

"Yes. He killed at least four of Malagant's men, and his master-at-arms."

"I hope he killed the trackers, too."

"Yes."

I itched to set my horse to a gallop. I knew we needed to get further from the fortress, lest we attract unwanted attention. It was nearly dawn: once the sun rose, we would be all too easy to see. Medraut did what he could, picking a route that passed as much as possible through trees. But as we rode they thinned, until at last we were out onto open land. Birds called their morning greetings around us. The horses' hooves kicked up slush. I said, "How much further till we're out of Malagant's lands?"

"A mile or two, I think." Medraut pointed. "You see the river? We need to get to the other side. There's a ford." I nodded, and forced myself to keep to a steady trot. And all the while the sky brightened and the sun climbed higher. We curved down to the ford, then upwards, towards a ridge.

Something soft brushed against my cheek. I looked up, expecting more snow. Instead, a black feather drifted downwards, first one, then three, then ten, fifty, a rain of feathers falling all around us, obscuring the sun. Medraut held out a hand, mouth open, wondering. More and more feathers fell, swirling on every side, to come to rest, one upon the other, upon Gaheris's body, where he lay over the packhorse.

Once, long ago, when we were young and sure of our own immortality, we had seen such a thing before, Heris and I. A broken castle on the sea's edge, a beautiful treacherous lady and her vengeful brother. I had killed the lady, all through cruel mischance, and her brother pursued us to slay us both, as the castle collapsed about us. Gaheris had got us out, somehow, and back to safety inland. Yet, when we woke the next morning, we found ourselves surrounded by feathers.

Black feathers, raven feathers, like the bird for whom that castle's lord had been named. Brandelys. He was long dead, alongside his golden-haired sister, but there had been another, a maid who was more than she seemed, a slight brown girl who called herself Thorn. I had shrunk from the memory, until the day, a decade and more later, when Gaheris came back from errantry with a new tale of that castle, and a damsel beside him who made his face soften and his eyes light with joy. I had knelt before her, knowing the harm I had done her, and she had forgiven me for his sake.

A woman from the borders of the world. Rhanillt had been one such, and for her, trees had come into leaf in winter. Before, the feathers had been a warning. Now, they fell until Gaheris' form was completely muffled, and then, with a gust, a swirl, they, and he, were gone. Only the packhorse remained, cropping grass, completely unconcerned.

Medraut said, "That was magic."

"Yes."

Overhead, three ravens circled.

Three ravens. Three knights. As we came down the last rise at the far end of the ridge, I saw three armoured figures riding towards us. "Throw your sword away, and take off your cloak," I said to Medraut, and he gawped at me. "Those are Arthur's men. Our men. But we're wearing Malagant's livery." As I spoke, I followed my own directions, letting cloak and sword fall to the ground. The three figures conferred for a moment, then one of them rode forward, a hand on his sword-hilt.

I knew him, from the set of his shoulders and the way he rode. I slid off my horse, and called, "Gareth! Gareth!" For moment, he stared at me through his helmet, then he lifted his visor and a wide smile spread across his face. He came to a halt beside me, and dismounted.

"Gavin." He clasped my elbow. He twisted round, waving his companions forward. "It's a relief to see you. And Mouse." And he turned to embrace our youngest brother. "I thought you'd been captured. Or worse."

"We were," I said, just as the other two joined us. Lancelot, looking tired and anxious, and calm, solid Aglovale de Galis.

"The king's about three miles back down the road, with our forces and Marcus of Cornwall." Gareth said. "We were scouting."

"The queen?" Lancelot said.

"Captive in a fortress belonging to Malagant of the Summer Isles. But she's unharmed. We couldn't reach her. If we could have…"

"I know you would."

"And the others?" Gareth said. "Heris and Agrin?"

Lancelot, too, had dismounted. I looked at him, searching for words. I could not bear to look at Gareth. From behind, Medraut said, "Gari, there's…. That is…" He swallowed, then started again. "Agrin's the one who planned all this. He's allied himself with Malagant. Brian and Claudas, too."

"I brought Claudas to Camelot yesterday," Lancelot said. "He stayed there; he said he was too tired to ride again so soon. But Brian's with the camp. Arthur needs to know."

"Llinos is still at Camelot," Gareth said.

"I'll take the news," said Aglovale. "I know the land round here, and I'm more rested than either of you. You follow with Gawain and Medraut." And he clapped his heels to his mount, and was off down the road at a gallop.

Gareth said again, "But, Heris? Where's Heris?"

I still couldn't look at him. I stared at Lancelot, and felt the earth begin to tilt. He said, "Gavin?" and put out an hand to steady me.

A voice, my voice, from impossibly far away, said, "Luned… He tried to help her and she stabbed him. Heris is dead."

I remember almost nothing of the ride to Arthur's camp. I think, at last, I wept. I remember Lancelot riding beside me and from time to time taking my hand or murmuring words intended to comfort. I remember Gareth, crying and holding on to Medraut. I remember the arrival; a pavilion, blankets and hot water and wine. I remember

Kay, handing me the cup, then turning his back abruptly, so that no one should see his tears. I remember the king.

He came into the tent and sat beside me, holding me as I had held Heris. "Dear Gavin. This is a bitter day." I think I nodded. I had no words. No words could ever encompass what I had lost. Arthur said, "Medraut has told me what happened. All of it. Agravaine will pay, I promise you."

"Let me be the one to exact that payment," I whispered.

He sat back a little, and studied me in silence, for a time. He said, "Are you sure? He's your brother."

"No. Not any more. I only have two brothers, now."

And so, here we wait in our new camp outside the walls of Malagant's fortress. Its name is Camlann, apparently. Here we wait, while the engineers pound at his defences with our siege engines, and the sappers dig their way to mine under a tower. By day, his men take shots at us from the height of the wall-walk, and we respond with arrows and ballistae. Twice, Arthur has offered parley, and been refused. The news from Camelot is good: Aglovale and Gareth led a force back, and had Claudas arrested before he could do much more than bluster. Llinos is safe and unharmed.

No one has seen Thorn since that morning of ravens and grief.

Yesterday, Agravaine brought the queen to the top of the wall, holding her as his shield as he attempted to throw taunts. She looked pale, but her head was high, and she called to us to have courage. I think Agravaine wanted to hit her, but not even he could bring himself to do such a thing under the force of her gaze.

Safere tells me that the corner tower will fall today. I asked him if he had foreseen that through some magic art, and he laughed, and said, "No, merely engineering, Prince Gawain."

"Call me Gavin," I said.

Medraut has begged the king to let him lead the van when we attack tomorrow. I think he hopes to find death in combat, to somehow make amends for his misdeeds. I intend to ride beside him, and do what I can to prevent that. I will not lose another brother that I love. I will not let him die.

And I... Last night, I had the dream again, of the race and the thorn bushes with their clinging, stinging branches. Gaheris is ahead of me still, on the path, smiling as he looks back at me, holding out a hand. There are others with him, Lavaine and Astamore and Amran and Tristan and Lamorak. But I am trapped here, at the cliff's edge, held down while the thorns hiss and entangle and climb. As draw level with my eyes, they twist, each one claw-handed, each one wearing Agravaine's face.

EXPLICIT: An Afterword

The Arthurian legends hold a very particular place in Western (and to some extent Southern European) culture, and, like most people in the UK, I grew up with them. I don't remember not knowing at least the most familiar stories – the sword in the stone, the grail quest, Lancelot's adventures and love for Guenever. Modern readers tend to think of the stories either in terms of an Arthurian canon, focused around the versions of Sir Thomas Malory and Geoffrey of Monmouth, or as an accretion on a real historical figure who can be recovered somehow underneath the verbiage. But this is not how most of the mediaeval audience would have perceived them. It's far from clear whether they considered Arthur a 'real' historical king: most readers of Geoffrey would have recognised the amount of invention and embroidery in the account (and the degree to which it was shaped to reflect the political ambitions of his own time). Contemporary references show that while the so-called Matter of France (focused on Charlemagne and his warriors) was known to have its roots in history, the Matter of Britain was mainly considered as fantasy and story. And, despite the name, it was a story that belonged across multiple cultures and languages – not only French and English (and Latin, in which the very first elements were written) – but Italian, Spanish, German, Dutch, Norwegian, Welsh and others – and most of those who added to the corpus of stories felt free to add new details, adventures, characters and interpretations of their own. Far from being a set legend, from its beginnings, the tale of Arthur was flexible and open. Some versions became popular – Geoffrey's original ending was altered and displaced when Lancelot became a prominent character, though most versions that include Lancelot retain some elements from Geoffrey, including Mordred's treachery. But there were also stories and characters who did not catch on: Cliges, Moriaen, Loholt. The story of Gawain and the Green Knight is famous today, but it survives in a single manuscript and does not seem to have been widely known in the middle ages; the adventure does not appear in Malory, nor in the vast French post-Vulgate cycle. To mediaeval writers, Arthur was a hook on which to hang stories, existing in a timeless and vague landscape, and that is one of the reasons for the success of his legend. He and his court can be repositioned to allow multiple interpretations and voices and ideas. In some sense, Arthurian legend is a huge corpus of creative commons open to anyone.

Writers have continued to use the legend to explore new ideas about society and culture. Where mediaeval authors used Arthur's court as a place to discuss ideas of kingship, knightly duty, love and religious conduct, modern authors have explored feminism, esotericism, satire, pacifism, environmentalism, race and sexuality. The material is flexible enough to allow all these readings (though I have yet to find a really convincing socialist version – this is one area where there is perhaps not enough give in the story). Most of these writers have, however, tended to stick to the 'main' version of the legend – the one familiar from Malory (who took it from the French Vulgate cycle), even where they present more sympathetic versions of Mordred, say, or Morgan. (This reworking of villains is not new: Scottish chroniclers presented Mordred as the hero in the 13th and 14th centuries, and in most of the verse tales, Morgan is more strange than wicked, setting out to help the hero grow by challenging then rewarding him).

My Gaheris stories started out as a writing exercise for a writers' group – I wanted a framework to explore the relationship between three specific characters and I didn't have time or space to give a full back story. The obvious place to go to find a familiar set of people and background was Arthuriana. But I had never found the Tristan story appealing, and Lancelot-Guenever-Arthur felt overdone. So I chose Lamorak-Margawse-Gaheris. The only one of the characters I really knew anything about was Margawse, and then only via T.H. White and the story of Mordred. So I dug out my copy of Malory and started looking.

In my other life, I'm a mediaeval historian. I find it hard, once I start looking into something, to stop. For the purposes of my writing exercise, all I needed was the outline of the story. But historian brain noticed something: in Malory and to a lesser extent in the Vulgate and post-Vulgate, there is a big contradiction in the character of Gaheris. This isn't unusual in Arthuriana – many characters are inconsistent even in the same work – but Gaheris was particularly interesting to me, because I had always had a soft spot for the Orkney brothers and because – in historian mode – I have an interest in feud and its effects on society. I went looking for Malory's sources – which led me to the Prose Tristan (which is where most of what we know of Lamorak comes from), then the Vulgate, as well as the more familiar works of Chrétien de Troyes and Geoffrey. Most of the time, even in the Prose Tristan (whose author hated Gawain and denigrated both him and his brothers) Gaheris is positively presented as courteous, kind and largely honourable, and is Gawain's favourite brother. He also acts as a kind of conscience to both Gawain and Arthur in the early sections of the Vulgate, post-Vulgate and in Malory. But he murders his mother. Gawain's brothers first appear in the work of Chrétien, where they are background figures. But Gaheriet– or Gaheries – seems to have been the most interesting to other writers, while Agravaine and Guerrehet remain minor. It is also likely that Gaheris and Gareth were originally one character, who became two due to scribal error or the needs of poetic metre. (The original names as given in Chretien are virtually identical – Guerehet and Guerehes). Modern interpretations have tended to associate the 'good' actions of Gaheriet with Gareth and the bad ones with Gaheris, but this is down to Malory, and not the earlier version of the Vulgate. Gareth as we now know him is Malory's own invention, taking the name of the shadowy Guerehet in the Vulgate, and giving him all the positive aspects of Gaheriet (aside from the conscience, which occurs in the story before Gareth arrives at court).

Both as a writer and a historian, I have a weakness for underdogs. Gaheris interested me. Like Gawain, his character had been subjected to a gradual degradation in the tales as the focus moved to newer characters, but in his case he had also been displaced from his personality. I decided to give it back. Which led me to wonder why such a man would kill his mother; which led me back to Lamorak, the feud between the sons of King Lot and the sons of King Pellinor and, well... Writing – like historical research – is often a matter of 'what if'. I started with 'what if Gaheris and Lamorak were friends?'

I wrote the first version of *Serpent Rose* in 1991 or 1992, mostly by that point, for fun. Initially, I didn't intend to do any more with the characters, but I had come across an episode in the Prose Tristan where Lamorak sends a chastity test to the ladies of King Mark's court. I was also, around this time, teaching a course on the Arthurian legend, and therefore still reading some of the less well-known tales. One of these is the French *Lai du cor*, the Lay of the Horn, about a chastity test administered, for a change, to the men of Arthur's court. I was interested, too, in the women of the Arthurian world – not the famous queens and sorceresses, but the damsels who are rescued or won by knights and then seemingly forgotten. And that was the core of what became *Rose Knot*. I had no idea what to do with two linked novellas, so I put them in a drawer, occasionally revising them a little, or playing with ideas for other works continuing Gaheris' story. I wrote an opening for what would be the final section, and tried out various ideas for the third, mostly based around a section in the First Continuation to Chrétien's *Perceval*. But none of them really worked, and, apart from a short piece about how Lamorak first encountered Gaheris, written in 2005 for a different writers' group, I didn't add new words.

Then, in 2019, Ian Whates asked me if I had a novella lying around, specifically one on a knightly theme. So I sent him *Serpent Rose*, and he liked it, publishing it as part of a set of novellas from Newcon Press. *Rose Knot* came out as a standalone novella, also from Newcon Press, in 2021. In 2022, I was asked to be a guest of honour for the 2023 British National Science Fiction Convention, Conversation, and Ian suggested to me the idea of a collection of my Gaheris stories to come out at the convention. So I dug out my file of notes and ideas and extracts from mediaeval texts and started thinking.

All of the novellas have roots in existing Arthurian stories, though I often reshape, deviate and refocus. *Knotted Thorn* is perhaps the most reshaped of the four. From the original idea to use the First Continuation of *Perceval,* I ended up keeping only Gaheris on a solo quest, to which he has been partly summoned and which involves some bad memories, plus the empty halls and gardens that he and Gawain encounter in the flashback. Thorn and her siblings are partly based on the children of Llyr in the Second Branch of the Mabinogi, and partly on elements of the Fourth Branch, though the character of the invisible knight Garlon is from Malory, and Alaw and Brandelys are a mixture of the Mabinogi, the Brandelys' sister episode in Chrétien's *Perceval,* the quest of the Hart in Malory, and an incident in the Vulgate of a damsel who likes to murder knights. Thorn is based on the Damsel of the Blanche Lands, a character who never actually appears in any of the tales but is described as loved by Gaheris in the Vulgate. As a historian, I don't believe that the Arthurian tales preserve much – if anything – of pre-Christian Brythonic religious practices, but as a writer it makes for interesting material (and I wanted to explain Garlon, because he is so unlike the rest of his family).

My original idea for *Thorned Serpent* stuck close to Malory. I'm not entirely sure why: possibly because both Malory and T.H. White write of the last days of Arthur so movingly, but focus on Lancelot rather than Gawain (and I had always intended him to narrate this section). But I didn't want to use the adultery story or the Roman war (which are the two usual contexts for the rebellion and the death of Arthur and his main knights). Agravaine had been a consistent antagonist from the first novella, though, and plays an important role in engineering the downfall in several versions of the legend. The abduction of Guenever by Malagant comes originally from Chrétien's *Le Chevalier de la Charette* (which is also the first occurrence of Lancelot), but I have added Agravaine to the tale, and given to him the responsibility for Gaheris' death and Gawain's hunger for revenge which in Malory lies with Lancelot. The earliest known reference to Mordred comes in a Welsh chronicle text from no earlier than the 10th century, which says simply that he and Arthur fell at the battle of Camlann. It doesn't say that they were on opposing sides: that element entered with Geoffrey of Monmouth, where Mordred is Arthur's nephew. (He isn't specified as being Arthur's son until the Vulgate cycle in the 13th century). I felt I had been inconsistent with his character in the earlier novellas, so tried to resolve that here, as well as giving a nod to the Welsh chronicle.

Most of the characters come from some version or other of the Arthurian legend, though I have played around with their personalities and in some cases used the Welsh versions of their names. The only ones who are my complete invention are Thorn's eldest sister and second brother, Gaheris' squire Evan, Llinos' maid, and the Camelot librarian. As far as I know, Safere does not practice magic or medicine in any of the mediaeval tales and his sexuality goes unmentioned. I chose him as Lamorak's lover because he is such an obscure figure and has no particular baggage associated with him. Luned/Lynette originates with Malory, but belongs to a type – the Proud Damsel – who appears in various forms across the material, and is not always either good or redeemable. Modern retellings usually present her in a positive light: the same retellings often make Llinos/Lyonesse silly or weak. This juxtaposition of female characters where 'active' (often described in quite masculinised ways) is good and 'passive' (often described as engaged on traditionally female-identified activities like embroidery or running a household) is bad both irritates me and strikes me as inherently misogynist and patronising, as it reinforces patriarchal ideas of the value of particular activities. There should be a place for women who run households and sew as heroes, too. And I thought Lyonesse deserved more attention after marriage. I don't like Tristan and I don't like the ways he justifies his behaviour, so King Mark is rather nicer in my version than in the legend. Lamorak is usually portrayed as either the oldest or second oldest of Pellinor's legitimate sons: aside from his love affair with Margawse and his seeming prowess as a knight, we have little material surviving about him. I made him the youngest because it suited the story I wanted to tell.

I don't claim any authority: as I said, the Arthurian stories are communal property, a vast shared world that crosses time and space and culture. As a historian, I regard the search for the historical

Arthur mostly as a distraction; insofar as he may have existed at all, he is most likely a composite character based on many different leaders over a considerable period (ranging from the 5th century c.e. to the 19th) as well as borrowing from legendary heroes. Films and novels that try to present the 'historical' Arthur are my least favourites (with the exception of Rosemary Sutcliff's *Sword at Sunset*, which is a fine book, even if the history is wrong). Legends are not static: they change and grow and react to the needs and anxieties of each era; they don't belong on tramlines, nor should they always and everywhere be treated with respect. Mediaeval writers changed the material as they saw fit, whether to talk-up a favourite character, address an issue that they considered critical, or just to have fun. Most traditionally-published modern writers hesitate to go as far (with a few honourable exceptions, including YA writer Gerald Morris, who is one of the very few to introduce a brand new character to Arthur's world and make him interesting, believable and necessary and whose books I recommend). There are also those who police Arthuriana, trying to claim it for only one set of people, one culture. Across the corpus there have always been people using the legend to preach a particular set of values, but they have always existed alongside others who opened it up to include characters and ideas and places from outside Europe. The context in which the mediaeval stories were written mean that they tend to be Christian, but Christianity is not essential to them (as more recent novels by Susan Schwartz and Elizabeth Wein have shown).

There's space for everything and everyone in legends and they can encompass anything. They belong to us all.

About the Author

Kari Sperring is the author of *Living with Ghosts* (DAW 2009), (winner of the 2010 Sydney J Bounds Award, shortlisted for the William L Crawford Award and a Tiptree Award Honours' List book) and *The Grass King's Concubine* (DAW 2012). As Kari Maund, she's an academic mediaeval historian, and author of five books and many articles on early Welsh, Irish and Scandinavian history. With Phil Nanson, she is the co-author of *The Four Musketeers: the true story of d'Artagnan, Porthos, Aramis and Athos*. She's British and lives in Cambridge, England, with her partner Phil and three very determined cats, who guarantee that everything she writes will have been thoroughly sat upon.

Her website is http://www.karisperring.com and you can also find her on Facebook.

ALSO FROM NEWCON PRESS

The Wild Hunt – Garry Kilworth

When Gods meddle in the affairs of mortals, it never ends well… for the mortals, at any rate. Steeped in ancient law, history and imagination, Garry Kilworth serves up an epic Anglo-Saxon saga of swordplay, witches, giants, dwarfs, elves and more, as a young warrior wrongly accused of patricide sets out to clear his name and regain his birthright.

The Double-Edged Sword – Ian Whates

A disgraced swordsman leaves town one step ahead of justice. His past, however, soon catches up with him in the form of Julia, a notorious thief and sometimes assassin. Thrust into an impossible situation, he embarks on what will surely prove to be a suicide mission. "A cheerfully brutal story of betrayal and skulduggery, vicious fun." – *Adrian Tchaikovsky*

The Chinese Time Machine – Ian Watson

A new collection from one of science fictions most inventive writers; a volume released to celebrate the author's 80th birthday. Features ten stories published over the past five years in *Asimov's, Analog*, and elsewhere, plus a new 34,000 word novella that is original to this collection. Ian Watson at his entertaining best.

The Queen of Summer's Twilight – Charles Vess

A mysterious man on a black motorbike rescues a rebellious teen from the streets of Inverness, setting in motion a series of events that will see contemporary Scotland clash with the realm of fairy, in this stunning tale inspired by the ballad of Tam Lyn.

Night, Rain, and Neon edited by Michael Cobley

All new cyberpunk stories from the likes of Gary Gibson, Jon Courtenay Grimwood, Justina Robson, Louise Carey, Ian MacDonald, Simon Morden, DA Xiaolin Spires ++.
"Three hundred pages of thought-provoking cyberpunk that will give many hours of pleasure." – *SF Crowsnest*

www.newconpress.co.uk